MALAFORMED
REALITIES

VOLUME ELEVEN

THOMAS M. MALAFARINA

**HELLBENDER
BOOKS**

an imprint of Sunbury Press, Inc.
Mechanicsburg, PA USA

an imprint of Sunbury Press, Inc.
Mechanicsburg, PA USA

Copyright © 2025 by Thomas M. Malafarina.
Cover Copyright © 2025 by Sunbury Press, Inc.

For information about special discounts for bulk purchases, please contact Sunbury Press Orders Dept. at (855) 338-8359 or orders@sunburypress.com.

To request one of our authors for speaking engagements or book signings, please contact Sunbury Press Publicity Dept. at publicity@sunburypress.com.

FIRST HELLBENDER BOOKS EDITION: June 2025

Set in Adobe Garamond Pro | Interior design by Crystal Devine | Cover design by Lawrence Knorr | Edited by Lawrence Knorr.

Publisher's Cataloging-in-Publication Data
Names: Malafarina, Thomas M., author.
Title: Malaformed realities volume 11 / Thomas M. Malafarina.
Description: First trade paperback edition. | Mechanicsburg, PA : Hellbender Books, 2025.
Summary: Thomas Malafarina strikes again with 13 spine-tingling tales of horror.
Identifiers: ISBN 979-8-88819-337-2 (softcover).
Subjects: FICTION / Horror | FICTION / Short Stories (single author).

Designed in the USA
0 1 1 2 3 5 8 13 21 34 55

For the Love of Books!

For my incredible wife, JoAnne.
Thank you for all you do.
You are my reason for everything.

CONTENTS

INTRODUCTION

Here we are at Volume 11 of Malaformed Realities. I truly enjoy being able to present this series of my short story collections to you. I was once asked if I would stop at Volume 10, and I explained that as long as the ideas keep coming, the volumes will also keep coming. As a writer, I find myself engaged in all sorts of projects. I am often contacted by websites, online magazines, print anthologies, and so on, requesting I contribute to their latest endeavors. I seldom turn down one of these opportunities. I'm a writer; I'm supposed to write whatever is needed. I love the challenge as well.

On occasion, but rarely, I am given what we call "the bible," which is a detailed description of the premise of the type of story to be written. For example, the publisher might have a particular character or a group of characters they want included in the story. The "Bible" gives you a description of those characters and their personalities. From there, I am tasked with developing my own story, including those characters. This can prove to be a unique challenge.

Often, I am simply given the germ of an idea. Sometimes, I am offered no more than a word or two. I'm perfectly fine with that. That type of direction allows me the freedom to run wild with my ideas, not bound by any requirements. It gets my creative juices pushed into high gear, and that's what this is all about. Most of the time, these stories find their way into publications. Sometimes, I write these stories and submit them, and for whatever reason, the project never comes to fruition.

When I give an occasional live presentation, usually to a library or literary group, I am asked if I create an outline for a story or novel before starting one. They often look at me like I am from Mars when I explain that I plan nothing, I just start writing. I tell them I write a bit, then ask myself a series of questions, and then write some more. One example I like to use is my novel, *Burner*. That started as two simple paragraphs, meant to be nothing more than a description of a man walking into a strange antiquities store. If you read the book, those two paragraphs I originally wrote are still the same at the beginning of the first chapter. From there, I started asking myself questions, and the story began, continued, and eventually ended. When complete, I had a novel that I had never initially planned on writing, but one that was nonetheless written.

As with Burner, I have no idea what it will eventually become when I start a story. Sometimes, an idea will become a short story; sometimes, the story will evolve into a novella and occasionally into a novel. I never plan what direction an idea will eventually take; I just let it become what it needs to become. Sometimes, an idea never becomes a story at all and gets tucked away in my idea vault until the day my muses choose to stimulate me to dig it out and develop it.

Although I primarily write horror fiction, my favorite genre, I have delved into the world of sci-fi, fantasy, humor, non-fiction, and even cartoon books. We have, for example, published a series of five strange cartoon books, all with the title *Yes, I Smelled It Too*, Volumes 1 through 5. I hate to put labels and the restrictions such labels carry upon me, so I try never to do so. I'm a writer, and writers write . . . whatever is needed.

As with the previous 10 volumes of Malformed Realities, Volume 11 is a nice collection of short stories (some not so short) and even a novella. As with all my collections, I try to add a bit of everything to the mix: stories to terrify and even stories to make you laugh.

I hope you enjoy Volume 11. For your information, Volumes 12-15 are already in process, so there will definitely be more to come.

Thomas M. Malafarina
June 2025

THE WITCH'S TREE

The tree was a massive, serpentine growth clinging to the corner of the decrepit ruin of what was once a cozy two-story cottage with a pointed cedar shake roof. Such an inviting appearance was quite deceptive since cozy was not a word that could accurately describe the inhuman things that had occurred inside that house many years earlier when the tree was only a twig planted by the cottage's unholy resident. In those days, the home appeared much more welcoming, which was how it was meant to look, despite its location deep in the forest, where few dared to venture. If someone braved the forest, the resident wanted to ensure the visitor would feel comfortable approaching the house. She had many reasons for this deception, and all of them were evil.

However, now the house stood in ruins, its windows gone and its door hanging open on a single hinge. The chimney that once produced plumes of smoke from the stone fireplace below now protruded from its roof, broken, a useless remnant of what was. The owner of this dilapidated structure was also gone and had been for decades.

The house sat below a huge canopy of tall age-old oaks and maples with roots large and twisted jutting far above the surface, making the trees look as though they might come to life at any second and pulling their massive root legs from the ground, plod like gigantic monsters through the forest. However, the gargantuan trees remained fixed in their forest beds, casting shadows onto the forest floor below.

The disturbing tree that stuck to the house twisted and turned in a series of "S" shapes, climbing, vine-like, from its six-foot round base to its spreading serpentine branches all along its winding length. Looking at this lumpy, lizard-like behemoth, its gripping branches embracing the deteriorated house, made one think that the creeping monstrosity might be the only thing keeping the house from collapsing. Such a thought would be more accurate than one realized.

Once a century passed, a witch occupied the cottage when the house was new. She, a woman named Grizelda, was the one who first planted the twig that eventually would grow to be the massive thing known to nearby villagers as "The Witch's Tree." The wisest occupants of the town learned to steer clear of the dark forest and the Witch's cottage. Many who dared to venture closer and lived to tell about it claimed the air in that forest was almost palpable with evil. One holy man swore he felt the earth tremble beneath his feet from the Hellish horror rising from its unholy soil.

In those early days, it was said among the villagers that those who did not return were vexed and captured by the Witch. Then, their bodies were ground to a pulp and used as fertilizer to feed the Witch's Tree. People believed the reason the tree had grown so huge, so quickly, and was so terrifying was because it contained the lost souls of dozens of the Witch's victims. Rumor had it that if you got close enough to the house and the tree, you could hear the mournful wailing of the dozens, perhaps hundreds of lost souls that fed the monstrosity. They also claimed that the tree wrapped its unholy branches around the house so that the structure would remain decades after its occupants had perished.

Other legends said that if anyone got close enough to the tree to touch its surface, they would die instantly and collapse to its base, where thousands of insects would arise from the corrupted soil and savagely break down the corpse to fine particulates for consumption by the Witch's Tree. So much lore surrounded the Witch's Tree that it is hard to determine how much of it was true, but as with such things, one must decide for himself.

/ 2 /

In the early 19th century, two curious boys from the village ventured into the forest searching for the Witch's house. By this time, the witch had died and passed on to wherever such wretched creatures go, and the house had been abandoned. The boys didn't believe in sorcery or other superstitions commonly accepted by their parents. The friends, Jacob and Isaiah, had even acquired the reputation of being "odd" since they were free thinkers who didn't follow common beliefs despite their biblical names.

They didn't mind the criticism. In their eyes, the American Revolution was over, the country was new, and it was time to introduce new ideas and possibilities. They had no interest in the old ways and wanted to prove that witches didn't exist and legends were nothing more than fictional tales, or in their words, "Poppycock."

After several hours, the two were certain they had gotten off the beaten path somewhere along the line and were lost. When they thought they might not find their way home, they came upon a clearing in the woods under a canopy of large trees. In the center of the clearing, in shadows, they saw the abandoned house with a tree climbing up the corner, with its branches stretching out to the sides. It was perhaps twelve inches in diameter at the base and almost reached the top of the house. Isaiah approached the tree against Jacob's admonishment and pressed his palm against its bark.

What happened next was Jacob's account, which he told the village constable, Mark Welton, after Jacob had spent several years in the county insane asylum. The boy had been found wandering aimlessly through the woods, screaming and crying madly and mumbling gibberish no one could understand. When Jacob had been cured sufficiently to speak coherently, he told a story that was not only unbelievable but one that the constable didn't dare share with the superstitious townspeople.

Jacob no longer had the mental capacity to present his story articulately, as his mind was in disarray, causing him to speak in short, disjointed sentences. Constable Welton patiently took Jacob's erratic descriptions in the visiting room at the asylum. Then, he put them into his report in a cogent fashion as if Jacob had presented them himself rather than in the young man's rapid, almost incoherent ramblings. According to the constable's report, Jacob said, "When Isaiah pressed his palm against the tree, he began to tremble and shake from head to toe. His hair seemed to stand on end as if by some force I could not comprehend. I shouted to him to remove his hand and come back, but it was as if he were paralyzed and unable to move. Then he collapsed to the ground. I didn't know if he was dead or still alive, but for his sake, I hoped death had already taken him because what happened next was something no human should suffer while alive.

"Before I could try to help Isaiah, hundreds of small branches rose from the soft soil and wrapped themselves around him. Then thousands of insects, worms, flies, spiders, and the like crawled from the ground and swarmed Isaiah's body. The branches squeezed his body tighter, and God help me; I could hear his flesh tearing and his bones being crushed beneath the tightening branches. I'm certain those sounds will haunt me for the rest of my days.

"At one point, his eyes bulged out of his skull, popped out of their sockets, and rolled down his bloody cheeks, dangling there by thin filaments. As his blood came forth from the ripping skin, thousands of insects swarmed onto his body, drinking his blood and devouring Isaiah's flesh. Within seconds, all that remained were bones that had been picked clean. Then, the snaking branches crushed the bones to a powder that was quickly absorbed into the tree. It was unlike anything I had ever seen. For a moment, I saw Isiah's face appear as if carved into the tree bark, then it disappeared. I have never relayed this account to anyone, not even the doctors at this place. I was afraid they would never leave me out of this place if I did."

Constable Welton knew that Jacob's fears were a waste of the young man's time as he would never be released from the insane asylum, whether he told his story or not. Welton had spoken with the Head Physician at the hospital, who told him Jacob would likely be in the facility for the rest of his life. Two days after Welton's visit, Jacob hung himself with his bedsheet.

/ 3 /

At the turn of the twentieth century, it was said that a recent immigrant to the United States from Italy had been seeking employment in the village, which had since grown to be a small town. He needed a place to stay for the night and was unsuccessful at finding any lodgings. He was unaware that the closely-knit locals despised all newcomers in town and especially detested those from foreign countries. As a result, every boarding house in town had claimed they had no vacancies. This would have posed a problem for Angelo, but it would not necessarily be an insurmountable challenge. He had already noticed that the town had several nice parks, and since the weather was mild that summer, Angelo felt confident he could sleep under a tree for a night, hoping to find proper lodging the following day.

Angelo was a naturally kind, considerate young man with a jovial, friendly personality. It was a trait that had benefited him so far in his time in the U.S. He genuinely liked people and found that most people instantly took a liking to him. He was also trusting of others because he was a trustworthy, honorable person. Angelo was always willing to give someone the benefit of the doubt. However, that trait would not serve him well in this particular town.

Unfortunately, Angelo was unaware of how much the townspeople hated strangers. Nor could he know the level of bigotry and hatred the town's residents had toward foreigners. At the final boarding house where Angelo was turned away, he had the misfortune of encountering the owner, Mister Jebidiah Smith. Jeb hated all foreigners because of their funny accents, weird ways of dressing, and strange habits. He especially detested those of Italian descent for reasons all his own. Apparently, a year or so earlier, Jeb had lost a fight with an Italian gentleman in the local pub. Since then, all people of Italian extraction instantly made it to the top of his hate list. He decided it was time to repay those "danged foreigners" once and for all, and this "I-talian" nobody would suit his needs just fine.

Jeb pointed Angelo toward the dark forest just before sunset and told him of a nice abandoned house there that would provide him protection from the elements for the night. Then Jeb gave Angelo specific directions to ensure he would find the place quickly.

"It ain't purty, and it ain't perfect, but it'll do ya in a pinch," Jeb told the eager Angelo. "You'll recognize it by the large tree growin' next to it. You can't miss it."

But inside, Jeb was laughing his most evil of laughs, knowing that some horrible fate would befall the immigrant interloper at that accursed place with the Witch's Tree. The unfortunate Angelo had no idea that the man who presented himself as caring and who seemed to have given him such helpful advice was actually a horribly hateful man who was banking that he was sending Angelo to his death.

Angelo found the house with the tree right where Jeb had told him it would be. It was almost nightfall when he arrived, and Angelo could barely see the tree. He walked past it and entered the abandoned structure. Although it was a warm night, it was surprisingly chilly inside the house. Angelo had a jacket in his suitcase, but it had turned too dark for him to see what he was doing. He would have to make do with the clothes he was wearing.

From a dark corner of the room, he heard a ragged voice say, "Who dares to enter my house?"

Angelo was surprised and confused as the nice man at the boarding house said the place was abandoned. He thought perhaps someone else who could not find lodging had taken residence there. The voice sounded like that of an old woman.

"Mi scusi? I meana, excusea me?"

"This is my home. Why are you in my home, uninvited?" the voice asked.

Angelo said, "The nicea man at thea boarding house ina town, hada no rooms, and hea said thisa place wasa empty."

The voice replied, "There are no nice people in that town. They all think they are better than me but are not worth the space they take up. I should kill you for being here, but I have a better idea. Here is what I want you to do, my strange foreign friend. I want you to sleep here this evening and know that no harm will come to you. In the morning, you will find ten gold coins waiting for you. Take the coins into town and tell the man who sent you here that you want to rent a room. When he asks you where you got the money, tell him you found the coins in my house. Then tell him you believe there are probably many more coins hidden here and that you hope to come back sometime to look. Do not mention seeing me here or speaking to me. If you do that for me, I will let you live and reward you with the gold coins.

Angelo said, " Yesa, I cana do that. Grazie . . . I meana tanka you."

Then, the strange old woman was gone. Angelo did as he was told and slept in the house that night, although his sleep was fitful. As the odd woman had promised, ten gold coins were next to his head when he awoke. As she had instructed him, Angelo brought the coins to Jeb at the boarding house. Jeb's eyes bulged with excitement as he stared at the treasure before him. Miraculously, Jeb suddenly had a vacant room available, and he told Angelo he could have it for as long as he needed it. Jeb even provided him with a nice, warm breakfast.

Angelo told Jeb about the abandoned house in the woods. In his broken English, Angelo explained that he hadn't slept well the previous night and would go to his room to nap after breakfast. Then Angelo told Jeb how he had found the coins inside the cottage and was certain there were many more coins in the house just waiting to be discovered. Angelo said he hoped to return to the house after he slept to look for more coins. Jeb pretended to be uninterested but devised a plan to get to the coins before the little foreigner did.

Later that afternoon, Jeb and two friends went into the forest to the abandoned cottage, hoping to find the rest of the coins. None of the three would-be treasure hunters were ever heard from again. Locals assumed they had fallen victim to the Witch's Tree, which was said to have had a significant growth spurt that year.

/ 4 /

Young William Engelton was sixteen years old in 1965 when he disappeared from the newly built suburbs outside of town, bordering the woods. His parents were heartsick when he failed to return home one day after spending the afternoon; they assumed he was playing with other neighborhood boys. However, his friends had a somewhat different tale to tell. His best friend, Harvey Montgomery, told investigators that although young Billy had been hanging out with the gang earlier in the afternoon, he had left them sometime after 1:00 P.M.

"Billy was obsessed with finding that Witch's Tree we have all heard people in town talking about," Harvey told local police. "We tried to tell him all those stories were garbage, and if there ever was a Witch's House or Tree, they were long gone by now. But Billy wouldn't listen and said he would go into the forest and find the tree. Maybe he did find it. From what I hear about the place, I hope not."

Several searchers went deep into the forest and found the battered house and the Witch's Tree. They took Polaroid pictures of both. However, no sign of William could be found. One of the police investigators examined the photos in detail with a magnifying glass a day later. He was shocked and confused by what he thought he saw. At the time, Officer Charles Dumont would have sworn on a stack of bibles that he saw the screaming image of William Engelton's face etched into the bark of that accursed tree. But after some serious consideration about what people might think of him and what that might mean to his job security or potential for promotion, Charles decided it would be better to chalk it all up to his imagination and burn the photo. William Engelton never returned home and was never seen again.

It is believed the house still stands, hidden in the woods, shrouded by the canopy of trees. It is also said that the Witch's Tree still clings to the dilapidated structure, keeping it from collapsing into rubble. Is the tree cursed? Does the Witch's ghost still haunt the house, and does the tree continue to suck the souls of unknowing strangers who touch its bark? Many believe it's all a fabrication, a legend. Others know the truth.

WAR PIGS

Authors note: In late 2024, I was approached by Nocturnicurn Press to write a story based on Black Sabbath's song "War Pigs" for a charity anthology called Hand of Doom; A Literary Tribute to Black Sabbath. *As a teenager, I wore out the Black Sabbath* Paranoid *album, trying to learn guitar parts for all the songs. Since I am always up for a challenge and willing to help a worthy cause, I offered them this story.*

"In the fields, the bodies burning.
As the war machine keeps turning."
—Black Sabbath, "War Pigs"
Buttler, War, Osbourne, Iommi

Now, in darkness, world stops turning.
Ashes where their bodies burning."
—Black Sabbath, "War Pigs"
Buttler, War, Osbourne, Iommi

Stan Klingaman was a hard kid to nail down. At least, that's how his English Literature teacher, Mister Frank Grace, would have described him. Stan had always been that way. He was like that as a small child, and now, in 1971, just two years before high school graduation, he was, if anything, even harder to get a fix on. Stan couldn't be pigeonholed into any particular group or clique. He seemed to move seamlessly from one to the other as if he were readily accepted wherever he went. Although Stan wasn't one of the smartest kids in the class, he could hang with the brainiacs and geeks. He had no athletic abilities whatsoever but had no problem spending time with some of the most popular and often most aggressive jocks in the school. As far as Frank Grace knew, Stan did no drugs of any kind but could fit right in with the dope heads and stoners. If he were to try to define Stan, Mister Grace would probably steal a line from Winston Churchill describing Russia in 1939 and say Stan was "a riddle wrapped in a mystery inside an enigma." No one seemed to know exactly what made Stan tick, and they seemed to be ok with that. God knew Stan was.

Stan loved music, just about all types of music. Perhaps it was his love of such a wide variety of music that allowed Stan to move so easily from one social cluster to another. Or maybe it was his artistic and creative nature in general. Stan was able to draw and paint like nobody's business and had a reputation for being the "guy who could draw whatever you needed." He was also known to be a fairly good all-around guitar player. His love of music spanned a variety of styles from Iron Butterfly, Steppenwolf, Chicago, Santana, The Beatles, and Three Dog Night to what would soon be his latest favorite discovery, Black Sabbath.

Stan was told that Sabbath was much heavier than any of the other bands he enjoyed and was most certainly much darker. Stan suspected most of what they professed through their music was fabricated for their "Satanic" image and album sales, but he had no problem with that. Stan was a fan of the horror movie genre and years earlier had seen the 1963 Boris Karloff film of the same name, *Black Sabbath*, and thought that was pretty cool. The band seemed to have a mystique about them. Stan found it fascinatingly hard to explain, but they definitely had something. Stan was about to sample in his first Black Sabbath album, *Paranoid*. It was the band's second studio album, released in the U.S. in 1971, but it would be Stan's first exposure to the group.

Stan played rhythm guitar in a local band that had gained a good deal of popularity, playing dances in the area. His lead guitar player and best friend Dennis had turned Stan onto the album by telling him to listen to a track called "Iron Man."

"I'm telling you, Stan, when you hear their guitarist, Tony Iommi laying down that intro riff, you may crap yourself. I'm not kidding, either. Crank it up. It will transform you." Dennis had cautioned him, and he had not been wrong. Those heavy chords following the disembodied voice growling, "I am Iron Man," were life-changing. After hearing the tune, Stan sat awestruck, headphones cupped around his ears, his mouth hanging agape. He was completely taken by the song. He felt out of control but in a good way. It was how he felt the first time he listened to "In-A-Gadda-Da-Vida" by Iron Butterfly. He did not doubt that if there was any song that would make this band super-famous, it would be Iron Man. Everyone would love it.

Stan had to admit, as much as he loved Tony Iommi's guitar playing and the magic rhythm section of bassist Geezer Butler and drummer Bill Ward, he was not immediately won over by lead singer Ozzy Osbourne's vocals. He felt such a cool band should have a lead vocalist with a deeper, more sinister and ballsy voice. Then again, who was he to argue with the band's obvious success. Despite his minor misgivings, Stan was certain "Iron Man" would go right up the charts. He believed he had a nose for such things.

But Stan was never one to pick the low-hanging fruit. Some might think of him as something of a music snob, but he didn't care. Stan knew any band that could move him in such a way had to have another tune on the LP, less noticed by the great unwashed, but one he could discover that would move him in an even greater way. Stan did the first thing he always did at moments of indecision like that; he flipped over the album to read the liner notes to learn everything he could about Black Sabbath. In doing so, he quickly scanned the song list and saw some interesting titles, such as the title track, "Paranoid," along with "Hand of Doom," "Electric Funeral," and "Rat Salad." Then Stan noticed the title of the first song on the LP, which stood out for him called "War Pigs."

"War Pigs." Stan thought, "What an interesting title. Two simple words, yet they say so much." Before even listening to the tune, Stan suspected it would be his favorite song on the album. Maybe it was because he had just survived the tumult of the late 1960s in the U.S. and all the uproar the Vietnam War brought. Or perhaps it was that he was almost 16 years old, a sophomore in high school. That meant the military draft, with subsequent deployment to the jungles of Vietnam, was just a few years away. When Stan turned 18, he would have to register for the Selective Service; then his future would literally be tossed into the life and death machine of the dreaded "lottery," where he would have to watch live television and pray that his number wasn't called.

He had already gone through this mock exercise during his freshman year and this past year, and the results were never good. His birthday always came up in a way that he knew he would be called to service. He would watch again the next year, and finally, when he turned 18, it would be too late. He already had a plan of action in place, at least theoretically. If his number was one of the first to be called, he would go out the next day and enlist in either the Air Force or Navy, hoping these might be the lesser of the various evils. Neither choice would be ideal for him as Stan was not fond of taking orders from anyone, even in the best of situations. He supposed he would have to find some way to adapt or, more likely, get in trouble and find himself with a dishonorable discharge. He wondered if he got kicked out of the Navy or Air Force, would that automatically keep him out of the Army? Interesting thought; perhaps this could be his Plan B?

Of course, Stan knew that when it came to things as insane as war, there were never any guarantees. It wouldn't necessarily matter what military branch he wound up in. He recalled a friend of his father who had been thrilled to learn that his son, who had been drafted into the Army, had been sent to Thailand rather than Vietnam. Where he was stationed was far from the action. It was about the best of a potentially bad situation. Unfortunately, during routine jungle practice maneuvers, a Bengal tiger attacked, killed, and ate the unsuspecting soldier. What were the odds of that?

Stan's older cousin, Jim, had enlisted in the Air Force and thought he had been fortunate to be stationed in Turkey. Stan figured nothing ever happened in Turkey. But Jim had been robbed and killed, his throat slit, outside of a bar in Istanbul. These were indeed dangerous times and dangerous places; there were no guarantees.

"War Pigs," Stan thought again. "I think this is going to be a winner." He put on his headset and positioned the needle for the first song. He closed his eyes and prepared for what he suspected would be an exciting and possibly frightening experience. However, he had no idea just how right he would be.

The song opened with Tony Iommi striking dark, sinister minor chords, not unlike those opening chords on Iron Man, which rang deliberately long as Geezer Butler's bass plucked over top of the ringing chords, with Bill Ward's drums providing perfect somber accompaniment. Being a guitar player, who was simultaneously learning bass, Stan knew and appreciated the symbiotic relationship that had to exist between the drums and bass. In War Pigs, these two, Butler and Ward, flawlessly created such a relationship. It was the type of playing capable of generating goosebumps. When this magic was combined with the abysmal sounds of air raid sirens, Stan felt as though he had plummeted into a mood darker than he could have believed possible. Then the guitar struck two sharp chords, and over what Stan assumed was a high-hat cymbal, he heard Ozzy Osbourne's voice sing, "Generals gathered in their masses. Just like witches at black masses." Whatever misgivings Stan had originally held concerning Ozzy Osbourne's vocal styling were now gone. In fact, everything was gone. He could not have possibly been prepared for it; the world he knew was gone.

Stan opened his eyes to find himself lying on the cold ground in the ruins of a city he couldn't begin to identify. It at least appeared to have once been some city but was no longer recognizable as its previous incarnation. The air was pungent with more vile and rancid odors than Stan would have believed was possible. He could smell all kinds of objects burning: wood, fuel, paper, rubber, and something he feared might be the stench of burning human flesh.

Stan looked at his clothing and saw he wore a dark green uniform of some type, but it was filthy, caked with mud, coated with dirt, and was no longer much more than rags, scarcely clinging to his equally filthy, gaunt frame. Stan was thirsty and felt weak, understanding he hadn't eaten or had anything to drink in a very long time. How could that possibly be? What the Hell had happened to him?

He felt as though he could hear a dark, somber melody with driving guitar, bass, and drums inside his mind, but it was so faint and distant that it might be nothing more than a faded memory of something he had heard. His body ached, wracked with pain from head to toe. Stan didn't believe he had any broken bones but felt severely cut, bruised, and perhaps burned. He tried to sit up, finding the screaming pain throughout every fiber of his body, making the attempt agonizing. Stan wondered what he was supposed to do? He couldn't simply lie on the ground waiting to die. Then Stan heard a voice in the distance. He lifted himself slightly on his tattered elbows to see if he could tell where the voice originated. The air around him was thick with smoke and ash. His eyes watered and burned, and he felt short of breath. Perhaps he had cracked or broken his ribs. He prayed he hadn't punctured a lung.

About ten yards away, Stan saw a large pile of debris. Focusing and looking closer, Stan discovered with horror the pile wasn't the detritus of collapsed buildings but was something much worse and much more horrifying. It was made up of the ruins of broken lives. The mound stood more than ten feet high, thirty feet around, and was composed of human remains. Severed arms, legs, heads, and torsos in varying stages of decomposition were piled high upon each other, some no more than bone with scarcely a fragment of flesh remaining, others practically complete although gray and pallid with decay. Hundreds of thousands of blow flies swarmed the stinking pile, making homes for their maggots in the insulting remains of what was once a small part of humanity. Crows and buzzards feasted on the decaying meat remnants, looking like dark-suited diners waiting for a table at an upscale restaurant.

At the top of the putrefying pile of wholesale death, an ancient, yellowed television sat at a slightly skewed angle, its rabbit ear antenna pointing off in odd directions. A program was being broadcast in black and white over its flickering screen. The rapidly moving program featured quick flashes of horrifying scenes, some too terrible to see. Many of them Stan had witnessed before as newsreels he had seen at the Saturday movie matinee when he was a kid. Others he had never seen before and hoped never to see again. Some were of planes dropping bombs on jungles; others showed helicopters spraying napalm and Agent Orange in an attempt to defoliate an area thick with trees.

Once, the message "War is good for business—invest your son" appeared briefly on the screen. A second later, a shot of what would become known as "napalm girl" appeared on the TV. Little did Stan know this picture would not actually be taken for at least another year into his future. More messages soon appeared like, "Hey, hey LBJ, how many kids did you kill today?" Soon, newsreels of Stalin, Mussolini, Khrushchev, and Hitler appeared, along with the assassinations of Martin Luther King and the Kennedys.

Then the scenes changed to groups of overweight, wealthy-looking cigar-smoking men drinking whiskey, shaking hands, and passing bundles of money back and forth as in another scene, thousands of disheveled young men in tattered uniforms walked hopelessly into burning cities to join the legions of the dead. The most unacceptable thing was like lambs to slaughter; the soldiers kept coming, one after another, thousands by thousands.

They continued marching onward to their deaths, as in another scene, money continued to change hands. The rich got richer, and the poor just kept dying. As the bodies piled higher and higher, more of the cities burned. The same handful of rich men continued passing money, smoking expensive cigars, laughing, drinking, and enjoying the show as the never-ending dying continued uninterrupted.

Suddenly Stan awoke in a cold sweat. The song "War Pigs" had ended, but not for Stan. This had become much more than a song to Stan. It had become a turning point in his young life. He had made up his mind; he would never allow himself to be part of the War Pigs' machine, to be chewed up and spit out for their profit. Rich, greedy old men started wars for their own greed but sent the young men from the poor families to be ground up like raw hamburger in their insatiably hungry war machine. All the while, the War Pigs got fatter and richer off the sacrificial flesh of the uneducated poor.

Stan didn't know how he would avoid being caught up in the mess, but he knew somehow they wouldn't get him. If it meant fleeing the country, he would do that; if it meant permanently crippling himself, so be it. He was ready to do whatever he had to do. Fortunately, the future changed for Stan in a way he couldn't know at the time. The war in Vietnam ended a year later, and the draft was finished shortly before Stan's eighteenth birthday.

But none of that mattered any longer. Stan knew now how the system worked; he had been shown the truth of the War Pigs that fateful day. There would be more money to make, more wars to fight, more people to die. The usual false excuses would be given, such as "they're taking our freedoms," or "we're the good guys, they're the bad guys," and so on. But Stan would know the truth. He would know to follow the money. The insatiable financial appetite of the War Pigs could never be satisfied. They ate the innocent souls of the unsuspectingly willing living to feed the overflowing coffers of the damned. It's how things were and always would be, and there was nothing Stan could do about it but watch, wait, and never let the War Pigs have him.

BE CAREFUL WHAT YOU WISH FOR

"Be careful what you wish for because you just might get it."
—UNKNOWN

"The only suitable gift for the man who has everything is your deepest sympathy."
—IMOGENE FEY

"Protect me from what I want."
—JENNY HOLZER

It had been yet another in a seemingly endless series of monotonous days, just like every other boring day of late, and Stephen had become frustrated beyond his ability to reason. He had had enough of walking about aimlessly with no destination, plan, rhyme, or reason. Was this truly to be how he would spend the rest of his natural life? He felt as if he might lose his mind and scream with insanity just thinking about how miserable his life had become. It consisted of the same old tiring routines day after day, week after week, for what seemed like so many years.

This was all the more frustrating because Stephen knew he had enough money to control every aspect of his life completely, much more so than most people. Nonetheless, he continued trudging the same mundane daily routine without deviation. Although Stephen hated his life, he did nothing to try to change it because he knew it was of his own making, and emotionally, he could no longer change anything. An outside observer might say he had everything, but Stephen knew, in reality, he had nothing, at least nothing that mattered to him any longer.

Stephen had fallen into an exceptionally deep pit of depression, having no idea how he might dig himself out and no longer caring if he ever did. He had been depressed several times over the years, but it seemed much worse this time. The creeping bouts of malaise had slowly begun several years earlier, shortly after it had all happened after his pitifully bad luck had done an abrupt about-face, that is to say, at least from an economic standpoint.

Now Stephen had the kind of financial good fortune most people only dreamed of. He had never even imagined having such vast amounts of money. However, he knew if he could be granted just one wish, that is to say, one more wish, it would be for everything to return to the way it had once been, and all of what he now possessed would simply disappear. But Stephen knew there would be no more wishes for him; those days were long gone. If he were going to find a way out of this miserable pit of despair, he would have to do so of his own volition.

However, Stephen understood that he had to devise some means to put some sort of distraction or excitement into his life, something new, something to stimulate him, even if that was out of his control and potentially dangerous. He needed to find some activity that might alter his normal mind-numbing practices, any sort of change whatsoever.

Stephen no longer worried about death or injury; his luck was much too good to allow something as trivial as physical injury to occur. He had tried all the most hazardous activities he could think of, from mountain climbing to sky diving, bungee jumping, and walking down a dark alley with one-hundred-dollar bills hanging out of his pockets, but he realized his good luck would not allow him to be hurt.

During one of his past bouts of depression, he had considered trying to commit suicide, but he instinctively knew no matter how hard he tried, he would never succeed; his good fortune simply would not permit it. He was destined to live a long and healthy life of great wealth, a life he no longer wanted.

As he stepped onto his enormous mansion's elaborate brick and stone porch, Stephen thought about all he had acquired and lost and how foolish and naïve he had been. God, he missed his wife and daughter so much, and no matter how much money or good fortune came his way, it would never even begin to make up for their loss.

He inserted his key into the lock on the finely hand-crafted front door and, with a click, walked into the darkened hallway. He switched on the overhead hall light and then turned on a small lamp on the oak hall table. He knew he should have put the table lamp on a timer, but Stephen had no interest in bothering with such things. The dense mist of apathy that had overtaken his psyche like a creeping fog of malcontent was most likely responsible. It could also have been that he simply found technology to be more of an annoyance than a benefit. This was also why he could enter the home without hearing the blaring of an alarm system in desperate need of resetting. He didn't feel like dealing with the hassles of owning such devices. Besides, he knew he had nothing to worry about from any living being, including himself.

Stephen casually approached the hall table and placed the large grocery bag he was carrying on top of the table. Then, he reached into his coat pocket, pulled out a wrinkled lottery ticket, and laid it next to the bag. He took off his coat and hung it in the hall closet, deciding to walk down the hall, past the living room, and out to his kitchen. Perhaps he could make himself something exciting for dinner. Stephen was not much of a cook, but maybe the distraction might be good.

He knew he could simply select any one of hundreds of phone numbers in his smartphone, and he would be able to order whatever he wanted from wherever he chose anytime, day or night. If he so desired, Stephen could simply hop on a plane and fly to France, Italy, or even China to have an interesting meal. His vast stores of money no longer meant anything to him, as neither did life itself.

"I think that's about far enough." Stephen heard a gruff voice say from inside the living room as he attempted to pass by the wide-arched opening. He looked up and saw a trace of shadowed movement from deep within the darkness. A few seconds later, he glimpsed two dark eyes reflected in the light from the hall and a flash of something metallic located approximately waist-high.

"A gun." Stephen thought. "There's an intruder in my home, and he has a gun." Yet he remained surprisingly calm as if the sight of a weapon pointed in his direction was a daily occurrence, which, of course, it was not.

It was just that Stephen had realized the intruder, who, although intent on something nefarious, might be exactly what he was looking for: the answer to his unending plight. He tried to see back in the gloom to determine what the prowler might look like but could only see the man's pale extended hand, the one holding a very menacing-looking pistol.

"You know." The mysterious stranger said. "Owning a house like this and not bothering to install a security system is pretty damn stupid, in my opinion."

Stephen didn't reply but stood staring into the darkness. The intruder continued. "I could have simply come up behind you and slit your fool throat if I was so inclined. You are either extremely naïve or very stupid. If you hadn't come home just now, I had every intention of robbing you blind. Oh, and for the record, I still plan to do just that." Then, the robber was suddenly caught off guard when, instead of appearing terrified, Stephen shrugged his shoulders as if he didn't care one way or the other. Stephen stood quietly for a moment before shaking his head as if disbelieving in the strange situation he was now in. And then, to make matters worse, Stephen chuckled aloud, apparently unable to control himself.

"I don't see what you find so funny." The stranger said with rising indignation and a significant amount of confusion. "In case you haven't noticed, I have a gun here, Einstein, and that means I hold your life in my hands and can end it at any time I choose with the simple pull of this trigger." Stephen was perfectly aware of the severity of his situation, but the intruder didn't realize that this entire state of affairs was exactly what Stephen had found so oddly amusing.

After a few more moments of silence, Stephen finally decided to speak up and said with surprising calm, "Yes, I see your gun. And yes,

I can also see it's pointed directly at me. But I think I need to let you in on a little secret. If you truly believe you hold my life in your hands, you are sadly mistaken, my friend, because you do not. However, if believing in such fairy tales makes you happy, go ahead and shoot." Then Stephen waited for a beat, expecting to hear the crack of gunfire, feigning nonchalance while hoping against hope that his amazing luck would suddenly fail him, he would be shot, and finally, he could once again be reunited with his family. But there was no gunshot.

Although Stephen couldn't see the man's face, he was certain he must have worn an expression of utter astonishment at this last audacious statement. After all, what sort of madman would boldly suggest to someone pointing a gun at him that the attacker should pull the trigger? But Stephen knew many things that the intruder did not know. And even without that knowledge, Stephen was fairly certain the man was not even an experienced burglar and certain by his actions so far, he was not a murderer by nature. Had the intruder been so inclined, he would have already knocked Stephen unconscious or killed him rather than stopping him and issuing what Stephen was certain was an idle threat.

"No, I didn't think so. I don't believe you're a killer, my new mysterious friend." Stephen said, now standing in a surprisingly relaxed pose as if nothing were out of the ordinary.

"Look, buddy." The man replied nervously, growing more nervous, "I'm not your friggin' friend. And maybe you're right. Maybe I'm not a killer; at least I may not have been a killer when I walked in here, but that don't mean I can't become one." Although the man was still hidden in the shadows, Stephen could see by the way the gun was fidgeting in the reflective light that the man was getting anxious and uncomfortable. "Look . . . I'm a very desperate man . . . and desperate men have been known to do things they might not normally consider . . . especially if they are pushed too far. And for your information, you are beginning to push me too far."

Stephen said, "Although you may not believe it, I honestly do know where you're coming from, and I understand your situation completely."

The man menacingly waved his gun and replied with frustration, "Understand? Understand? How in the hell could you possibly understand what I'm going through? Look at this place. It's a mansion, a friggin' palace. You're obviously filthy rich, and you want for nothing, while every day for me is a struggle just to try to survive."

Stephen insisted, "Look, despite outward appearances, I understand more than you realize. And I can empathize with you. Please allow me to help you. Just tell me what happened to you that drove you to this. And considering that you plan on robbing me anyway and have already threatened my life once, I think you owe me that much. Wouldn't you agree?"

"What? Agree? Are you insane? I don't owe you a damned thing." The man shouted, "I'm here to take your money, and that's all you need to know. That, and the fact that if you don't tell me where you have hidden your cash, I'm gonna splatter your guts all over the wall." He lifted the gun shakily and shouted, "And don't think for one second that I won't do it either!"

Stephen tried again to reason with the man using a calm voice, "Easy now, my friend. I intend to give you everything you want, possibly even more than you anticipated. All right? For starters, why don't you come over here and look in this grocery bag? You can have everything inside if you want it. Go ahead. Take a look. It's all yours."

"What? Groceries?" The man screamed. "I'm not here to beg for food, you idiot, and I'm not looking for your charity either. I am here to rob you . . . R . . . O . . . B . . . rob! So, give me your money. NOW!"

"Well then," Stephen replied, still sounding strangely calm. "Then look inside the bag, and I promise you won't be disappointed.

Furiously, the man waved his gun, ordering Stephen to step aside. Then, forgetting himself, the robber stepped out from the shadows, and Stephen got a good look at him for the first time. He was a tall, thin, relatively good-looking man with dark hair and surprisingly intelligent eyes. Stephen had expected a thug or, at the very least, some sort of street-smart tough guy. But what he saw before him was someone who was very much like he had once been. The man was inexperienced in his newly chosen profession. Stephen was suddenly excited at the potential the man offered him. This man really could be the answer to all of his prayers.

Keeping the gun trained on Stephen, the robber slowly approached the large paper sack and quickly peeked inside, immediately turning his attention to Stephen. Then he did a double-take, looked back into the bag, and for a moment froze with amazement, his eyes growing wide with disbelief. The hand holding the gun began to tremble slightly, and for a moment, Stephen worried it might accidentally go off. Then, realizing the absurdity of his worry, he brushed the thought aside.

"What the hell!" The man shouted. "What is all this? Some kind of joke? The bag is full of money. There must be several thousand bucks in cash in here."

"Yeah. I know." Stephen replied. "Based on experience, I would say maybe twenty or thirty grand, give or take a few."

The burglar, whose real name was Thomas Stewart, stared at Stephen momentarily with perplexity, and then recognition appeared on his face. He thought to himself, "Oh . . . Yeah . . . Now I think I get what's going on here. This guy isn't just some rich a-hole who inherited a ton of money. He's a thief, a crook just like me." Then, just as quickly, Thomas realized that if his would-be victim was a robber, he was much more successful at the trade than Thomas had been so far. The house was incredible, so there must be more to the man than he had originally assumed.

Keeping his gun trained on Stephen, Thomas asked, "So what did you do, rob a bank or what?"

Stephen realized the intruder had misunderstood and mistaken him for a fellow criminal. He laughed, "I didn't rob anyone. I found the bag along the highway, just as you see it there."

Thomas would not fall for such a preposterous lie, "Yeah. Right. Do you mean to try to tell me that you were walking down the street and found a grocery bag full of cash? Just like that!" Thomas snapped his fingers to accentuate his statement. "What do you take me for, some kind of idiot? Nobody has that kind of good luck."

"I do," Stephen replied matter-of-factly. "I have that sort of amazing financial luck all the time. Do you see that lottery ticket I found?"

Thomas looked down at the crumpled ticket. "Yeah, I see it. What about it?"

Stephen replied, "Well, I also found that while walking. And although you interrupted me before I had time to check the website, I'd be willing to bet it is a winner, not just a winner, but a really big one."

"Uh-huh!" Thomas replied with disbelief, "You must take me for a real chump, expecting me to believe this load of crap you're shoveling. Do you know the odds of anyone winning big on the lottery, let alone winning with some wrinkled-up, old discarded ticket you found along the road?"

"The odds are probably astronomical." Stephen admitted, "Nonetheless, I guarantee the ticket will be a major winner. That's just the way things work for me."

"Look. I don't know exactly what your story is, my friend, but you said you were a desperate man," Stephen continued. "Once, I, too, was an equally desperate man. Now I have all of this. But I'm going to venture into your current situation. I suspect you once were a fairly successful upper-middle-class professional earning a good living. Then the economy went bad, you lost your job, and you either lost your home or are about to lose it. How am I doing so far?"

Thomas looked at Stephen with shocked surprise, wondering how this stranger could have possibly gotten his story so correct. He had never met the man before, but somehow, he knew about his job loss and the fact that the bank was about to foreclose on his home. Thomas could not reply, so he just stood staring slack-jawed at Stephen and slowly nodded in agreement.

"I would also speculate that you have a wife and family, and although your wife has stood by you so far, things are getting rough on the home front," Stephen said. "And you're afraid if you lose your home, your wife will leave you and most likely take the kids with her."

This was all so bizarre. Thomas had no idea how this man, with his oddly confident manner, could know so much about his life.

Stephen continued. "Yep. I think I nailed your situation down perfectly. And although I know you may find this hard to believe, just a few years ago, I was in the same boat as you were, or perhaps sinking ship might be a better description, then everything changed for me overnight."

Finally, Thomas found his voice and asked, "Overnight? Not possible! What do you expect me to believe? Did you find a magic lamp with a Genie who granted you three wishes? What sort of fool do you take me for?"

"Well. It was not exactly like that, but something along those lines." Stephen said. "I was like you. I had a wife and daughter but lost my job and could not find another. The bill collectors were banging on my door and ringing my phone off the hook. The bank was about to take my home."

"Alright." Thomas said, "Suppose I buy into your cockamamie story. Where did all of this come from?" Thomas waved his arm to indicate the opulent surroundings of Stephen's home.

Stephen replied, "Someone offered me the opportunity to change my financial luck, and I took it. This was the result. And if you think you'd like to have what I have and more, I can arrange that for you as well."

"And why in the hell would you want to do that for someone like me who came here to rob you?" Thomas asked suspiciously. "What is this, some kind of con? Is it some ridiculous get-rich pyramid scheme? Look, buddy, I've been approached by all these types before, and I'm not about to fall for such crap and head down that particular road to ruin."

"I assure you," Stephen said. "It's not a scheme or business. And although it may seem like I'm doing you a favor, I guarantee my reasons are purely selfish; I am doing this only for myself. You probably won't believe me, but the truth is that I am tired of all of this. When I was in trouble like you were, I thought money would bring me happiness, but it has not. All it has brought me is sorrow." Stephen said. "You and everyone else might think I should be the happiest man alive, but I'm far from it. So, the only way for me to truly change my life is to get someone like yourself to voluntarily take my place."

Thomas asked, "Take your place? What is that supposed to mean?"

Stephen explained, "All this amazing good fortune can only belong to one person at a time. Before me, it belonged to another man, and before him, someone else. I have no idea how far back in time it goes, but I suspect centuries. The important thing is that I have it now and am offering it to you."

Thomas once again looked perplexed and said, "This is insane. But just assume for a minute that I'm desperate enough to be willing to play along with you. How in the hell do you propose making this supposed good luck transfer happen?"

"It's quite simple, really." Stephen said, "All you have to do is ask me. If you just tell me you wish you could have all the luck I currently possess and all the money you could ever need, and I agree, then it will be yours. What will happen is that good fortune will leave my body and go into yours. And from that moment on, you will never want for money again. But you have to be sure this is really what you want. And I must warn you to be careful what you wish for because you might just get it, as I did."

Thomas was sure this stranger was out of his mind, some kind of rich eccentric wacko. And what was that last cryptic statement supposed to mean? "Be careful what you wish for?" What was that all about? The guy was some kind of nut job, Thomas was certain. But as he said earlier, he was a desperate man, and desperate men tend to do things they normally would never previously have considered. So, he decided to play along with the lunatic. The worst-case scenario was he might get some cash out of the deal. "Not that it matters to me, but what is supposed to happen to you if I make this wish and take away all of your good fortunes? What will become of you?"

Stephen said, "That's a good question. Here's how it works. When you make your wish, all of my luck will become yours. When the transfer is complete, this house and everything in it will be yours. I'll simply leave, and you will never see me again."

"Wait a minute! Hold your horses! I get this now." Thomas said distrustfully. "You're trying to con me into letting you go. Then, as soon as you walk out that door, you'll go around the corner and call the cops. They'll bust in here a few minutes later and haul my sorry butt off the jail. Well, fat chance, buddy! If you honestly think I'm going to let you walk out the front door like that, you're crazier than I thought." Thomas raised the gun and pointed it straight at Stephen's chest.

Stephen never flinched or showed the slightest sign of fear. Instead, he said, "Then I suppose I have to prove it to you. I have to convince you that what I am saying is true. What do you suppose the odds are of a bullet missing me from your current distance?"

"What?" Thomas again asked, caught off guard, "What the hell are you saying? From this distance, a blind man wouldn't miss. Are you telling me you want me to shoot you from this point-blank range? Are you suicidal or what?"

"No, not really," Stephen said. "I have to admit, at one time, I was, but no longer. I also believe even at this proximity, if you shot at me, you wouldn't hit me. You have no idea how powerful all of this is. Look, I realize you don't consider yourself the murdering kind, but I assure you that you won't harm me if you pull that trigger."

Thomas said, "Ok. Wait a minute here. Maybe you're just out of your friggin' mind or something. I don't know. But I have no intention of killing you unless I have no other choice. So I'm not about to pull this trigger just because you say so, ok? How's about this . . . why don't I just take this bag of money and leave?" Things were getting way too weird for Thomas, and his gut told him to get out of Dodge and pronto.

Stephen retorted, "If you think that will satisfy you, then please just take the bag and go. And feel free to take the lottery ticket as well. But I don't think that will be enough for you; I suspect you want more. And if you do, then I have a better idea. All you have to do is tell me you wish you had all my luck, and I was left with none. If you do, all the riches you ever imagined will be yours. But the key is that you can't just say the words; you must mean them."

For a moment, Thomas stood silently, staring at Stephen as if studying his expression for signs of deception. There were none. Thomas thought, "This guy believes everything he is saying. In his mind, he thinks he's telling me the truth." Then Thomas suddenly realized it didn't matter whether he believed in wishes or good luck because the man standing before him most certainly did. What that meant to Thomas was that if he could convince this strange man that he believed what Stephen was saying and would accept Steven's proposition, the madman might be crazy enough to sign over his house and all his money. Thomas decided to do his best to gain the man's confidence.

"What is your name?" Thomas asked Stephen, figuring that was as good of a place as any to start.

"Stephen." The man replied, "Stephen Albright is my name. And yours? If I may ask."

Thomas hesitated for a moment, then decided to be honest with Stephen. If he would pull this off, he had to be truthful. He said, "My name is Thomas Stewart."

Stephen said, "Very well, Thomas Stewart. May I assume you are considering taking me up on my offer? Are you ready to assume my place and claim your financial fortune?"

"I am," Thomas replied, but still somewhat warily. He was playing all this interaction by ear, and since he had never dealt with a crazy person before, he had no idea what might happen next. There was also something so very odd about how this Stephen character was in such a hurry to give away his fortune that, for the first time, Thomas began to feel apprehensive about everything. Although he was not prone to superstition, something did not seem quite right about all of this. He thought of something his father had once told him, "Tommy, if something sounds too good to be true, it probably is."

But Thomas needed to believe Stephen was nothing more than an eccentric crackpot. And since Thomas still held the gun and had it pointed directly at Stephen, there was little the man could do to harm him. Yet he felt something was still a bit wrong with the entire situation. All sorts of internal alarms seemed to go off immediately, warning Thomas to grab the money bag and flee. But Thomas was certain these feelings were unfounded, and he decided, why should he settle for a bag of money when he could have it all? This crazy man was offering him a whole new lease on life.

"Ok." Thomas acknowledged, then asked, "What should I do? I mean . . . how do I make all of this happen?" He didn't want to screw up what could be a very sweet deal.

"Stephen explained, "Just say aloud that you wish you had all the luck I currently have and that I would no longer have any of it. It's as simple as that. But once again, I have to warn you to make sure you really mean what you are saying and that deep down in the very pit of your soul, this is really what you want."

Thomas realized such a declaration would not be a problem for him because he and his family had been struggling just to stay afloat for so many years. Things had gotten about as bad as he felt they could ever get, so bad that he had stooped so low as to try to rob Stephen's home. He even realized that if it had become necessary, he could have murdered the man and shot him in cold blood. That was exactly how bad things had become. Thomas loved his wife and family and would do anything in his power to help them. He would have sold his soul to the devil if it meant helping his family. So unbelievable as it might be, what Stephen offered could be his last chance to save his family.

"Yes," Thomas said. "I'll do it." He braced himself for what he was certain would be a major letdown, took a deep breath, and said, "I want what you have. I want all the luck you possess to leave your body and come into mine. I want your riches. I want your good fortune. And I want you to have none of it any longer."

For a second or so, nothing seemed to happen. Slowly, Thomas noticed a sparkling white vapor seeping from Stephen's body as if every pore of his flesh was emitting a haze. Soon a cloud-like fog hovered above Stephen's head, and he seemed to swoon a bit on his feet as if the strength had been sucked out of him, and he looked as if he might pass out.

Then, the sparkling mist slowly traveled between the men and surrounded Thomas's body. He felt his skin tingle, and the hair on his arms seemed to stand on end as if he were in the middle of an atmosphere charged with electromagnetic energy. Next, the vapors entered his own body through his pores, and he became filled with a strange, satisfying warmth.

Thomas could see Stephen standing across the room watching him, watching the spectacle with calm reservation and what appeared to be a look of relief as if he had been somehow freed from some horrible curse rather than having just given away a fortune. Once again, Thomas began to sense a deep discomfort in the pit of his stomach, as if all of this perceived good luck might suddenly go very bad.

After a few moments, the tingling of his flesh stopped, as did the deep heat he felt inside. Those sensations were replaced with a sudden euphoria, the likes of which Thomas had never experienced before. His previous thoughts of concern vanished amid all of his happiness. Thomas realized he had never felt so strong, positive, and self-assured in his entire life. He believed he could do no wrong as if anything he ever attempted would be successful, and every thought he would ever have would be deemed a pure genius. Thomas could not comprehend why Stephen would have ever become tired of such feelings or why he would have willingly given up the incredible sensations. He felt as if he was on top of the world.

"Open the top drawer of the hall table," Stephen said, still sounding a bit weak from the ordeal. "There are some documents in there for you."

Still, under the positive influence of his newfound euphoria, Thomas didn't even question why there might be anything in this house specifically meant for him. Instead, he opened the drawer and withdrew what appeared to be a large legal document and several smaller documents.

Stephen said, "That top document is a deed to this house and the surrounding land. There are also copies of all of my active financial accounts and investments, or should I say, your investments now."

Still stunned, Thomas opened the top document and was astonished to see the name on the cover sheet begin to change right before his eyes. Stephen Albright began to fade and was simultaneously overwritten with his name, Thomas Stewart. As he leafed through the remaining documents, the same thing happened to each of them. His name was now on every single financial certificate. He had seen numbers totaling in the millions flashing by as he skimmed the papers.

"You mean to say it's true? All of this? Everything? It's all mine?" Thomas asked with utter disbelief.

"Yes," Stephen replied. "Everything, all of the wealth and riches you could imagine, will be yours for the rest of your life. That is unless you choose to offer it to someone else, as I have done with you."

Thomas looked aghast. "And why would I ever want to do that? Just because you were stupid enough to give it all away doesn't mean

I am equally as crazy. This is everything I've ever dreamed about all of my life. It's more wealth than I could spend in several lifetimes. What amazing luck! I'd never give away such an incredible gift. All of my troubles are officially over. My wife, kids, and I will have everything we ever dreamed of. She won't believe me when I tell her. Speaking of which, I have to call her right now and tell her the good news."

Stephen said nothing. He just looked knowingly with pity as Thomas tucked his gun behind his back and pulled out a cell phone. Thomas's face filled with joy at the thought of telling his family of his newfound fortune. But Stephen stood silently, knowing what was about to happen next.

Some laws governed the universe; some were known by man, others unknown. There were physical laws as well as spiritual and economic laws. One such law, which Stephen knew far too well, stated that there was only so much of everything available, and for everything you chose to get, you must give up something else. If you, for example, had two hours of spare time available and had to decide between going to dinner or a movie, to choose the one, you must sacrifice the other. This rule was one Thomas was sadly about to learn.

"Jenny? It's me." Thomas said into the phone. Then, after a bit of hesitation, he said. "Excuse me? Who is this? Where's my wife, and what are you doing with her cell phone?" Then, a dark shadow seemed to pass across Thomas's face, and he replied to the voice on the other end of the line. "Oh my God! Which hospital? Saint Luke's, you say? I'll be right there."

Stephen didn't ask what the problem was because it didn't matter what the particular circumstances might be; he understood the result would be the same. He already knew Thomas's wife and family were dead and that the policeman simply hadn't wanted to break the news to Thomas over the phone. It was a similar scenario to that which he had been through several years ago when his wife and daughter had been killed within a few seconds of his taking ownership of the very same gift.

"That . . . that . . . was . . . he said . . . he was . . . a . . . police officer." Thomas stammered. "He said there was . . . was . . . an accident. My wife and kids were injured . . ." His voice caught in his throat.

". . . and they are on their way to the hospital by ambulance. I had better get right over there."

"If you feel you must," Stephen said.

"Of course, I must!" Thomas shouted. "It's my family, for Christ's sake. They've been injured. They need me."

Stephen said, "You mean they needed you? And you weren't there because you were here claiming the most important thing in your life: money."

Thomas said, "How dare you! Screw you, Stephen. You know that's not true. I was only here trying to secure my family's future."

"And it appears you did just that. Now your family has no future." Stephen said. "I might as well tell you there's no need to hurry to the hospital. It won't do any good. By the time you get there, they will all be dead if they aren't dead already."

Thomas looked confused, "What? How . . . how can you pretend to know that? What the hell are you talking about?"

Stephen said, "Remember I warned you to be careful what you wished for. But apparently, you were so busy thinking about all the money you'd have that you didn't think things through. I understand completely because, as I said, I was once as desperate as you are."

"But this . . . this thing . . . was supposed to bring me good fortune." Thomas pleaded, "And now you tell me my family is dead. What kind of good luck is that?"

Stephen said, "A simple law of the universe is that you can't have everything. For each thing you choose to have, you voluntarily or involuntarily choose to give up something else. And you have made your choice."

Thomas asked tearfully, "Are you trying to tell me I caused this to happen to my family by choosing to make one stupid wish?"

Stephen said, "I promised you that you would have more money than you could ever spend, and you would never have to worry about being injured and killed for all of your natural life. I said you would live a long, healthy life and someday die of natural causes as a very old, wealthy man. That is what this particular good fortune is about. And now you have all of those things."

"But my wife and my children! How can they be dead?" Thomas shouted as best as his sobbing voice would permit. "What good is all the money in the world if everyone I love is dead?"

"That might have been a good question to ask earlier. I tried to warn you to be careful." Stephen repeated, "But you didn't. And now what was mine is yours." Then Stephen slowly turned to leave.

Thomas shouted, "Where the hell do you think you're going?" He reached around his back and brought out the pistol, pointing it menacingly at Stephen.

Stephen replied, "I told you before I was going to leave, and now, I will do just that. You have what you came here for, and now I'm going to try and start a new life, and maybe if I am truly lucky, I will find some semblance of true happiness before I die."

"You bastard! You knew this would happen!" Thomas said accusingly, "You said you had a family once. They probably also died because of this horrible wish, this curse. You tricked me into this devil's bargain, and now I'm all alone in the world." He began to sob uncontrollably. "It's all your fault! Don't you dare move another step closer to that door, or so help me, God, I will shoot you!"

"I'm truly sorry about your family." Stephen said, "As I was sorry about my own. I've hated myself every day since I made the same bargain you just made, and I'm quite certain you will be wallowing in misery for many years to come. But that's no longer my problem. It's yours. So, if you will excuse me, I will be leaving. So, unless you are truly prepared to shoot me, I suggest you accept your good fortune and make the best of it."

Thomas shouted with insane rage, "Die, you bastard!" Then he pulled the trigger, and the room echoed with the deafening blast from his handgun. Stephen was slammed against the wall as the bullet entered his stomach. He involuntarily reached down to where he had been shot, and his hands came away covered with the blood pouring from his wound.

To Thomas's shock, Stephen didn't cry out or look in pain. It looked to Thomas as if the man was happy; he had just been mortally wounded, evident by the expression of satisfaction Stephen had on his dying face.

"You . . . you . . . wanted me to shoot you," Thomas said. "That was your plan all along. Oh my God, you wanted to die and got me to kill you. You played me the whole time."

Stephen seemed to be staring into space as if seeing and smiling at something or someone invisible to Thomas. Then he slid down the wall, landing on his backside on the floor, still sitting and staring joyfully at the same seemingly empty space.

Thomas dropped the gun to the floor, then fell to his knees and buried his face in his hands, allowing the tears to flow freely. He had been desperate and greedy and had not listened to his subconscious's warnings. Thomas had been a fool. He now had all the money he could ever imagine, yet like Stephen, he had nothing. He stared at the bloody corpse of Stephen Albright and mumbled, "Be careful what you wish for . . . you just might get it."

DEATH PATROL

Author's Note: In late 2024, Twisted Pulp magazine asked me to write a story based on a series of photos depicting three maniacs in a setting reminiscent of the movie, "The Purge." They called themselves The Death Patrol. Here is that story.

The once prosperous city, a testament to man's creativity and design ingenuity, now lay in ruins, a twisted decaying maze of crumbling buildings and pitted streets that formerly overflowed with prosperity. The previously awe-inspiring skyline was now nothing more than a stark black painting in silhouette on the canvas depicting the smoldering crimson sky. This devastating backdrop served as a haunting reminder of the pure horror that had befallen this once monumental metropolis.

The foul air was redolent with the stench of decay. The only sounds one could hear echoing through the desolate streets and alleyways were the howling of the stagnant wind blowing through the ruined streets and the distant moans and cries of the remaining savages as they preyed upon each other, struggling for survival in this pure Darwinian world, exploding with insanity. In this post-apocalyptic dung heap, where even former preditors now lived in fear, where rats and other scavengers thrived on the corpses stacked high in the streets, a veritable wasteland, any sort of hope for civilization was a faded memory, replaced by a desperate struggle for survival. This was a world that had long since forgotten the meaning of peace, love, and caring and had traded for kill or be killed.

Amid the chaos and destruction, three Godless souls could count themselves among those who endured. They were survivors of the holocaust that had wiped out most of the population of the world. They banded together as like minds, albeit minds of the twisted variety. The only reason they still existed was because the three were probably the most vile, soulless people remaining on Earth. So much so that referring to them as human might be a stretch. They were all three insane beyond imagining. There was not one among them with a thread of decency or the capacity to even comprehend the sanctity of human life.

They called themselves the Death Patrol, as death was the currency they dealt with. This tribe of mobile mayhem consisted of one man and two women. The man, who called himself JP, was the de facto leader of the trio simply because of his size and strength. When asked, JP would say the initials stood for Justice Personified. His real name had been Jerome Purdy, but that was not a very intimidating moniker. Despite these threatening traits, JP knew never to push the two women further than they would allow, as he had no desire to awaken some morning with his manhood missing, only to see rats feasting on it.

JP was a big man, just over six feet tall, with sleeve tattoos on both arms, accentuating the muscles bulging from his tightly fitting gray tee shirt. He wore canvas work pants, black suspenders, and brown boots. His most intimidating feature was the hideous pig mask, which he seldom removed. As frightening as the mask might be, the horribly disfigured face beneath the mask was far worse. JP carried a machine pistol for distance killing and a crowbar or pick ax for when he needed to get up close and personal.

Eva was a strong girl who fancied black boots, red, white, and blue American flag shorts, and a black tank top with an orange skull stenciled on the front. Depending upon her murderous moods, she favored either a cat mask or a clown mask. Her weapon of choice was a razor-sharp ax with a long wooden handle. Eva was by far the most angry of the crazies on the team and, as such, made sure all her kills were close. She always said she loved to see the fear in her victims' faces and watch the light leave their eyes as they died.

Pari was the smallest member of the Death Patrol, wearing a black dress, pink sneakers, a beaded necklace, and pigtails in her long hair. Sometimes, she wore a pumpkin mask, and other times, a white death mask with the eyes and mouth stitched shut. Pari's main weapon was an AK-47, but she could always rely on her handy baseball bat when needed. If one were to try to pick which member of the Death Patrol was the least insane, chances are Pari would be everyone's initial choice. That is until they saw the rotting severed head she carried with her on a rope for good luck. Once they found out the head belonged to an ex-lover, all bets would be off.

The Death Patrol ruled the ruins of the City of the Dead, so named because more than 95% of the population had been killed. Life in the city was without rules, laws, or consequences. It was like every day was a scene from the movie The Purge. Instead of twelve hours of mayhem in the City of the Dead, it was nonstop. This Death Patrol wandered free, knowing that even the toughest of the surviving lunatics were not crazy enough to take them on. A few other small gangs were struggling to survive, and on occasion, they might take a run at The Death Patrol, but that would be their fatal mistake. Being tough was one thing, but being certifiably insane was another thing entirely. How do you instill fear into someone who knows no fear? How can you threaten to kill someone for whom death has no meaning? The answer is simple, you can't.

One day, the trio came upon a car trapped under a fallen electrical pole. There was no danger from live wires since electricity had been extinct for more than a year. JP approached the car and heard someone moaning inside. He tore open the door and saw a man trapped behind the steering wheel. The collision had pushed the wheel deep into the driver's stomach. His innards were dribbling out from the rip the wheel had made in his guts. The man looked up from hooded, exhausted eyes and said, "Please . . . Help me."

Pari laughed and said in her high-pitched, crazy voice, "Help you? Help you? There ain't nobody in this whole damn world can help you, Honey."

Eva looked at the injured man and said, "Ooowee. You is a dead man who don't even know it." Then she chuckled knowingly.

The man said weakly, "Please . . . Help . . . I have money."

JP laughed and said, "Money? Money? What the Hell are we gonna do with money? Run down to the bank and open an account? What do ya say, ladies? Shall we open a savings account? Maybe a 401k or an IRA account is what we need."

"How's about we try our luck in the stock market?" Pari cackled.

Eva said, "I want me one of them black credit cards that's got no limit."

JP leaned into the car and screamed like the madman he was, "Your money is worthless. Money don't mean Jack around here!" Then he turned to Pari and said, "Pari, do me righteous and put this moron out of my misery! His stinking guts are offensive to my delicate olfactory senses."

"I'll be happy to, JP," Pari said, raising her AK-47.

Eva said, "Now, Pari, don't you go wastin' yer bullets on some dumb nobody who's got one foot in the grave and 'tother on a banana peel." And without hesitating, Eva stepped forward with her ax and severed the dying man's head from his neck. It fell out of the car and rolled across the ground to JP's feet.

He said, "Hey, Pari. Y'all want this one? The one you're carrying around on that rope is starting to stink to high Heaven."

Pari laughed and said, "I don't want no damn fool nobody's head. If I'm gonna drag some dead head around with me, it better have some significant meaning for me, like old Henry here."

"I know that ex-boyfriend's head is important to you, darlin', but it's really getting rank, as you may have noticed," Eva said. "Maybe it's time to trade up to a fresher model."

"Thanks for your concern, Eva, but I'll just keep Henry here with me a little while longer." Pari insisted. JP and Eva noticed that Pari was starting to get that wild look she usually got right before she wigged out. Neither of them wanted that to happen. Pari may have been the smallest, but she was by far the craziest. So, JP kicked the head over to Eva and said, "Cranial soccer, anyone?" He and Eva kicked the head around for a few minutes as Pari calmed down, returning to as close to "normal" as she ever got.

They heard a man's deep voice from the alleyway behind them say, "Well, what do we have here? A couple of wannabe soccer stars. I see youse two are trying to get a 'head' start on today's game."

The three turned to see a group of ten menacingly large, muscular men armed with pistols, knives, and homemade spears surrounding them. The leader of the group was a big man with a shaved but tattooed head who had to weigh close to three hundred pounds of solid muscle. He wore a sleeveless shirt revealing his own series of prison-style tats. The rest of the band were almost as big as this man and equally as ugly and likely as dangerous.

The man pointed his pistol at JP and said, "How's 'bout youse all put down yer weapons, so's me and da boys kin get a closer look at these here lovely ladies. It's been a while since any of us has had us some gen-u-ine good lovin', and we think them two right there might suit us just fine." Then, pointing at JP, he said, "And you, pig mask. Maybe we'll take a turn at you as well. Ya see, us beggars can't be too choosy. So, maybe I should say beggars might be buggers." The group of renegades all laughed at their leader's joke.

There was no movement from the three members of the Death Patrol; they were studying the situation and waiting until the time was right. JP could see that Pari was getting that crazy look again and sensed the moment was just about at hand when the big bald leader said, "Well, is you gonna put down your weapons or not? We can just as easy have our way with your corpses. It wouldn't be the first time, but we really prefer warm bodies to cold ones. Come on now, alls you have to do is . . ."

The leader never got to finish his sentence as Eva's ax flew through the air and sank into the man's skull with a sickening thwack sound. The big man stood for a second before falling face-first onto the battered asphalt street. When the ax handle hit the paving, the ax popped out of his skull, along with what little brains he had. Before the other nine men could react, Pari went into full nuclear meltdown mode and opened up on them with her AK, as JP did the same with his machine pistol.

The men who weren't immediately gunned down returned fire. Eva ran directly into the gunfire, retrieving her ax and swinging like the mad woman she was. Having run out of ammunition, Pari joined the chaos, swinging her baseball bat and crushing skulls. With a pick ax in one hand and a crowbar in the other, JP, also out of bullets, got up close and personal with the last two attackers. When the fighting was done, the ten attackers were dead, lying in a stinking river of their own blood and released bowels.

JP stood panting momentarily, looking down at the carnage they had created, and said, "Well, ladies. How did we make out today in our latest adventure?"

Eva said, "I do believe I'm fine, JP. A few bullets grazed me, and I think I got a through-and-through in my left shoulder, but I've had worse."

Pari reported, "Yep, I got me a few of them near misses, too. Hell, one of them put a new part in my hair." Then she laughed hysterically with her patented insane cackle.

JP said, "So, all-in-all, except fer a few scrapes, we done good. Chalk it up to another successful day for the Death Patrol. What say we strip these fellas, take their guns and ammo, and see if they got anything else we can use."

With that, the Death Patrol gathered the spoils of their battle and then returned to their hideout under one of the fallen buildings to rest, recover, and be ready for their next day of killing in a world of endless butchery.

SEEING IS BELIEVING

/ 1 /

The two old men sat next to each other on the wood and concrete park bench, with a bag of unsalted peanuts open between them. A small squirrel stopped a few feet in front of one of the men, got up on its hind legs, and chittered. It was like the little creature was trying to tell the man what he wanted, even though it couldn't speak. The man reached into the bag and retrieved three peanuts, which he promptly tossed to the squirrel, who grabbed them off the ground, tucked them into his mouth, and scurried away.

The man, whose name was Sid, turned to his bench mate and asked, "Man, Harry. It's so great to see you up and around. I was starting to think I might not be able to recognize you without beeping machines all around you and tubes coming in and out of every orifice you own, plus a few extras the doctors took the liberty of creating."

"Yeah, Sid. It's equally as great for me as you might imagine. Probably greater. Except for one thing."

Sid said, "What thing, Harry? You know me, brother. I've always been here for you and always will be. Tell me what's eating you."

Harry briefly summarized the problem to his friend, who looked so shocked that he might no longer be able to speak coherently. With a shaky and concerned voice, Sid asked, "So, my oldest friend and comrade, do you really expect me to believe that demons exist and are walking around among us right now?"

Sid was a thin old man in his early 70s with a mostly bald head, sporting a fringe of long, sparse, white hair tied back in a sad excuse for a ponytail. He wore two gold rings in his left ear, hearing aids in both ears, thick glasses, and a full beard and mustache combination, which were in dire need of a trim. The day was mild enough for his faded Santana concert tee shirt and worn jeans. On his feet, he wore sandals and white socks. If you were looking to paint a caricature of an aged remnant of the Woodstock generation, Sid would be your ideal model.

Harry replied, "You know me, Sid. I expect nothing, and that way, I am never disappointed. But trust me when I say I'm telling you true."

Although the two had known each other since childhood and had been through many of the same life journeys together, somewhere along the line, Harry had given up his Woodstock ways in exchange for a more conservative, albeit casual look. He had neatly combed salt and pepper hair, which was visibly thinner where it barely covered a recent scar that still appeared puckered and tender. His mustache and goatee were neatly trimmed and went well with his designer glasses. Harry wore a flowered Hawaiian shirt and tan cargo pants. His feet were in white low-top sneakers with no socks.

To look at the pair sitting together on that park bench, one might think that a well-to-do gentleman was offering advice to a down-on-his-luck street person, but that observation would be far from accurate. The two friends had started a software company at the beginning of the information revolution, which had become one of the top ten software companies in the country when they sold it to a mega-conglomerate more than three decades earlier. Since then, neither of them had needed or wanted to work. Harry had always given most of the credit for their success to Sid, who seemed to have an almost supernatural ability to make decisions that would result in a great influx of cash.

Sid said, "Maybe so, Harry. But the way you talk about it, you truly believe these demons exist." He was uncertain why he and his friend were having this discussion. It was not part of their typical conversations, which leaned more toward reminiscing about people they once knew, which old acquaintances had recently died, girls they had known in their youth, and the "good old days" in general. They seldom spoke of business as it was a topic they were both happy to have put behind them years earlier. They never spoke of things like this.

"Of course I do, Sid. Seeing is believing, as they say." Harry replied cryptically.

"Then please explain why you believe or what you've seen." Sid wanted to get to the bottom of why they were having this unusual discussion.

Harry took a deep breath and explained, "It's like this, Sid. The creatures I'm referring to as demons presently walking the Earth originated in the outermost circle of Hell. You've heard of Hell, right, Sid?"

"Heard of it? You know I've been divorced four times. I've lived it." Sid replied with a laugh. He had indeed been married and divorced four times, each wife having gotten a generous portion of Sid's money. Harry married his wife before becoming wealthy and lived faithfully with her until her passing two years earlier.

"Nice one, Sid. But these creatures come from a place where there is a fragile membrane that separates the world of the living, that is to say, us, from the realm of the damned is at its thinnest.

Sid said, "I assume this is where you tell me that portions of this membrane, as you call it, are so thin that demons can find their way through. Right?"

"Right, you are, Sid. There is nothing these horrible creatures want more than to cross over and start wreaking havoc."

"You mean, that's all they want? Just to cause trouble?"

Harry replied, "Yep. They love causing chaos and despair. Remember, these are damned souls, former evil humans who have died and been banished to Hell. They get their pleasure from causing anguish and great suffering to living humans. We have what they can never have again; we're alive."

"But, Harry. Another thing that I find confusing about what you're saying is, wouldn't we notice them walking around? I mean, aren't they hideous little creatures with horns, pointy ears, and tails? Don't they run around with pitchforks and things like that?"

Harry said, "Man, Sid. Either you watch too many horror movies or read too many graphic novels. Here's how I believe it works.

These demons can't just pass through this barrier, no matter how thin it might be. If they could, the scenario you described would become a reality. We'd be overrun with monsters. No, they have to find a suitable host whose body they can inhabit."

Sid asked, "You mean like demonic possession, like in The Exorcist?"

"Yeah, something like that. Something must attract the demon's attention as a good potential host. The person could be a criminal type whose soul is already corrupted. Or, it could be someone completely innocent and free of sin."

"Well, that just doesn't seem fair!"

"Sid, remember that we're not dealing with schoolyard games here. We're talking about damned souls trying to find a way out of the eternal torment of Hell. I don't think they're the best beings to discuss what's fair and what isn't."

"I suppose you've got a point there, Harry."

Harry continued, "Anyway, once someone attracts a demon's interest, intentionally or accidentally, the victim's hope of avoiding possession is lost. If a demon locates a desired host near a place where the membrane is thin, it's all over but the shouting."

"And the projectile puking pea soup," Sid interjected.

"Nice one, Sid. You're a laugh a minute."

Sid replied, "Sorry about that, Harry. Sometimes, I can't control my own mouth. A goofy idea pops into my brain and right out my mouth before I even realize it."

"Yeah, I know, Sid. I've known this for over sixty years since we were little kids in grade school."

"Has it really been that long, Harry? It seems hard to believe."

"It has been, Sid."

Sid asked, "So, how come after the sixty-plus years we've known each other, you're only bringing up this demon nonsense now? In all those years, you never mentioned it. In fact, when we both went to see The Exorcist movie back in the 70s, you acted like it was all a bunch of crap. Now, all of a sudden, you're a believer. What gives?"

Harry hesitated, "As I said earlier, Sid, seeing is believing."

"And you've seen?"

"Oh yeah. I've most definitely seen Sid. You know that accident I had a few months ago?"

Sid said, "Sure, how could I not? You almost bought the farm, my friend. I can still see remnants of that on your noggin."

Harry explained, "True. But I didn't die. I thought I was lucky to have survived that. Now, I'm not so sure."

"What do you mean, Harry?" Sid asked, sounding genuinely concerned.

Then Harry told his tale.

/ 2 /

His story began several months earlier, almost two years after his beloved wife, Diane, passed. Harry had been crossing the street not far from the park where he and Sid now sat when a drunk driver ran a red light and struck him. Harry had flown twenty feet through the air and landed, hitting his head on a curb, and was knocked unconscious. He had lain in a coma for more than a week before eventually regaining consciousness. Harry complained to his doctor about feeling strange. Harry couldn't explain what he felt; he just felt like something was different. The doctors ran dozens of tests and scans for the next several weeks, and there were no signs of any problems. In fact, they admitted they were shocked that he had survived at all.

Still, something felt odd to Harry. He seemed to have trouble focusing for long periods. His thoughts felt muddled, disjointed, and disorganized. He was, by nature, a meticulously organized person, so this new feeling was foreign to him. During his extended hospital stay, Harry had been seen by many different doctors. Many nurses had also treated him. Most he couldn't remember, but one he would never forget, not because of any kindness she might have bestowed on him, quite the opposite. Her name was Nurse Peters.

Harry had taken an immediate dislike to the woman. While the other nurses were friendly and happy to engage him in conversation, this woman was cold, unfriendly, and all business and she could be mean. If the woman was rough when handling Harry and he complained, she always apologized, but Harry sensed her apology was as false as the smile on her distrustful face. It felt to Harry like the woman got pleasure from causing him discomfort. He had spoken to a few other patients who had similar complaints about the woman. Then, one day, something happened that made Harry question his sanity.

A polished metal mirror hung on the wall next to his bed. Harry couldn't see in it most of the time because he had been lying in bed. One day, as he returned to bed after a trip to the bathroom, Nurse Peters walked into the room. As she passed the mirror, Harry's breath caught in his throat. He couldn't believe his eyes. Gone was the miserable-looking nurse with gray hair and wrinkles, and in her place was one of the most hideous creatures Harry had ever seen.

Although the glimpse he got in the mirror was brief, his mind had captured an image he knew would haunt him until his dying day. He saw a repulsive monster with leathery, greenish-brown skin. It had huge eyes bulging from dark, baggy sockets. Its nose was snout-like, with large black nostrils that seeped a disgusting green ooze. The creature's mouth was large and seemed frozen in a rictus grin of hundreds of long, sharp fangs. Two large tusks, more than six inches long, rose upward from its huge jutting bottom lip. Two ram-like horns curled back from its bald forehead on each side of the monster's skull, glistening with sweat. Long strands of greasy hair hung in patches from the back of its horrid skull.

"Is everything alright, Sir?" Nurse Peters asked.

Harry looked in the direction of the voice, expecting to see the hideous creature from the mirror, but instead found himself looking into the miserable but human face of Nurse Peters. She was looking at him strangely as if concerned about his behavior.

Harry said, "Yes, I'm, um, fine . . . I'm just a bit tired. Thank you for asking."

The nurse replied, "Then you'd better get back into bed and rest. I have other patients to see." Her tone was the same as always: brusk, business-like, and to the point. As she walked by the mirror, Nurse Peters stopped to check her appearance before leaving. Harry was certain the nurse would see nothing but her normal reflection. Harry was also sure that one hundred others, catching her reflection in mirrors all over the hospital, would only see an older nurse, not the hideous creature he had seen.

What, if anything, had he actually seen? Had he been hallucinating, or was this all a figment of his imagination? During the early days of his recovery, the doctors had asked him repeatedly if he had seen anything he couldn't explain. He had told them he had not and answered them truthfully. But after what he had just seen, Harry didn't know what to do. If he told them, he might never get out of the hospital. If he didn't, what would become of him? Was this strange vision the result of his head injury?

Harry had decided to keep what he had seen to himself. Every day, he became more convinced that what he had seen reflected in the mirror was some type of demon. From the first, he knew something had been off with Nurse Peters. Once he saw the monster in the mirror, Harry was convinced that the nurse was possessed and that, for whatever reason, the mirror allowed him to know the truth. In movies, vampires can't cast reflections in mirrors. This might be something like that. The difference is that no one can see the demon inside except him. His head injury must have triggered something in his brain to allow these creatures to be seen.

After being released from the hospital, Harry began to research. He needed to know what was happening to him. Harry started to obsess with learning all he could about Hell, demons, and possessions. He kept his studies a secret, not even sharing them with his best friend, Sid, until he was ready. During this research, Harry read about the belief that a thin membrane separated our world from the world of demons. When he got to the part about possessing a host, Harry realized he had somehow seen an actual demon in that hospital mirror, and Nurse Peters was its host.

Suddenly, it all began to come together and make sense. Harry now understood why Nurse Peters seemed off and was so cruel to her patients. There was a Hell-spawned demon living inside her. Harry believed the nurse was chosen because she was a naturally angry, mean-spirited woman, which the creature had been seeking. Then Harry realized if that woman could go through life with no one suspecting that she was nothing more than a flesh puppet for a demon, then there had to be others. Unfortunately, for whatever reason, he was the only man who could see them.

/ 3 /

A month after his release from the hospital, Harry sat at the counter of a local diner, eating breakfast. He planned to meet his friend, Sid, later in the park. Harry planned to tell Sid everything he had learned since his accident and about his apparent newfound gift of sight, as unpleasant as that might be.

As Harry sat deep in thought, a man walked into the diner holding a sawed-off shotgun and shouted, "Nobody move, or somebody's gonna get their guts splattered all over this place."

Harry hoped the robber would empty the cash register and leave, but if he chose to rob the customers, Harry would happily give up his wallet. He only had $40 in cash, and his other cards could be replaced. It would be a hassle, but it was better to be alive and inconvenienced than dead. Harry found it odd that the would-be robber did nothing to hide his face. It was as if he didn't care. The diner had cameras all over the place. The guy must have been high on drugs or something. Then Harry looked in the wall-length mirror running along the counter before him.

He no longer saw a man with a shotgun but a hideous creature. Where the man had been almost six feet tall, this monster in the mirror was no more than four. It had brownish-green, leathery skin, and its flesh was coated with a slimy film. The creature had the same hog-like snout, wide fangs, tusk-filled mouth, bulging eyes, and ram's horns. It had a long mane of hair that hung down to the center of its back. The monster's arms were ape-like, and its hands and feet were enlarged with talon-like claws on its fingers and toes. The demon's hands gripped tightly on the sawed-off shotgun.

Harry realized now why the robber cared nothing about disguising its identity being discovered or protecting it from witnesses and the cameras. The body holding the weapon might be human, but the thing controlling that body was a demon. But if that were true, and it obviously was, why would a demon want money? Harry supposed that under normal circumstances, in Hell, for instance, a demon would not need cash. However, in the world of the living, money makes the world go around. Harry knew that better than most people. It's much easier to cause problems and disrupt lives if you have a boatload of cash rather than being broke. Causing trouble was what these demons were all about.

For the moment, none of this mattered as the man/demon was pointing a shotgun and threatening to kill people, and Harry was one of them. As Harry watched in the mirror, a man stood and approached the demon. He wore a black cassock and a white color. Harry was curious about the effect, if any, this man of the cloth would have on this demon. The priest held out both his hands to show he presented no threat and offered to help the man if he would just put down the gun.

The man smiled with an insane grin that looked even more treacherous when seen in the mirror from that mouth full of fangs. Then, with no other emotion, the robber pulled the trigger and cut the man in half with a single blast. Before Harry could begin to process what had happened, another man got out of his seat with a pistol in his hand and blew the top of the murdering criminal's head off, sending blood, brains, and bone in all directions. Harry felt something slap against his foot and saw a chunk of something gray and crimson stuck to the side of his shoe. He kicked his foot and flicked it off.

When Harry looked in the mirror again, the demon was gone, and the robber, minus half his head, lay dead on the floor as blood puddles beneath him. Although he knew he should stay and give a witness statement when the police arrived, Harry was keenly aware there was nothing of value he could offer, and anything he might say would likely get him committed to a loonie bin.

As Harry walked away from the scene, he wondered what had happened to the demon. Was it sent back to Hell on the express train, or was it floating around looking for another host? Harry realized that, for now, none of that mattered. One thing, however, that did concern him was his finding a way to rid himself of this newfound and unwanted ability to see what others could not. Perhaps when he talked to Sid about it, he might have some recommendations other than mental counseling.

/ 4 /

"All I can say is, wow! That's some story, Harry!" Sid said.

Harry asked, "So what am I supposed to do, Sid? I can't just go blurting this out to the doctors or police. They'll think I'm nuts, and even if they did happen to believe me, there's nothing they can do about it anyway."

Sid thought momentarily, then suggested, "Maybe if you tell your doctors, they'll find some way to shut this thing off. I mean, look around the park. Can you see any little green monsters running around?"

"You're not funny, Sid. I came to you because you're my best friend, and I thought you would understand, even if you didn't completely believe me."

"I'm sorry, Bro. That was my stupid mouth running off at the wrong time again. I haven't ever been able to control it."

Then Harry said, "Besides, if you were paying attention, I already told you they only appear as reflections in mirrors. For all I know, the park could be crawling with demons, and without a mirror, I'd have no more idea than you would."

"Didn't you say these demons could be killed? You saw that guy this morning at the diner, right?"

Harry said, "Yeah, I did. And the demon went away afterward, but so what? I can't go around checking people out with a mirror and then killing them. From what I've read, most of the time, these possessed people are victims themselves. A lot have no idea they've been taken over. How long do you think it would be until I was caught, tried for cold-blooded, premeditated murder, and given a lethal injection?"

Sid thought, then said, "Yeah, you're right. No matter how you look at this, it's a lose-lose situation."

"So, what am I going to do, Sid? Pretend none of this has happened to me and everything's right with the world, even though I know it isn't?"

"All I can suggest is what I think I'd do if I found myself in a no-win situation like yours," Sid said.

"And what's that, Sid?"

"I would embrace my new talent, Harry. I would keep it secret and never tell anyone about this gift."

"What good would that do."

Sid said, "It would be like a sort of superpower. You will be able to know who is possessed and who isn't. Let's say you're some poor working slob whose boss is being a real jerk; in fact, he's always a jerk. You check him out in the men's room mirror and see that he's got one of those critters inside him. Right? Now you know why he's the way he is. What you do with that information is up to you. Maybe you could find a way to undermine his authority and get him fired. Does that make sense?"

Harry hesitated while he thought it over, then said, "Yeah. I suppose it does. If I look at this as a gift and not a curse, I can see how it could give me an advantage. It could allow me to avoid any trouble any of these things might cause me. You're right, Sid. This is sort of a superpower."

"There you go, Buddy. Listen to old Sid. He always has your back and knows what's best for you."

"Thanks, Sid."

As the pair sat looking at the people in the park across the road, a large truck slowly passed by. It was one of those trucks that carried large panels of glass and mirrors. When it stopped at the intersection, Harry looked into the mirror and didn't see his friend, Sid, sitting beside him. Instead, he saw a hideous demon smiling its horrible grin of fangs. Harry now understood why Sid could never control what came out of his mouth.

"Thanks again, Sid. You've been more help than you realize," Harry said as he got up and walked away.

JURY DUTY

"When you go into court, you are putting your fate into the hands of twelve people who weren't smart enough to get out of jury duty."
—Norm Crosby

"Some people try to get out of jury duty by lying. You don't have to lie. Tell the judge the truth. Tell him you'd make a terrific juror because you can spot guilty people."
—George Carlin

"You might be a redneck if you missed 5th grade graduation because you had jury duty."
—Jeff Foxworthy

"It's rare to find someone excited over jury duty. If they're out there, I've never met them. Not a one. When the summons for jury duty arrives in the mail, how many people scream, 'Yes!' and run to clear the calendar? None. Our first and only reaction is, 'Oh, no,' quickly followed by, 'How can I get out of this?'"
—Regina Brett

/ 1 /

It had been a hectic week at work, and Greg's brain was fried. The last thing he needed was to come home, check his mail, and find a summons for jury duty. Greg Harrison hated being forced to show up to do his "civic duty." He had been through many such jury requests over the past thirty years, and most were annoying at best and unbearable at worst. Whatever the case, jury duty was always troublesome, and this one would be a major inconvenience.

Greg and his wife, Helen, desperately needed a romantic getaway. They had been planning a trip for months, trying to coordinate their busy schedules to find a five-day window when they were both available. Then, once they nailed down those dates, which happened to be a Saturday through Wednesday in late September, they had to call their kennel to ensure they had space for the couple's two dogs.

After booking the kennel, Greg had to make hotel, airline, and car rental reservations. After weeks of calling and online booking, all the reservations were made, and the couple was booked for their much overdue vacation. They thought nothing could spoil their good time. Then the mail arrived with a jury duty summons for Greg for the same Monday the couple expected to be in sunny Florida.

Helen was devastated, "I can't believe they scheduled you for our vacation week. Three hundred and sixty-five days, and they had to pick that Monday? You know how hard we had to work to make this happen, Greg. Can't you get out of it somehow?"

"You know better than that, Helen. When you get one of these, you have to show up." Greg insisted.

"But, Babe. Of all the weeks on the calendar, why that one, and why did your summons have to arrive the day after you made our final vacation plans? What can we do?" Helen asked.

Greg said, There's nothing we can do, and we won't know for sure if I have to report until the Friday evening before the Saturday we plan to leave."

"You mean you might not have to report?"

"I might not. It has happened twice to me before. About twenty-five years ago, I got a summons, called into the courthouse, and discovered my juror number did not have to report. If that happens, we will be clear to leave Saturday morning."

"And if your number is called?" Helen asked.

"Then I will have to show up on Monday. But first, we'll have to start making phone calls and logging onto websites to reschedule the kennel, the flight, the car rental, and the hotel. Luckily, I ensured we could reschedule or cancel at the last minute."

Helen said, "What a pain! And we won't know until Friday night?"

"That's right, Babe. And the most frustrating part is I could go down to the courthouse Monday morning, sit for several hours, and get sent home. They would have ruined our plans for nothing. These things are often settled on the courthouse steps, and a jury isn't needed."

"That would be awful, a total waste of our time."

Greg said, "True. But you know what would be worse?"

"No, what?"

"What would be worse would be if I got picked to serve on a jury."

Helen said, "Yep. I remember when you served before, you hated it. I forget why you hated it."

Greg said, "Well, it's not like on TV. Trials are long, boring, and repetitive. But the worst part is when we have to go to the jury room and decide whether the person is innocent or guilty."

"That's a big responsibility," Helen said.

"It is. And unfortunately, it's put into the hands of a group of morons."

"That's kind of harsh, Greg, don't you think?"

"Not really. I think some of the stupidest people I have ever met were those sitting in that room deciding the defendant's fate."

Helen said, "Didn't you guys vote to acquit that defendant when you served."

"I didn't. But the rest of the idiots did. I was the only holdout. I knew the guy was as guilty as sin, but the others refused to convict him."

"But why not?"

"They felt the prosecution didn't present enough evidence to convict. I believe the real reason was they didn't want to live with the knowledge that they might put a man in jail for a decade or more. It's easy to say you want to be tough on crime, but when you know you are going to be responsible for taking away a man's freedom, it's a different story. I, on the other hand, had no problem with it. I said we should lock him up and throw the key away."

Helen said, "But eventually, you gave in and voted to acquit."

Greg said, "You're right, I did. We sat locked together in that stupid jury deliberation room for two solid days. I knew they would never change their minds, and I felt I had wasted more of my time than I wanted to, so I finally gave up and said, 'Let's go home.'"

"Well, Greg. Let's hope for the best, and maybe when you call in on that Friday night, we'll get lucky, and you won't have to show up on Monday."

"Cross your fingers, Babe." Greg agreed.

Unfortunately, a month later, when it came time to call the courthouse, Greg heard the automated answering message call his number, and he knew he had to report promptly on Monday morning.

/ 2 /

The rest of Greg and Helen's weekend was ruined, as they had to spend it rescheduling their vacation. Fortunately, being the pragmatic people they were when Greg and Helen scheduled the original dates, they devised a series of potential backup dates in case something happened to cause them to cancel. Unfortunately, these dates were not ideal, but they would have to suffice.

After reporting for duty Monday morning, Greg sat in the county courthouse's jury pool room. Being a veteran of what he felt was a ridiculous exercise, he had come prepared with a book to read to help pass the time. He had thought about looking for a book with a title that might raise some eyebrows in the waiting room, like "How to Murder The Person Next to You" or "How to Disembowel a Judge," but thought better of it. He also brought a notepad for jotting down ideas and observations.

He sat through the mandatory orientation videos prepared by judges, explaining the importance of their charge as potential jurors. Then, he waited while two other groups were led out of the room. Greg was getting his hopes up as the clock got closer to noon. Even though his vacation was ruined, if he were sent home without being chosen, it would be several years before the judicial system would bother him again. Then his number was called, and he joined the shuffling group of about thirty people heading to a nearby courtroom for questioning. Greg knew this process was called voir dire from watching TV shows, but he considered it "how not to be picked."

Unfortunately, Greg was hopelessly honest, so his answers to the questions were true, even though he may have wanted to attempt to lie his way out of being chosen. As is often the case, no good deed goes unpunished, and Greg was selected. This was even after he gave the judge his honest opinion and said the jury system was a "useless joke." Now Greg supposed the joke was on him as he and his fellow jurors were led into another small waiting room, which would later become the jury deliberation room.

There was little conversation between the jurors. A few seemed to know each other, and they exchanged words. Greg was very good at reading people. Also, as an amateur fiction writer, he studied people and made up stories to accompany them. In no time, he had pegged most of the people in the room as "city people."

Greg did not consider himself a suburban snob and tried to avoid appearing condescending to other people. However, he was well edu-cated, as was his wife, and they lived in an upper-class suburban com-munity. They seldom ventured into the city except on rare occasions to catch a show or concert, after which they immediately joined the caravan of cars scurrying away like rats from a sinking ship. They knew the reputation the place had for robberies, rape, shootings, stabbings and murder.

The people in the room with Greg were not well-to-do suburban-ites. It was obvious to Greg that whatever crime this jury would soon learn about would be no stranger to most people in the room. He could tell they had seen it all, probably many times before. Whoever this criminal was, he would get a fair trial because this was mostly a jury of his peers. Greg felt as out of place in the jury room as he had ever felt in his life, and what was worse, he sensed that his fellow jurors could tell that he was not one of them.

There was one woman, an older lady Greg had determined might not be one of "them" either. She was well groomed and held herself in a manner that suggested she might be educated and of a different class than most present. Greg sensed that she might be on his side if he needed an ally in the confrontation that would inevitably follow the trial. Sadly, all of his assumptions proved to be true.

/ 3 /

The trial was over relatively quickly, with the defense and prosecution presenting their stories and witnesses. An abbreviated version of the trial was as follows:

A young defendant was alleged to have traveled to the city to buy marijuana from a locally known dealer. The defendant had been carrying an unregistered pistol for his own defense. As he was purchasing the cannabis, a police car approached. Both the dealer and the defendant took off in different directions. The defendant was wearing a dark blue hoodie and black gloves.

He ran down a side street where several people sat on their row house porches at ground level. Some kids were playing on the sidewalk. The defendant ran out into the street to avoid the kids and around a parked car. When he got to the rear of the vehicle, he dropped his gun in the gutter and ran on. The people on the porch saw the defendant and heard metal hitting the blacktop. Although they didn't see him drop the gun, they heard it hit the ground. They approached the rear of the parked car and found the defendant's gun.

The defendant removed his hood and gloves and dumped them into a trashcan. He walked away slowly, hoping to escape, but police caught up with him, and he was arrested. He was charged with trying to buy illegal drugs and carrying an illegal, unregistered weapon. The defendant had a long criminal record and had been on probation, living in a halfway house in the suburbs a few miles from Greg and Helen's exclusive neighborhood.

After hearing the facts about the young man, learning of his previous record, and hearing from witnesses who heard him drop the gun outside their homes where young children were playing, Greg had made up his mind that this character was going back to jail. Unfortunately, the rest of his jurors had a different idea of what should happen to the defendant. For the next two and a half days, heated arguments ensued in the jury room, with most of the jurors wanting to vote not guilty while Greg and the older woman, Jean Fredericks, was her name, voting guilty. They had taken over seven votes, and no one would budge.

They returned to the courtroom several times to tell the judge they were at an impasse and could not get a unanimous vote. The judge ordered them to go back and continue deliberating until they all agreed. He looked directly at Greg, certain he was the one who was keeping the vote stalled. Greg sensed the judge knew the others wanted to vote not guilty, and he wanted Greg to convince the others to convict.

An obnoxious woman, Sally Edison, who had somehow bullied her way into becoming the jury foreperson by intimidating most of the other jurors, was one of the loudest advocates for letting the defendant go. She had five female allies on the jury: Regina Kincade, Debby Usher, Jane Freshler, Kelly Sands, and Irene Jacobs. The four remaining jurors were male but had also aligned themselves with Sally. They were Bill Hess, Hank Yarborough, John France, and Gerald Snow. For some reason unfathomable, these apparently strong, supposedly independent men had essentially bent down and spread their cheeks for Sally, allowing her to dominate and control their opinions.

The back-and-forth arguments between Greg, Sally, and the others frustrated him and made him feel like an alien on a strange planet.

Sally Edison: "You only want to convict him because if he is set free, he'll return to the halfway house in the suburbs."

Debby Usher: "Yeah, that's right."

Hank Yarborough: "You just don't want him back in your precious burbs."

Greg: "But he admitted to coming into the city to buy weed, didn't he?"

John France: "So what?"

Greg: "Um, excuse me, but isn't it illegal to buy and sell weed."

Sally Edison: "Who cares? Everybody buys weed off corner guys here in the city. Isn't that right?"

Greg: "I don't. Do you, Jean?"

Jean Fredericks: "Of course not."

Bill Hess: "Look here. We got us a couple of goody two shoes."

Greg: "If that's what you call obeying the law, then consider me guilty. Speaking of quilty, the guy had a gun."

Sally Edison: "They can't prove he had no gun."

Greg: "Are you kidding me? Witnesses saw him run right past them. They identified him. They heard him drop the weapon, and when they went around the back of the car, they found the gun on the ground."

Bill Hess: "That don't mean nuthin. If they didn't see him throw the gun, then they can't prove he did. Maybe he bumped into the car, and it made a metal sound."

Greg: "Then, where did the gun come from?"

Regina Kincade: "The cops probably planted it. Our cops are all crooks."

Gerald Snow: "Yeah, they do stuff like that all the time."

Greg: "Hold on a minute. The cops couldn't have planted it; it was found by that couple who lived in the house before any cops even showed up."

Jane Freshler: "Maybe the cops planted it earlier."

Kelly Sands: "Yeah, that wouldn't surprise me."

Greg: "That's ridiculous. The cops would have had to know the guy was coming into the city and would run down that particular street and right past the gun, which is impossible."

Sally: "Maybe the gun was already laying there. There's guns layin' around, all over the city."

Irene Jacobs: "Yeah, they're like all over the place."

Greg: "Guns lying around all over? Well, that's great to know. You see, I have an uncle who collects guns. He pays good money for them at gun shows. I think I'll tell him to save his money and come to the city. I'll explain how guns are lying all over the streets, waiting for him just to come and pick them up. Hell, I'll tell him it rains guns in the city. I better warn him to bring a big pickup truck and a shovel to scoop them up because they're everywhere."

Sally Edison: "You know what your problem is? You live out in the burbs with your Richie Rich houses, and you think you're better than us because we live in the city."

Gerald Snow: "That's right, Burb Boy!"

Greg: "I don't think I'm better, but after listening to your blatant stupidity for the past two days, I know I'm smarter than all of you. Hell, my dog is smarter than you all."

Sally Edison: "You can't talk to us that way."

Bill Hess: "You're lucky we ain't out on the street, Bucko, or me and my boys would have something to say to you about that."

Greg: "I'm trembling with fear. Look, this known criminal wasn't breaking the law in the suburbs. His halfway house may be out there, but he apparently is smart enough not to crap where he sleeps. He came armed into your city, the place where you and your families live. He didn't come into my neighborhood; he came into yours. I'm trying to help you, but you folks insist on freeing this guy because you hate and distrust law enforcement, and you apparently hate people who live outside of your precious city. Fine, if that's how you want it."

Sally Edison: "What does that mean?"

Greg: "What that means is everyone in this room knows the defendant is guilty, no matter how you choose to convince yourselves otherwise. You morons have already wasted two full days of my life that I will never get back arguing to save someone who would rob and maybe kill anyone in this room and not give it a second thought. If you're too stupid to know that, fine. If you want gun-toating trash like that walking around your neighborhoods, who am I to stop you? I'm changing my vote to not guilty. You want this scumbag set free; he's all yours. Why should I care? A loser like him will find himself back in court in no time, or he may end up dead. Yes, I think as stupid as he is, he'll probably never see his next birthday."

Sally Edison: "Now, wait a minute, that's no way to talk."

Greg: "Well, Sally, hero of the stupid. Defender of the dopy. If you disliked what I just said, you're really gonna hate this. I hope and pray that after we let this bum back out on the street, my only wish is that each of you crosses paths with other criminals like him that you let run wild in the streets of your precious city. I hope they rob, rape, or kill each one of you. That would be fair payment for wasting my time."

Jane Freshler: "That was a horrible thing to say.

Greg: "You bet it was. Let's take another vote. I will vote to release him as soon as possible so he can roam free, hopefully in your neighborhoods.

Gerald Snow: "Hey, Dude, that's not right. You can't put no curse on us."

Bill Hess: "Yeah, man. You can't put no whammy on us. Take it off."

Greg: "You're right. I don't have the power to put a curse on you, folks. If I did, I most certainly would."

Kelly Sands: "You call us hateful. You're a more hateful person than we are."

Greg: "Whatever. I'm the worst person on Earth. Now, let's vote so I can go back home. I'll be watching the newspapers for your future assaults or maybe deaths. It will make pleasant reading over my morning Cheerios."

The vote was taken. It was unanimous to acquit. Jane Fredericks decided to follow Greg's and change her vote, too. When the verdict was read in the courtroom, the judge looked directly at Greg, and he could see the disappointment on the judge's face. Greg stared defiantly back at the judge as if to reiterate his original statement that the jury system was a joke. Greg felt vindicated, knowing he was right. The jury was dismissed, and Greg went home.

/ 4 /

A month or so later, Greg and Hellen returned from their long-awaited vacation, rested and ready to dive back into the rat race. Greg was sitting at the kitchen table, eating his bowl of Cheerios, when he noticed an article in the local newspaper. The headline read, "Women Killed In Cross-fire During Botched Robbery." Greg read the article and was stunned to see two names he thought he recognized. One was Jane Freshler, and the other was Kelly Sands.

"Helen? I think we might know these two ladies mentioned in this article."

"What are their names?" Helen asked.

Greg said, "Jane Freshler and Kelly Sands."

Helen thought for a moment, then said, "No. I don't recognize either of those names. What happened to them?"

"The article said they were shot and killed in a botched robbery yesterday in the city. Those names sure seem familiar to me. Maybe I met them at some business function. I meet so many people, but it's hard to say."

Greg continued to read the article until he reached the part where it described them as lifelong city residents, and then it suddenly hit him. "I know where I met them, Helen. They were on the jury with me."

"Are you sure, Greg?"

"Well, I'm pretty sure. I wrote all my fellow jurors' names on my notepad. It's on my desk in my office. I'll go and get it. I'll be right back."

Greg got up from the table and headed to his office. When he returned, he compared his juror list to the two names in the article. "It's them, Helen. It has to be them. It lists their ages, and that works with my memory of them. Holy cow! That's terrible. They were so young."

Helen said, "As I recall, they were part of the gang that made your life miserable for two and a half days."

Greg recalled returning home after his jury service ended, complaining about his time on the jury. He had told her everything, including how he had berated the jurors and reluctantly agreed to vote with them just to get home.

"Yeah, they all did. It was like they hated the cops, and they hated me for living in the suburbs. I have an idea. I'll be right back. I need to check on something."

Helen said, "You didn't finish your Cheerios."

"That's ok, Babe. This will only take a minute or so." But it took Greg much longer than he had planned, and he never got to finish his Cheerios.

Greg got on his computer and started a Google search for each of the jurors on his list. He began with Regina Kincade. He was stunned to read an article that appeared on the first day he and Helen were on vacation. Regina and her family had been the victims of a home invasion gone wrong. Her husband had tried to overpower the invaders and was shot and killed. Then Regina was raped, beaten, and killed as well.

"Oh dear Lord, I can't believe this," Greg said.

He searched for another name, Gerald Snow. He had been the man who had given Greg the nickname "Burb Boy." Apparently, Gerald had gotten into a confrontation with someone at a local bar. The bartender told them to take it outside, which they did. Gerald expected to have it out with fists and never anticipated the knife the other man carried. The result was Gerald had been stabbed to death.

Greg entered every name on his list, and each of them had died in some horrible and violent way since the day they completed their jury duty. Jane Fredericks, his only ally during the trial, was apparently unharmed as the search for her name revealed nothing. The only other juror still alive was Sally Edison, the jury foreperson and Greg's number one nemesis during the trial.

Greg was wracked with guilt as he recalled his heated statement during that last day of the trial. Could it be true? Had a stupid thing he had said in the heat of frustration somehow turned into a curse that resulted in all those jurors' deaths? No, that was impossible. It all had to be a coincidence. But Greg would never believe such a coincidence could occur by happenstance.

Greg returned to the kitchen to find Helen washing his breakfast cereal bowl. "They got soggy, Greg. If you want more, you'll have to . . ." Helen stopped mid-sentence. "Greg, are you alright? You look like you just saw a ghost."

Greg hesitated momentarily, then said, "Helen. I think I did something horrible. I didn't mean to, but somehow I must have."

"What, Honey? What do you think you did?"

"Remember when I got back from jury duty, how frustrated and angry I was with my fellow jurors?"

"Yes, I recalled. You told me almost verbatim how you chastised them for their narrow-mindedness and stupidity."

"That's true. But do you remember what else I said to them?"

"I suppose, Greg. I mean, I can't recall it word for word, but the jist of it was that if they wanted to live in the city with criminals and would rather set one free instead of putting him in jail, then they shouldn't complain when something bad happens to them."

Greg said, "Yeah. That was the essence of it. But I was much nastier in what I said. I said that I hoped and prayed something bad did happen to them, and I would enjoy reading about it while eating my morning breakfast."

"Well . . . yeah. That was pretty nasty. You're not typically that mean, Greg."

"I know, but I was pretty pissed. One of the guys on the jury actually accused me of putting a curse on them."

"A curse? That's a bit out there, Greg. You're a pretty talented guy, but I don't believe putting the whammy on somebody is part of your skill set."

"I would have agreed yesterday, but I'm not so sure today."

Helen asked, "Why Greg? What happened?"

"Almost every one of the jurors I told you about has died through some form of violence since serving on the jury with me."

"What? That's not possible."

Greg said, "That's what I thought. I was in my office, on my computer, searching for the names from my list, and every one of them except for two had died. In some instances, other family members have died with them as well. Helen, what the Hell have I done?"

"You didn't do anything, Greg. This is all some horrible coincidence. You said two jurors are still alive. Which ones were they?"

"One was an older woman named Jane Fredericks. She was the one juror who was on my side and wanted to vote guilty."

"And the other?"

"The other was the jury foreperson, Sally Edison. She hated my guts. Although this is nasty for me to say, if I were going to put a whammy on anyone, she would have been at the top of my list."

"And she is still alive?"

Greg said, "Yes, as far as I can tell. I couldn't find anything saying otherwise."

Helen suggested, "Maybe you should look up her address and go to see her. Maybe it will make you feel better and realize that there was nothing you did to cause these other deaths. Honey, these people obviously lived in bad sections of the city or hung out in places known for trouble. That has nothing to do with you."

"But what if it did, Helen? I was really angry when I said those things. What if I really did curse them and am responsible for their deaths? I don't know if I could live with myself knowing I had done such a horrible thing."

Helen said, "Listen, Greg. We'll figure this out. All we have to do is . . ."

She was interrupted by the sound of their front doorbell ringing.

/ 5 /

"I don't know who could be calling this early in the morning. I'll get it," Greg said.

Greg opened the front door and, to his surprise, saw Sally Edison standing there with a furious look on her face. What was worse, she was holding a pistol in her right hand.

"Get in the house now, Greg, and don't say a word, or I'll blow your guts all over the room."

Greg stammered, "S . . . S . . . Sally? What's the meaning of this? Have you lost your mind?"

"No, Greg. If anything, I am more aware than I have ever been. I know what you did, and you have to find a way to make it stop, or else I'll make it stop right here and now."

"What do you mean, Sally?"

"You know very well what I mean. You put a curse on us, Greg. I don't know how you managed to do it, but you did. Maybe you worship at some Satanic cult out here in the burbs. I don't know, and I don't care. But you have to take the curse off of me. I'm the only one left. Thanks to you, everyone else is dead."

"Sally. I told you before I don't have any ability to put a curse on anyone. If the others have died, it's all coincidence. I can't take off a curse I never put on you in the first place."

"But you did, Greg. You may not realize it, but you cursed us in your anger, and someone evil must have been listening. Now, everyone but me is dead, and that means you killed them."

"I didn't mean to do anything like that, Sally. But look, if it will make you feel better, then yes, I cancel the curse. I free you from anything bad happening to you. You will not be killed. Does that satisfy you?"

Sally thought for a moment, then said, "No, Greg. It doesn't. I believe the curse you put on us was so powerful that your simple statement can't undo it. The only way for me to cancel this curse is for me to kill you."

Greg began walking backward, trying to put some distance between himself and this crazy woman. Sally matched him step by step until he was backed against the wall with nowhere to go. She raised her gun and pointed it directly at Greg's heart.

"I'd like to say that I'm sorry it has to be this way, Greg, but I never liked you in the first place. You were belittling and condescending, looking down at us like we weren't fit to shine your shoes. It will give me great pleasure to end this curse and end you at the same time. Goodbye, Greg."

Just before Sally pulled the trigger, Helen rushed up behind her with a cast-iron skillet and slammed it against the side of her head, caving in the woman's skull. Sally collapsed and was dead before she hit the floor. Blood and brains spilled from her open skull and pooled on the hardwood flooring. Helen stood trembling in shock over what she had done to protect her husband.

Greg embraced Helen and said, "It's ok, Babe. She can't hurt me or anyone ever again."

Helen said tearfully, "The curse is over now, Greg. Isn't it? She was the last one."

Greg held Helen tightly, knowing that he would never know for certain if the curse was real, if he was responsible for the deaths of the jurors, or if it was all a horrible coincidence. But somewhere deep in his soul, Greg knew the truth; he knew what he had done and knew someday he would have to accept that realization.

HAIR OF THE DOLL THAT KILLS YOU

It had seemed like a great idea to Sarah at the time. Then again, how many times have you heard that said right before disaster strikes? The Senior Citizen Crochet Club met weekly in the Ashton Public Library, where they planned future projects, discussed various crocheting techniques, ate snacks, drank wine, traded local stories (gossip), and sometimes even crocheted. Although the wine-drinking and gossiping were in full swing that evening, the ladies seemed to be having some difficulty coming up with ideas for a new fund-raising project.

It was essential that they come to a consensus and decide on a project and that they do so quickly. Even though it was June, the group knew there was much to be done as the Autumn Christmas buying season was only a few months away. There would be designs to plan, materials to buy, and assignments to hand out. When the club finally began their work, they would perform like Santa's Elves on steroids. The ladies would form a cohesive production line that would rival the giants of manufacturing history. Or so they liked to imagine.

Despite their delusions of grandeur, the crocheting club could be quite efficient when they put their minds to it, with each member assigned a specific aspect of the final product. Then, when all the individual components were ready, the assembly phase of the project would take place, and the promotion and fundraising sales would begin. But before they could do any of this, they had to come up with a project.

The recipient of the profits from this year's fundraiser was a local nonprofit school for special needs children known as "Harmony

House," named for the home's founder and primary benefactor, Ms. Harmony Thompson. She was not only the richest woman in town and a real taskmaster, but she proved to be as generous as she was demanding. Once the project was agreed upon, the Harmony Foundation would provide funds for whatever supplies were required.

The Crocheting Club President Emma Burges reminded the others, "Ladies, we're under the gun here, and time is running out. If we expect to have this project ready to go by October, we had better get moving." Emma was a natural-born leader and was, hands down, everyone's choice for president. She was methodical, organized, and able to manage a project, usually without ruffling too many feathers, although she wouldn't hesitate to do so if she believed that was what was required. However, whatever outstanding management skills she brought to the table, Emma's creative abilities were unfortunately painfully lacking.

Betty Singleton offered her usual suggestion, "I think we should do scarves again this year. Those always seem to be big sellers." Then again, Betty always suggested scarves. If there was one thing you could count on with an assurance equal to that of the sun rising in the east and setting in the west, it was that Betty Singleton would always suggest crocheting scarves. It wasn't that Betty couldn't rise to the challenge of a more difficult undertaking; she certainly had the skill to take on whatever came her way. But Betty could crochet scarves in her sleep without thinking about what she was doing.

Some might argue that Betty had been crocheting scarves in her sleep for years or at least had done so while under the influence of greatly consumed quantities of wine at the crochet meetings. Betty certainly loved the fruit of the vine, as did most of the ladies in the group. However, if they chose some new and never-before-attempted project this year, the wine consumption would be relegated far into the background, and the group's crocheting skills would need to move to the foreground.

"No, I don't think scarves will cut it this year, ladies." Sarah Dugan offered. She was not among the group's favorite members largely because of her superior and condescending attitude. Sarah was somehow involved with Harmony House, although no one knew exactly what her role might be. It was also said that she was "as thick as thieves" with Harmony Thompson herself, although that relationship could neither be confirmed nor denied. Sarah added with her typical air of superiority, "Harmony is looking for something different this year, something challenging and exciting."

It drove the other women in the group crazy whenever Sarah called Ms. Thompson "Harmony." Although it might be true that Sarah lived in a social strata somewhat higher than the other members of the crocheting group, she was nowhere near as wealthy as Harmony Thompson. Nor could she pretend to be able to play in the same sandbox with the likes of Thompson money.

However, that fact never stopped Sarah from "putting on airs" whenever the opportunity arose. The senior women noticed that Sarah was always "dressed to the nines" no matter the occasion, whether the situation merited such attire. Although it might have been true that Sarah Dugan wasn't in the same financial league as Harmony Thompson, that didn't stop her from acting as if she were.

"So, Sarah, since you apparently have some insight into the workings of Harmony Thompson that the rest of us are painfully lacking, perhaps you can shed some light on what sort of project Ms. Thompson would want us to consider this year?" Emma asked, being sure to to get in every possible sarcastic dig she could along the way. She had already endured just about enough of Sarah Dugan's "wealthier than thou" attitude for one evening.

Sarah replied with equal smugness, "Well, as luck would have it, Harmony and I have spoken at length about this, and we believe we've come up with a prototype for this year's project."

"But of course you have," Emma replied, her tone dripping with sarcasm. Knowing Sarah Dugan the way she did, Emma suspected Sarah had just learned the word "prototype," likely from Harmony Thompson, and, as such, would be tossing it around many more times during the evening, acting as if she were as familiar with the term as her own name. It was a known pattern with Sarah. She would learn a new word or phrase, beat it to death for a week or so, and then come up with another. That alone wasn't a bad thing. It wasn't like anyone in the group had a problem with its members wanting to improve themselves. However, it was just that Sarah couldn't quietly enjoy her self-improvement; she had to be so "in-your-face" about it every time.

Emma inquired, "And what, Sarah, may I ask, is this mysterious project?"

"I have a prototype right here," Sarah said. And Emma couldn't help but note the second use of the word "prototype." In her mind, Emma heard an imaginary bell dinging, as if indicating each time Sarah used the word.

Sarah reached down deep into her oversized crochet bag. "Harmony created the prototype design herself; I just did the crochet work. The truth is Harmony couldn't crochet if her life depended on it. Don't tell her I said that." Sarah gave a twitter of nervous laughter as if to suggest any of these ladies were on a first-name basis with Harmony Thompson or that the woman would even bother to give any of them the time of day.

As Sarah pulled the project from her bag, an audible, simultaneous gasp filled the room, followed by shocked silence. What Sarah displayed was a crocheted doll of some sort. If Sarah had assumed her presentation was to be met with "oohs" and "aahs" of pleasure at seeing how "adorable" the doll was, she was going to be greatly disappointed. Because that was not at all what her fellow crocheting club members thought. It wasn't instantly apparent to Sarah that the group thought the "prototype" was the most hideous creation the ladies had ever seen.

The doll was meant to be a girl with obviously caucasian light tannish-pink crocheted skin, dark pink panties, and a yellow sleeveless top. In a pinch, under the influence of a sufficient amount of liquid spirits, much of the monstrosity might have been considered marginally cute. However, the face of the doll more than made up for that in its supreme uglyness. There was no amount of alcohol on the planet to make that face appear any less heinous. The thing's mouth was a red, gaping wound in its crocheted face, and what was supposed to represent its nose was no more than a slightly noticeable bump puckered into its lumpy skin.

The real horror was the doll's oval, puffy, baggy, bulging, creepy eyes that expressed all the emotion of a dead, rotting carp floating bloated along a river bank. Those eyes resembled the painted oval eye rocks called "eye amulets" that ancient Egyptians placed over the eyes of the dead. It was believed these painted rocks allowed the recently departed to see into the afterlife. However, recognizing this resemblance in the doll's eyes only served to make them creepier. As if this didn't contribute enough to the doll's heinous appearance, it had bright orange hair. This was not simulated orange crocheted hair but what looked like real human hair. The ladies wondered how much worse things could get.

Sarah smiled, oblivious to her fellow crocheting club members' revulsion, "Don't you just adore the doll? And isn't that hair amazing?"

Emma said nothing but thought, "Hidious, vile, disgusting maybe, but amazing? I think not."

Sarah asked, "Tell me honestly, Emma. Have you ever seen hair like that on a doll before? It's real human hair."

It was as if the "creep meter" couldn't register any higher; mentioning that little tidbit about human hair just pushed it upward. As if holding back an urge to puke her guts out, Emma reluctantly asked, "Um, Sarah? Where did that hair come from? Maybe from a wig?" Emma feared she didn't want to know the answer and was sorry she asked the question as soon as it passed over her now dry lips.

Sarah smiled proudly and said, "Wigs? Oh, Heavens, no. Harmony would never stoop so low as to allow something as tacky as that to be part of her doll."

Then Emma realized with horror why she had felt so apprehensive about asking the question. She remembered a relative of Harmony's in town and the type of business he ran. Because if the hair didn't come from wigs, then . . .

Sarah proclaimed proudly, "No siree! Harmony has a cousin, Frank Thompson, who is an undertaker, and all the hair we will use to make these dolls will be donated by the funeral director from fresh corpses. What a unique and incredible idea. Won't that be amazing?"

Betty Singleton appeared to be in a state bordering on catatonic as she stared at the hideous doll. Betty's eyes seemed to bulge from her reddened face, and her mouth hung open as if in a silent scream. Ironically, had Betty's hair been Bozo the Clown red, she actually might have resembled the wretched doll. Sarah noticed Betty's reaction and mistook her appearance for one of approval and perhaps even adoring rapture.

Sarah asked, "So Betty. Tell me what you think. Isn't this the most incredible doll you've ever seen?"

After a moment, Betty seemed to snap out of her stupor and said, "Incredible might not be my first choice of words in describing it. If you'll pardon my French, Sarah, I think that's the ugliest freaking doll I have ever laid eyes on."

Another of the ladies in the group named Jean Folsom, turned to her friend Anna Kilburn and whispered, "Did Betty Singleton just say 'freaking?'"

Anna whispered back, "Oh my, yes. She most certainly did. It must be the wine talking. Betty is obviously heading out of control. She normally wouldn't say 'boo' to a ghost."

Jean and Anna were probably the most timid members of the group. They could always be found huddled together, off to the side, whispering. Although that sort of behavior might appear rude to an unfamiliar onlooker, the rest of the group accepted and understood it. The truth was, had the two ladies not found each other, neither of them would likely ever speak at all. This was especially true with someone as hoity-toity as Sarah Dugan in the room.

Sarah was aghast, "Oh my, Betty. How could you say such a horrible thing? I spent hours developing this prototype."

Emma had lost track but assumed that had to have been the fourth or fifth time Sarah had tossed out her "prototype" word du jour. Assuming her leadership role as president, Emma said, "I'm sorry, Sarah, but I have to agree with Betty on this one. That doll is hideous by itself, and adding hair from recently deceased people is just worse than wrong . . . well, it's just beyond my comprehension why anyone would even consider such a thing."

Sarah immediately assumed a position of defense, taking on her typical air of smug superiority, announcing, "I have to strongly disagree, and I would be remiss if I didn't remind you all again that the idea for this design came directly from Harmony Thompson, herself, who fell in love with it. Do I have to also point out that Harmony House is financing the material cost for this project? Since they will be taking all the financial risk here and benefiting from the profits, I think it behooves us to follow Harmony's wishes.

Emma thought silently, "That's right, 'behooves' was Sarah's word of the day last week. God help us, I hope she's not bringing that annoying word back."

Jean Folsom timidly raised her hand and asked, "May I say something?"

Emma said, "Of course you can, Jean. And this isn't elementary school; you don't have to raise your hand."

"Oh, ok. Sorry." Jean apologized.

Sarah said in frustration, "For Christ's sake, Jean. Stop apologizing and say whatever you need to say." It was clear that Sarah was getting angrier by the minute.

Jean took a deep breath and said, "Anna and I have been discussing this, and we agree with Betty and Emma. As a collective, the Senior Crochet Club has a reputation and responsibility to maintain a higher-than-acceptable standard in everything we do. That doll, well, it's simply abysmal! No matter what Ms. Thompson may want, we can't, in good faith, risk our group's integrity on such a disturbing project."

Sarah started to spout off, "Why I never . . ."

Emma interrupted, "Look, Sarah. I know you and Ms. Thompson are tight, so you are eager to please her, but even without the hair, that doll is hideous. When you add the hair and consider where the hair comes from, the doll devolves to a new low level and, in my opinion, becomes an abomination. I think it's clear that none of us in this group want to have anything to do with this project. Look, if you don't feel comfortable telling Ms. Thompson about our decision, then I'll be willing to do so as president of our group."

Sarah was dumbfounded. "I . . . I honestly don't know what to say. When this meeting started tonight, we had no project. You were practically begging us for an idea. I presented an outstanding concept that our financial supporter loved, and you all rejected it. You're acting like I suggested we create an army of evil, murdering voodoo dolls or something."

Anna whispered to Jean, "That's not all that far from reality."

Sarah ignored the comment and then, in resignation, said, "Look. If that's how you feel, then I'll speak to Harmony and let her know that you refuse to do the project. However, I should warn you, Harmony doesn't take kindly to rejection, and it's quite possible, if not probable, that she may fire this group from the project."

Betty spoke up again and said, "Sarah. You seem to forget something important. We're a volunteer group. We give our time and skills for free. If your precious Harmony wants to try to find someone else willing to produce those friggin' hideous monstrosities, then more power to her."

Jean and Anna looked at each other, snickered, and Jean said, "Uh oh. She's escalated to 'friggin.' It might be time to cut off her wine supply."

Sarah addressed the group and said, "And what am I supposed to do with this prototype?"

Emma said with all the sarcasm she could muster, "I would suggest you do whatever the situation behooves you to do."

Jean suggested, "How about burial at sea?"

Anna added, "Perhaps burning it at the stake might be more appropriate?"

Betty said, "I'd recommend shoving it through a wood chipper."

Sarah grabbed the doll, turned from the group, and said, "Well, aren't we all just spilling over with humor this evening? Here's what I'm going to do, ladies, and I use the term 'ladies' very loosely. I'm quitting this group and starting another crocheting group. We'll be making these amazing dolls for Harmony House if I have to make every single one myself."

Emma suggested, "If that's what you want, Sarah, do what you must. But in all honesty, I'd recommend you didn't make too many of them. I don't think you will be selling many."

"Or any," Betty added.

Jean whispered, "I doubt they'll be flying off the shelves."

Anna chuckled and agreed, "Not unless they're riding on brooms."

Sarah turned in a huff and stormed out of the room, slamming the door behind her.

Emma sighed, then asked, "Next order of business?"

Betty chortled, "Pour more frickin' wine."

Jean and Anna just giggled and poured glasses for everyone.

* * *

Sarah sat in a recliner in the special crocheting room of her home, staring across the short expanse at the crocheted doll sitting on her fireplace mantle. She had been so proud of the thing. Sarah held a large glass of ice coated in a golden liquid unsteadily in her hand. Clearly, in her frustration, Sarah had opted to switch from wine to whiskey, knowing that after an evening like she had just experienced, getting from Point A to Point B as quickly as possible would be best. That is to assume that Point A is frustrated with disappointment while sober and Point B is blissful oblivion thanks to Ireland's finest golden elixir.

She couldn't comprehend how the group of women she previously considered friends could have turned on her so completely. Sarah was certain they would love the sample doll she had produced. She thought it was the sweetest thing she had ever seen, and having crocheted it with her own hands only made her love it even more. But not that coven of cackling witches. How could they have reacted so badly? It was just a damn doll. There was no need for them to be so callous or rude.

Sarah studied the doll as it sat leaning against the wall, its pretty pink crocheted legs dangling over the mantle's edge. Its scrunched-up face and staring eyes looking back at her seemed not to understand any better than Sarah did what the group found so appalling about it. The doll's red hair desperately needed brushing, as it stuck out wildly in every direction. Sarah had thought using real human hair for the doll was the greatest idea ever. She couldn't comprehend why the idea had repulsed the group. She imagined that special feature alone would quadruple the dolls' popularity. Yet, they had acted like it was Sarah who was wrong and didn't understand. It wasn't like she was asking them to create monstrous dolls or that using hair from the recently deceased could somehow mystically breathe life into inanimate objects. She just didn't get it.

Always thinking way outside the box, Sarah had already been planning far beyond the Christmas fundraiser before showing her prototype to the group and had discussed her ideas with Harmony Thompson, who was in complete agreement. Harmony, too, was a creative thinker and could imagine the potential money to be made from selling such dolls. Together, they envisioned a time when the dolls might become a worldwide phenomenon, a craze more popular than Cabbage Patch Kids or maybe more so than even Beanie Babies.

Since each of these dolls would be hand-crocheted, they could be special ordered, each unique. Yes, the labor would be initially intensive, but the sale price and profit margin could reflect that. Eventually, the labor could be exported to some cheap, third-world country, or with advances in modern technology, most of the process could be automated to reduce cost while maintaining each doll's customization and unique aspect.

Sarah and Harmony even had come up with a name for the product, "Harmony Honeys." The dolls could be individually built to the customer's exact specifications. Dealing with special needs children through Harmony House, Harmony Thompson had seen more than her share of sad and tragic stories. She knew bereft parents would do and pay almost anything to preserve the memory of their lost loved ones.

Harmony had told Sarah, "Imagine a family, distraught over the death of a young child. They are desperately looking for some way to keep the child's memory alive. Imagine if they could create a Harmony Honey to look as much like their lost child as possible and even use that child's actual hair in the doll's creation. Eventually, if we determined a market might exist, we could take it further and provide a containment unit inside the doll for the departed's ashes. I would think they would pay almost anything for such a doll."

Sarah approved but questioned, "I agree. That's an incredible idea, but what about the expense of creating the specialized dolls? As you also know, many of these folks are already suffering financially because of the astronomical medical expenses they have incurred during their loved one's illness."

Harmony said, "That's the beauty of this. Harmony House is a nonprofit organization. Using volunteer groups like the Senior Crocheting Club, we can produce the initial dolls as stock models. My cousin, Frank, is an undertaker. He owns Thompson's mortuary and crematorium over on Main Street. The bereft often want their deceased relatives to have their hair cut and styled before burial. He usually disposes of that hair. He can provide it to us at no cost for these initial dolls. We can sell them at fundraisers, with all proceeds going to Harmony House. We'll use those profits to buy materials for more dolls. Soon, we'll have several different volunteer groups crocheting dolls for us, all using the specifications and patterns we provide.

"We get publicity initially by using local news media, including TV, and start pitching the individuality and customized features of each. Eventually, we get national press coverage. Now, people who have money will want to buy their special, unique version of the doll. Maybe we give a few away to celebrities in exchange for their endorsements. The people who can afford to pay top dollar will do so, which will cover the expenses of those who can't afford it. Remember, Sarah, Harmony House is a nonprofit organization, so as long as all proceeds go back into the business and help those in need, it doesn't matter how much money we make. The more we make, the more people we can help."

That sounded amazing to Sarah, and at the time, she couldn't wait to share the idea with her crocheting group. But she had not been prepared for their extremely negative reaction. Although she might be willing to admit that her original prototype doll wasn't perfect, it wasn't as hideous as the group suggested. Minor modifications and improvements could have easily been proposed and implemented in actual production versions.

Sarah didn't understand why the ladies were upset about the doll having human hair. Perhaps she didn't know her "friends" as well as she thought. Apparently, they were all more superstitious than she realized. Why did it matter if the doll's hair came from someone who had died?

People died every day. She couldn't understand what all the fuss was about.

Then Sarah had a sudden, unpleasant revelation. She suspected their rejection of her doll idea had less to do with the doll itself than it had to do with her personally. She knew the group was jealous of her close relationship with Harmony Thompson, and it likely had more to do with how they reacted than anything else, including the doll or the source of its hair.

After she arrived home, before switching from wine to whiskey, Sarah called Harmony to give her the bad news about the group. Sarah expected Harmony to be furious but was shocked when the news didn't seem to phase her at all.

"That's not going to be a problem, Sarah. First, let me commend you for having enough faith in our product to walk away from that group of nay-sayers. It takes a lot of courage to take such a stand, and I truly appreciate how you stood up for Harmony Honeys. Look, I've been doing this a long time and know of several other crocheting groups who will be eager to volunteer to help us. If the Senior Crochet Club isn't interested, that's fine with me. I'll get you the necessary contact information so you can stop by these other groups' meetings to give a presentation to each of them. These people have been begging me to let them help us for years. They are just as skilled as the Senior Club but not as well known. They understand that teaming up with Harmony House will change all that."

That was an hour or so earlier, and at first, Sarah was thrilled with Harmony's reaction and happy to know their project still had a chance for life by using other groups. Then, after thinking about it for a while, Sarah felt stressed about presenting their idea to groups of women she didn't know. That was another reason she had started drinking the hard stuff. Now, a bit later, she was feeling no pain as she relaxed in her recliner, staring at the prototype doll across the room, her breathing getting evener and more relaxed.

Sarah's eyes started to close as the alcohol did its job, and soon she was slumped unconscious in her chair, mouth hanging open and snoring loudly. She was so far gone she wouldn't have been able to hear a rhinoceros charging through her home. As she slipped into oblivion, Sarah began to have the strangest dream. In this fantasy, she would have sworn the doll on the mantle had blinked its hideous eyes. But that was how Sarah knew she was dreaming.

So, when she saw the doll carefully climb down to the floor, she knew it must also be part of the same dream. Then Sarah was certain she heard the doll scamper into the kitchen, followed by a clattering noise, and then the sound of something crawling through the pet door into the backyard. Sarah had installed the door years earlier for her recently deceased dog, Sheldon. She missed Sheldon and had always meant to get another dog, but she had been too busy and never gotten around to it. As she fell deeper into dreamland, Sarah thought at least she still had the pet door ready for when she decided it was time for a new dog. Then, her dream changed, and all thoughts of the doll were forgotten.

* * *

The sound of Sarah's cell phone ringing seemed a hundred times worse than it actually was, partially because of how it had awoken her from a near-comatose sleep but mostly because of the pounding headache she had from her hangover. How much had she drunk last night? She couldn't begin to recall. Across the room, the prototype doll remained sitting on the mantle, just as it had been the previous night. Of course, it did. She gave herself a mental head slap. Why wouldn't it? She apparently had forgotten her dream of the previous night.

Reaching the side table, Sarah lifted the phone and saw by the caller ID it was Harmony Thompson. Despite her pounding head and dry mouth, Sarah did her best to sound as human as possible when she took the call.

"Harmony. Good morning. How are you today?"

At first, there wasn't a reply, but then Harmony said, "You don't know, do you?"

Sarah was becoming confused, which was not difficult since simply saying the previous seven words of greeting seemed to be the verbal equivalent of scaling Mount Everest. She looked at her phone again and saw the time read 2:17. Noticing that the room was awash with sunlight for the first time, Sarah realized it was afternoon. Looking at her phone again, the time changed to 2:18.

"I'm sorry, Harmony. I was up late last night planning our strategy for Harmony Honeys, and your call literally woke me." Sarah lied, trying desperately to sound much less incoherent than she suspected she did. "You said I didn't know. What was it I don't know?"

Harmony sounded extremely upset, which was unusual for someone as typically in control as she always seemed to be. She said, "Oh my Lord, Sarah. I'm just glad you're safe. You are safe, Sarah, aren't you?"

Sarah replied, "Yes, in fact, I'm sitting in the exact same spot I was in when we spoke last night. I must have fallen asleep in my recliner. Oh boy. I may be a bit stiff when I try to get up and move around."

"You have to listen carefully to me, Sarah. Something horrible has happened."

Sarah asked, "Horrible? What do you mean, Harmony."

"What time did you leave that crocheting group last evening?"

"It was early. The group made it clear that they hated our doll; I got angry with them, quit the group, came home, and called you immediately."

Harmony said, "Can anyone verify you were at home the entire time?"

"Well, I suppose you can since we talked for a while last night."

"That's not verification, Sarah. You have a cellphone and could have been calling me from anywhere."

Sarah was confused, "I don't understand any of this, Harmony. Why does any of this matter? What's going on?"

Harmony said, "Look, Sarah. I know you, and I believe in you completely. So I'm sending Bob Jackson, our corporate lawyer, to your house. If the Police arrive before Bob does, don't speak to them. It's your right. Do I make myself clear, Sarah? Do not speak to the Police for any reason at all!"

Sarah was beginning to panic, "Police? Lawyer? What the Hell is happening, Harmony?"

Harmony sighed briefly, then calmly said, "There was a tragedy at the Ashton library after you left."

Sarah asked, "Tragedy? What do you mean, tragedy?"

Harmony explained, "Shortly after you left the group, some crazed lunatic must have come into the library with a sharp kitchen meat cleaver and murdered the entire crocheting group."

Sarah shouted in disbelief, "Murdered? You mean all of them? Emma, Betty, Jane and Anna? All my friends? Dead? How can that be?"

"I don't know, Sarah. All I know is I heard it was a bloodbath. My cousin Charles is a detective with the city police. Every member of the club was killed, their throats slashed, and then they were dismembered and mutilated post-mortem beyond recognition. I was told the meeting room looked like a charnel house or an abattoir, with body parts, hair, and flesh scattered about so chaotically it could take months to determine what limb goes with what body. Also, apparently, every skull had been scalped."

Sarah thought she might vomit or pass out but managed to maintain control barely, "But you haven't heard who could have done such a dreadful thing?" Sarah asked.

"No, and as of this morning, the police don't exactly know either. They're just starting their investigation. But there's another problem, which is why I am sending Bob to your house, Sarah."

"What's that?"

Harmony said, "The Police said they found the murder weapon. It was a high-end custom meat cleaver. Charles told me it had the initials S.D. monogrammed on the handle. As I'm sure you recall, I gave you a set of monogrammed cutlery last Christmas as a thank-you from Harmony House, remember?"

Sara was stunned. "Yes, I remember; the wood block that holds the cutlery is on my kitchen counter. What should I do, Harmony?"

Harmony repeated, "When the police arrive, and they will, don't allow them into your house without a signed warrant. Do nothing, say nothing, and wait for our lawyer, Bob, to get there. I'm on my way as well and should arrive shortly."

Obviously numb, Sarah said, "Ok, Harmony. I'll wait for you."

Sarah disconnected the call and stood on legs that she was unsure could support her. She saw the whiskey bottle on the nearby coffee table and unscrewed the top. She raised the bottle and said, "As my grandfather Seamus Dugan was fond of saying, "Sometimes you need a bit of the hair of the dog that bit you to make things right." Then she took a healthy gulp of Ireland's finest, hoping her grandfather was right.

She slowly rose and stumble-walked into her kitchen. The first thing she noticed was that the wooden block that held her mono-grammed kitchen cutlery set was missing the meat cleaver. She felt weak in her knees and gripped her counter for support. As she did, Sarah glanced down at the floor near the pet door and saw a few traces of dirt, as if some animal had used the door, entering from the outside. Sarah grabbed a few paper towels from a roll and moistened them with water from the sink. She bent down and wiped up the dirt particles, looking at them briefly before tossing the towels into the trashcan.

Sarah glanced back into her crocheting room and saw the doll rest-ing on the mantle. She slowly walked into the room, never taking her eyes off the doll. When she got to the mantle, Sarah checked the doll's feet and noticed a few flecks of dirt similar to those she had found on the kitchen floor. Other than that, the doll appeared exactly as it had the night before. She shook the dirt from the doll's feet and brushed it into the fireplace.

For a brief moment, Sarah considered lighting a fire and tossing the doll into the flames. She had no idea why she would want to do such a thing. A little dirt was no big deal. But what had she thought she would find when she examined the doll? Had she thought to find the doll drenched in gore from a bloodbath? It must be the whiskey talk-ing. That was an impossible thought since dolls didn't come to life and kill people, no matter if the thing had corpse hair or not. A thought suddenly flashed into her mind. It was a revised version of her grandfa-ther's expression. She thought, "the hair of the doll that kills you," and an involuntary shiver slithered like a centipede down her spine.

Then the front doorbell rang, and Sarah saw a police cruiser parked at the curb in front of her house. As she turned toward the front door, Sarah could have sworn she saw the doll wink at her.

THE STARING BOY

Earning a living as a process server can often not be the most desirable way to turn a buck. The reactions of the people you have to present with legal documents can span the entire emotional spectrum. These responses can range from confused to surprised, to shocked, to angry, and even to violent. At one time or another, John Morgan had experienced people reacting in just about every way imaginable. Most of the time, he could read the people he was serving, but sometimes, their behavior was so far afield from what he expected that he was caught completely by surprise.

John seldom felt comfortable telling people he met in social settings what he did to pay his bills. He wasn't exactly ashamed of his profession, as the work he did was important to the judicial system, but he felt uncomfortable whenever it came to discussing his job with friends. He had seen the negative reactions of the few people he had told, and he didn't need to experience that sort of thing regularly. Their expressions were akin to someone who had just stepped in something foul a dog left on the sidewalk.

However, this was John's job, and as he stood in front of a beautiful three-story brownstone townhouse at 1124 Sycamore Drive with his latest summons clasped tightly in his left hand, John prepared himself for what would come next. He wasn't always told what sort of paperwork he was delivering, but he had served enough summons to know by their size and weight; that was what he was presenting today. He had no idea what the purpose of the summons might be, as it was sealed so only the recipient could read it. The recipient was Miss Margaret Elizabeth Madison, a name he had gotten from the address on the outside of the packet. He would simply knock on the door or ring the doorbell. If a woman answered, John would ask if she were Margaret Elizabeth Madison. If she answered him in the affirmative, he would hand her the summons and say, "You've been served."

Next, while Miss Madison was still standing in shock, probably with mouth agape, as was typical, he would quickly snap a picture of her holding the summons with his cell phone's camera and then walk away. Once he was far enough from the house, John would email the photo to the lawyer who had hired him, and within a few minutes, his payment would automatically appear in his bank account. John worked with many different lawyers from several of the city's top firms and, as such, was paid quite generously for his troubles. Today, he worked for Thomas Edmonton, Esq., of the firm Jackson, Wallace, and Blake.

Now, it was time for John to do what he did best. As John approached the house, he saw a young person sitting on a wooden bench positioned perpendicular to the front door on the concrete porch. At first, he thought the person was a girl because of its longish blond wavy hair and perhaps because of John's distance. But after looking a bit closer, he was certain it was a young boy.

The boy appeared to be perhaps as young as 15 or as old as 17; it was difficult to tell due to his slight stature. He sat on the bench, staring blankly into space, apparently not noticing John's approach. Although John couldn't quite put his finger on it, there was something off about the boy, something that didn't feel right.

John looked away for just a moment, and when he returned his gaze, the boy was gone. He had no idea where the boy might have gone. The porch was not exceptionally large, having a concrete base surrounded by brownstone pillars and sides. The only ways off the porch were by going in the front door or walking past John; he was certain the boy had done neither.

When John mounted the porch and rang the doorbell, he peripherally saw something on his right and turned to look at the source of the movement. He was surprised to see the same young man standing, partially hidden behind a decorative potted tree. It didn't seem that the boy was hiding in fear, as the look in his eyes reflected a completely different emotion, or perhaps lack of emotion would sum it up more accurately. The boy was pale as a sheet with dark circles under his eyes.

John was surprised to find the boy staring at him with a look of complete detachment. John didn't quite know how to react. He had never seen a stare convey such a total lack of emotion. He had difficulty meeting the boy's gaze and looked away momentarily. When he did manage to look back, the boy was still intently eyeballing him with that same dead, disturbing gaze.

A feeling of extreme discomfort rushed through John. He did not fear for his own well-being as this young man was a mere child compared to himself. Although he would only do so if necessary, he was certain he could defend himself. John was a muscular middle-aged man with a lifetime of experience behind him, so he was not concerned about whether or not the boy was a physical threat. But that dead-eye stare was another story. John was very much disturbed by that look.

John was not experienced in dealing with people who exhibited such odd behaviors. This boy certainly fell well into that category. Nor was John accustomed to handling people with mental issues or deficiencies. He was uncertain if the boy was simply screwing with him or if he truly was mentally ill.

In his most pleasant voice, John said, "Excuse me, young man. Do you live here?" The boy stepped slightly to the right, coming out from behind the plant, but said nothing, continuing to stare a hole through him. The boy was dressed in jeans and a sweatshirt. Both seemed worn and stained with something, perhaps oil or grease. It was likewise John's practice to dress in jeans, a sweatshirt, a tee shirt, and sneakers; his goal was to appear unthreatening to his target. Now, he was starting to wish he might have dressed in more intimidating clothes, like a sleeveless T-shirt showing off his guns. Although John had to admit, lately, those guns were more like slingshots since he needed to spend much more time at the gym, as did his former six-pack, which had evolved into a full case.

John couldn't explain why he was so unnerved by the boy or concerned about the threat level of his appearance. He was a grown man, and this strange staring character was just a kid. But the longer John looked into the boy's dead, glaring eyes, the more irrationally frightened he became. John suddenly found himself struggling with his emotions. The rational part of his brain told him everything was fine, while his reptilian fight-or-flight instinct was on high alert.

This distraction was not part of his planned agenda for the day, so weird boy or not, he had a job to do. John turned away from the boy and rang the doorbell again. Shortly after, the door opened to reveal an attractive woman in her late twenties. John found it strange how beautiful he felt the woman was despite her lack of makeup, casual dress, and bare feet. She bore a weary, confused, and distrusting look. Clearly, the woman had only recently awoken, perhaps from a nap, and John felt guilty for probably being the one responsible. But he had no time to worry about such things. This was his profession, and he had to finish this job.

"Are you Miss Margaret Elizabeth Madison, Ma'am?" John asked with his experienced businessman voice.

The woman hesitated, then said, "Yes, I am she."

With his left hand, John gave her the summons, saying, "Miss Margaret Elizabeth Madison, you've been served." Then he lifted his right hand, the one containing his cellphone, and he snapped a picture of the stunned woman with a move practiced a thousand times before.

He turned to walk away, expecting to see the strange, staring boy glaring at him, but the boy was gone. He headed toward the steps and heard the woman call after him, "Do you know what this is? Do you know what misery you've dropped into my hands?"

John avoided interacting with someone after serving them; it was a bad business practice. But when he looked at those beautiful, tired eyes, John was moved in a way he had never been before. He asked, "Ma'am?"

Miss Madison stared down at the summons in her hand, shaking her head, and then said, "You've just done me in, and you don't even know it. Just . . . just go away. You've done enough."

Although he wanted to know more, John decided it would be best to leave. As he walked down the porch steps, he felt someone watching him. He turned to see the boy standing in the shadows, staring at him. Only now, that stare was one of extreme rage. That look sent chills down John's spine. He hurried to his car, parked down the street, and once inside, he opened his email and wrote a quick note to the lawyer who had hired him. Periodically, John took unconscious furtive glances in his rearview mirror. He mentally chastised himself for being so paranoid. John attached the last picture in his library and then sent the email. Typically, he would check the picture for content and quality before sending it, but he was uncharacteristically nervous, having been severely disturbed by the encounter with the staring boy.

Once John was several blocks from the Madisons' home, he began feeling better until his cell phone rang with the number for the law firm displayed. He answered the phone, saying, "Thomas, my man. Did you get the pic I sent?"

Thomas answered angrily, "What the Hell are you trying to pull, Morgan? Is this some kind of sick friggin' joke?"

John was caught off guard, "I don't know what you're talking about, Thomas. What do you mean, joke? I'm sorry, man. I honestly don't understand."

"The picture, Bud. Did you even look at the picture you sent that you say you allegedly took?"

John admitted, "Well, no, I didn't. I usually do, but I messed up this time. What's the problem, Thomas? Is the quality not up to par or what?"

"Oh no, John. Not that. The quality is perfect. In fact, it's so perfect I might not sleep again. Look at the picture, John."

"I'm gonna pull over and put you on speaker. While I check it out." John said.

"You do that!" Thomas said angrily.

John pulled into a parking space, called up the picture from his phone, and was stunned into silence. The photo showed the confused Miss Madison holding the summons in her hand. But there was more. Standing behind her, staring directly at the camera, was the strange boy John had seen hanging around the porch.

"What the Hell?" John asked. How did that weird kid get into my picture? I thought I saw him hanging around outside the house earlier. I swear he wasn't behind her when I took the picture."

"If you say so, John. Now, tell me how you managed to pull that off."

"Pull what off?"

"That boy in the picture. Did you Photoshop that kid's image in or what?"

"Photoshop? Geeze, Thomas. You know me. It took me a month to learn how to use email on my phone. I have no idea how to use Photoshop. What's this all about? What was in that summons I gave to Miss Madison?"

"Well, John. I usually don't discuss their contents with the servers, but considering the situation . . ."

"Ok, so?"

The lawyer hesitated, then said, "It's like this. Miss Madison is a high school guidance counselor. We need her to testify in a case, and she refused because it will affect a separate trial, her own criminal trial. So, we had to issue a subpoena forcing her to testify in our civil trial."

"Sorry, Thomas. Now I'm even more confused."

"It's like this, John. Miss Madison has been accused of having sexual relations with a minor, a student she was supposed to be counseling."

"Ok . . ." John prompted.

"That same student went berserk and then shot and killed three classmates and a teacher before police killed him. I'm sure you heard about that."

"Yeah. I read about it in the paper."

"That boy, William Edward Davidson, is the same boy Miss Madison was accused of having relations with. We want her to sit for a video affidavit describing in detail her relationship with the boy and his mental state."

John said, "That explains why she . . ."

"Why she what, John?"

"As I was leaving, she said I had just done her in and didn't even know it. She said I had no idea how much misery I just dropped into her hand."

Thomas said, "Well, that's certainly true. But that still doesn't explain the boy in the picture."

"Are you suggesting what I think you're saying?"

"Yes, John. The boy in the picture is William Davidson. The boy who was killed months ago by the police."

John looked again at the photo and saw the boy's eyes staring at him with such malevolence he could scarcely comprehend it.

Thomas interrupted John's thoughts, saying, "Could you hold on for a minute, John? I have a call coming through that I think I should take."

"Yes, I'll hold."

John continued to examine the photo. Miss Madison stood, shocked and surprised, looking at the summons in her hand. And behind her, that boy stared out, making John feel like the boy was staring a hole in his soul. After a few minutes, Thomas clicked back onto the line.

"I don't know how to tell you this, John, but I just got some terrible news."

"What news?"

"The police called and said that a few minutes ago, the Madison woman jumped from the third-floor window of her brownstone and fell to the ground, killing herself."

"What but I . . . oh God help me, no."

"I know what you're thinking, John. But it's not your fault. You were just doing your job."

John was stunned. In a monotone, detached voice, he simply said, "Yeah, just doing my job."

Then he hung up the call and sat in his car, staring out the windshield for a time before taking another look at the photo on his phone. His heart skipped a beat, and a scream caught in his throat as he looked in horror at the picture. Now, both Margaret Madison and the boy were staring at him with a boiling anger that was almost palpable. The pair now looked like maggot-infested zombies. Their angry eyes bulged from baggy, dark-encircled sockets, and worms dribbled from their slack-jawed lips. Their grayed faces were pitted with blisters and holes, many of which spewed puss and blood. Maggots squirmed in and out of the holes as well.

John threw his phone out the window, unable to stand the sight of it for another second. He started the car, intending to drive away with no destination in mind. John knew he would have to quit his job; he simply could no longer do this. He would flee the city and start anew. John felt he had no choice. He looked in his rearview mirror and gasped in terror. Two sets of insanely angry eyes stared at him from the back seat. Then he felt two icy, cold hands wrap around his throat.

GRUNDIES

"Adapt or perish, now as ever, is nature's inexorable imperative."
—H. G. Wells

"Nature does not hurry, yet everything is accomplished."
—Lao Tzu

Chad looked out through the windshield onto the dark, slick expanse of highway ahead of him and suddenly realized he had absolutely no idea where he was. Up ahead, a road sign reflected in his headlights through the fog and misty rain, becoming only a bit more visible the closer he got. The sign read "Erie 50 MI." Chad was suddenly perplexed.

The last road sign he remembered seeing indicated that he still had eighty miles to travel. And now this sign said only fifty miles. He wondered if the previous sign had been wrong, or perhaps he might have read it incorrectly. But he was almost certain the sign had said eighty miles. If he were right, it meant that he had been essentially driving on autopilot for the last thirty miles or roughly forty minutes, completely oblivious to his surroundings. Chad looked at the clock on the dashboard display and confirmed that forty-five minutes had passed.

He was not completely surprised by such a concept since Chad was quite certain that everyone found themselves driving on autopilot at one time or another. He assumed nothing had happened of any noteworthiness, or most certainly, he would have snapped out of his trance; at least, he hoped that would be the case.

He remembered having experienced similar events on several occasions in the past. But this was the first time in his many years behind the wheel that he had zoned out so extremely as not to be able to recall one single detail of the past three-quarters of an hour. He was beside himself with confusion.

Chad supposed it was his own fault. Usually, when he drove from eastern Pennsylvania to the far northwest side of the state, he traveled via the turnpike, taking it past Pittsburgh, almost to the Ohio border, before heading north toward Erie. This route took him on all main highways, most of which were set up to accommodate four lanes of traffic or better.

That particular route was longer in terms of miles traveled as it formed the left and bottom sides of a right triangle. The higher speed limits those expressways offered with such an open roadway often made the trip go quickly; however, it was also an extremely boring driving experience. Chad usually listened to audiobooks to help him deal with the monotony, but sometimes, it just got to be too much for him.

For that reason, Chad had chosen not to take the turnpike on this trip. He had instead gotten the not-so-ingenious idea that it might be more interesting to get off the turnpike after Somerset and head northwest along the hypotenuse of the triangle, thereby taking the theoretically shortest route to Erie. At the time, it made perfect sense to him because everyone knew the shortest distance between two points was a straight line. However, although it may have been more straightforward in terms of miles traveled, the trip ended up being much longer in terms of hours spent on the highway.

Unlike the turnpike, most of the roads Chad took along the scenic route were country two-lanes that wound through rural areas, small towns, and vast forestlands. He couldn't recall how long it had been since he had seen a typical fast-food restaurant. There were few gas stations along the route either, and those he did see appeared to be of the Mom and Pop variety, looking frighteningly like those run-down shacks often depicted in horror movies about deranged hillbillies. He suddenly had a flashback to a scene from the 1970s movie *Deliverance,* which caused his stomach to tighten.

Chad recalled with displeasure how he had stopped at a local combination gas station and general store just before he zoned out. It was the sort of place that kept fish bait in the same cooler as popsicles. He remembered the deplorable condition of the store, with peeling paint on its exterior and the well-worn dusty wood plank flooring inside. The place had a dank and musty smell common to such old buildings.

And the old man working behind the service counter was equally as disheveled in appearance. That character had been a scrawny old coot in a stained and yellowed wife-beater T, wearing a soiled camouflaged trucker's cap with a brim blackened from filthy finger smudges. The old-timer looked as though he had not showered for days or shaved for weeks, apparent by the grizzled white stubble covering his face in irregular patches.

Across the room from the service counter, an odd-looking overweight young man, perhaps thirty-five, was precariously perched on a rocking chair and staring slack-jawed at Chad, who stood sopping wet, dripping water onto the aged plank floor. When Chad first walked into the store, the rocker had been in motion, but it stopped as soon as he approached the counter.

From the odd man's demeanor, it was apparent to Chad that he was a dullard, perhaps mentally retarded. Although Chad knew both terms were considered politically incorrect, they seemed to fit that particular individual. Chad thought to himself in words that would be regarded as even less socially acceptable, "What a bunch of inbred web-toed mutants." This idea solidified Chad's earlier *Deliverance* impression even further in his mind, making him very uncomfortable. He recalled how that single movie had bothered him in ways no other film had ever done before or since.

But despite his many misgivings and discomfort with the place, Chad completed his transaction without incident. However, he could not seem to shake the unusual sensation slithering down his spine as he walked out of the store. Even though he didn't bother to look back, Chad was certain the owner and his subhuman associate, perhaps the man's offspring, were still staring at him. He could almost feel their eyes boring holes in his back. Chad had climbed uneasily behind the wheel and then quickly drove away, deciding not to stop anywhere again until he saw some signs of real, honest-to-goodness civilization.

For Chad, the word 'civilization' meant areas of the state with familiar places like McDonald's, Burger King, Wendy's, Pizza Hut, or any of the other national franchises, which he knew he could usually count on to be clean and have a staff of cordial, friendly workers. Those were the sorts of places that would ensure him he had truly left the untamed wilderness and had safely made it back to at least some semblance of normalcy. That is to say, someplace much less bizarre than and much more socially acceptable than what he thought of as Clem and Bubba's Inbred Uncle Daddy Emporium.

Chad usually didn't consider himself a snob, a bigot, or a discriminatory type of person. But the more he thought about it, the more he realized that most of those people likely seldom thought of themselves as such. So, unfortunately, maybe he was more of a bigot than he realized. This made him feel momentarily guilty for having had such negative feelings toward the odd pair in the gas station. He didn't know the two people and had no business prejudging them. But when he recalled how all of his internal alarms had seemed to go off at once in their presence, he decided perhaps his displeasure was not necessarily the result of bigotry but was some natural built-in early warning system.

He had driven away from the store as quickly as possible, perhaps a bit over the posted speed limit, extremely anxious about putting as much distance between himself and the strange pair. He had started to imagine a scenario picturing the two weird characters leaving the store, climbing into a beat-up, rusted Ford pickup truck, speeding after him to force him off the highway, taking him prisoner, and doing whatever those sorts of creepy people did whenever they kidnapped someone. Once again, he recalled *Deliverance* and the scene where the character played by Ned Beatty was being raped by a group of mountain psychos. Another cold chill ran down his back as he repeatedly took quick glances into his rearview mirror to ensure he was not being followed and was still alone, which he was, fortunately.

He remembered looking up at the wet roadway and saw a sign stating "Erie 80 MI," and he had breathed a sigh of relief. He knew he would arrive at his destination in less than two hours and hoped to find more signs of civilization long before then. But that had been the very last thing Chad could recall. One minute, he had been driving along the rainy roadway, replaying the strange scene from the gas station. Everything went blank until he passed the sign proclaiming that Erie was now fifty miles away. He had no idea what had happened to the last thirty miles, more than forty minutes of travel.

Shortly after passing the most recent road sign, he entered another heavily forested area with trees towering so high and thick over the roadway, creating a blanket of shade so dark it was almost like night. The rain did not seem to fall heavily under the canopy of greenery but dripped steadily. The misty fog was just as dense as ever. Chad, once again, could feel himself starting to zone out, and he tried turning on the radio to help him stay alert, but all he got was static.

He fiddled with the tuning button for a few seconds before finally giving up. When he looked up from the radio, he was suddenly startled. Something, a creature of some sort, possibly a dog or cat, scurried out from the underbrush and ran directly into the path of his car. Chad swerved in a desperate attempt to avoid hitting whatever it was and almost overcompensated, which might have resulted in his crashing the vehicle into a tree. Swerving to avoid the creature, Chad missed the thing with his right front tire. But then he felt a thud under his car on the left side as he realized he had unfortunately struck the creature with his left rear tire. He also heard the animal let out a high-pitched screech, and then he knew he had hit it.

Chad pulled over onto the sparse shoulder of the highway and sat breathing rapidly as he looked into his rearview mirror. With the minimal light coming through the canopy of trees, he could see whatever he had struck lying near the middle of the road just on his side of the double yellow line. And it appeared to be still moving.

"Oh, man!" Chad exclaimed with frustration, realizing he was now faced with the decision of whether to drive off or to go back and see how bad things really were. He had hit and killed animals on highways before, small rabbits or squirrels that had wandered onto the road, and in every case, he had simply driven away—this time, he had not.

Although he could tell it was fairly large, he could not say whether it was a wild animal or perhaps someone's pet. He recalled passing several rural mailboxes along the road, and someone's dog or cat might have strayed onto the highway. Chad hated when people accidentally ran over pets and then fled the scene. It seemed so wrong to him, and for a very good reason.

When he was a young boy, perhaps five or six, he had a pet beagle named "Rascal." That dog had been struck and killed by a car, but the driver never stopped to tell anyone; he had just driven away. Chad had been out playing with his friend when they came upon the ravaged remains of his once-beloved pet. Young Chad had no idea who had killed his dog, but he wished the man had not just driven away, leaving Rascal unattended. He often wondered if his dog might have just been badly hurt and not killed immediately. Maybe his pet could have been helped and didn't have to die. But he would never know for certain.

Reluctantly, Chad slowly opened the door to his car and placed his left foot on the roadway. As he did so, he caught another reflection in the side mirror, and between the patches of fog, he could see the creature moving slightly once again. Apparently, he had not killed it but perhaps only stunned it. In the darkness of the shadowed and misty highway, he still couldn't identify what type of animal it was. Although he was quite concerned about the creature, he was equally uncomfortable approaching the unknown animal to render assistance. Yet he understood he couldn't just drive away and leave it where it was. He was certain another car or truck would eventually come by and hit it again, possibly finishing it off.

If he got to the creature in time, it might still be alive, and there might be a chance for him to do something to help it survive. He reached into his pocket and checked his phone, only to see there was no cell service available. He thought again about getting back into the car and driving away, then recalled how badly he had felt as a child upon finding his own dog dead along a highway. The rain had picked up because there was even a steady drizzle under the canopy of trees.

He stood next to his car, and after a brief hesitation, he drummed up the courage to cautiously walk up the road toward the injured animal. As he got closer, Chad heard a rustling in the underbrush along the side of the road and momentarily was startled, wondering if some other animal, perhaps a wild one, might be lurking in the underbrush. Maybe it was a predator or a scavenger eager to take advantage of the wounded animal.

Then Chad thought he saw the bushes moving in several spots along the highway as if some small unseen creatures were scurrying about just out of sight. Once again, he considered running back to his car, jumping inside, and driving away no matter how much he felt obliged to stay, but he realized he could not. He looked at his watch, realizing he would most definitely be late for his appointment in Erie and would likely have to reschedule it until later in the day.

He shook his head with frustration and walked toward the quivering mass of fur lying in the middle of the roadway. As he got closer, he heard it make a low guttural growl as the thing began to raise itself upright to the best of its limited ability. To his surprise, it was not a dog or cat or any sort of family pet. The creature he had struck was a large groundhog.

Chad suddenly had a memory from his childhood about how his father called groundhogs "whistle pigs" because of the way male groundhogs would stand on their hind legs and utter a whistling sound to attract the attention of females. He was told they also issued the whistling sound to warn other groundhogs of impending danger. Although Chad had never seen or heard of such a display, he assumed they must do something like that, or else his father would never have referred to them as such. He had forgotten the term until he saw the thing trying to stand upright.

Then another name suddenly popped into his mind; "grundy." His wife and several Berks County friends referred to groundhogs as grundies. Not being a native of that area of Pennsylvania as his wife had been, he assumed it to be a local colloquialism.

"A grundy!" Chad said aloud. "Now, what in the hell am I supposed to do?" He knew groundhogs were herbivores and, as such, didn't eat meat, but that didn't mean it wouldn't attack him if it felt threatened. Meat-eater or not, it still had teeth and claws.

He had originally been concerned about dealing with a wounded pet, but now that he knew the creature was a wild, feral animal, he was even more unsure how or if he should approach the thing. Then he heard the beast moan a mournful cry in a way that could only be the result of intense pain.

Chad carefully walked around the creature, trying to get a better view to determine the extent of its injuries. He was quite certain it could not crawl away, or surely it would have done so already. Then, as he crossed over to the opposite side of the double yellow line, his stomach clenched with disgust at the sight before him.

The back third of the poor creature was completely decimated, having been squashed flat by Chad's tire while the remaining two-thirds of the animal writhed in agony. The groundhog's back legs were no longer recognizable, having become part of the shattered jumble of fur, blood, and entrails smeared along the highway's centerline.

The upper part of the creature's body was vertical as the thing thrashed about, slashing with its clawed forepaws while hissing and growling and snapping its jaws savagely as if even in the throes of imminent death, it was still trying to fight off its human adversary. It issued a high-pitched whistling noise so loud it hurt Chad's ears. Then, he heard a series of similar whistling noises coming from the rustling underbrush.

Chad found himself wracked with conflicting emotions: pity for the poor dying groundhog, guilt for being the one responsible for its pain, fear that he might end up scratched or bitten himself, the knowledge that he would remember this unspeakable nightmare for as long as he lived, and an understanding of what he had to do next.

He could tell by the level of damage his car had done that the creature was as good as dead. The thing was obviously suffering from unimaginable pain. The only right thing for him to do was somehow put the pathetic creature out of its misery as quickly as possible. But how could he?

For a moment, Chad considered perhaps backing his car over the creature and finishing it off. Still, the idea of the additional mess it might make on his undercarriage revolted him. What could he do?

Then, he had an idea, not the best solution, but one he believed to be a workable plan.

If he could just find a large rock, he could sneak up on the creature from behind and bash in its skull, killing it quickly and humanely while keeping himself out of harm's way in the process. Chad was fairly certain with its squashed lower body stuck fast to the highway; the creature would not be able to turn around to attempt to attack him when he got close enough.

He slowly walked back to the side of the roadway to find a rock of sufficient size to do what had to be done. As he did so, the creature continued growling, hissing, and whistling until Chad passed beyond its field of vision. Then the animal went back down into a crouched position where it began pathetically licking its bleeding wounds.

Since there was little light under the dense trees, Chad had to squint in the darkness to find what he needed. The rain trickling down his face and into his eyes made the chore even more difficult. There was no doubt the wretched groundhog was beyond healing, but Chad had no idea where he would find the necessary courage to put the creature down in such an up-close and intimate fashion. He suddenly felt like a murderer planning a crime.

As he searched for the rock of the proper size along the side of the road, Chad once again heard the rustling in the undergrowth. He did his best not to let the strange sounds unnerve him as his groping hands finally found what he needed. Chad pulled hard on the stone, wrestling it from the damp, muddy soil. His hair was flattened to his head, and rain streamed down his face. Chad shook his head to try to shoo away the water droplets. His clothing was likewise sodden.

He lifted the large rock, carefully holding it on an area free of mud and debris to maintain a sufficient grip. Chad believed the stone was heavy enough to accomplish the task at hand, but it was unfortunately not quite as smooth as he hoped. It had numerous sharp outcroppings, which he realized might make the job messier than he would have originally preferred. He began to walk slowly back toward the mortally wounded creature, plastered to the middle of the road. He tried to steel himself for what was to come next as he did so.

As Chad got closer, the creature sensed his approach from behind and sat up once again, whistling while making a futile attempt to turn its body to see what was approaching from his blind spot. Chad lifted the heavy rock high above his head and then brought it down hard upon the wounded creature's skull. He heard a sharp cracking sound as simultaneously, some foul-smelling liquid, likely blood and brain matter, shot from the thing's head, flew in his direction, and coated his shirt, pants, face, and hands with a disgusting, musky-smelling stench.

His stomach turned over from the vile smell and the idea of the nature of the substance that was now all over him. He turned his head and vomited on the highway. The animal fell to the roadway as Chad dropped the deadly stone, and it rolled a few feet away from the creature's corpse, landing next to the steaming puddle of vomit.

Chad was bent over, waiting for his uncontrollable retching to stop. After it finally did, he stood momentarily, taking in the horror before him. The grundy was most certainly dead; its ruined body was now just a mass of glistening, unrecognizable fur. He had killed it, although he could scarcely believe it himself. Chad knew if he returned to this same spot in a few days after the scavengers had done their best to decimate the corpse and numerous other vehicles had run over the remains, there would be nothing left but a flattened mass.

"Road pizza" is what he had often jokingly called such a sight. He had seen such similar creatures squashed flat countless times before. He picked up the large rock and turned to return it to its original location, as there was no point in having some other car strike the stone and blow out a tire or perhaps cause an accident. As he did so, he heard a chorus of wild hissing, chittering, and whistling coming from the woods beyond. He also thought he saw many sets of glowing eyes staring at him from the underbrush.

Grundies! He thought, realizing that the now-dead creature likely had been part of a larger community and perhaps even had left baby groundhogs behind. Seething with anger and frustration at the unpleasant situation he had found himself forced into, Chad hurled the boulder with all of his strength toward the woods, secretly hoping to hear one of the things screech in pain as the stone found its mark.

However, all he heard was the creatures scattering with fear. It gave him a great deal of satisfaction.

Chad was no longer feeling quite like himself, at least not the man he thought he was. The day's events made him feel very different, as if he had earned his rightful place at the top of the food chain. Despite his earlier reservations, Chad now felt some deeply hidden recessive and primal adrenalin rush, which he assumed primitive man must have felt when hunting for food.

He could smell his sweat mixed with the raw, woodsy stench from the felled creature, and it made him feel savage and alive in a way he had never felt before. His breathing was deep and seemed to echo in the now-silent woods. Then the rush faded quickly, and Chad's momentary emotions of being master of all he surveyed likewise dissipated.

Now he suddenly realized he was returning to being just regular white-collar Chad standing in the middle of a highway with stinking groundhog gunk all over him, wild-eyed like a madman panting and sweating like a rutting hog. Although he still felt the slight remnants of the previous euphoria, he was rapidly coming back to reality.

His mind returned to its proper perspective, and Chad realized that as soon as he could find a cell phone signal, he would have to reschedule his meeting, likely changing it to the following morning. After the trying day he had experienced, Chad was certain he would need to find a roadside rest stop or somewhere to clean up to the best of his ability and then find a hotel to crash for the night.

He planned on taking the longest and hottest shower he had ever taken in his life and then would find a way to dump all of his soiled clothing in a trashcan or dumpster somewhere. He had no intention of bringing them home for his wife to wash, not with all the grundy gunk on them. Next, he planned on finding a bar and drinking very heavily before heading back to his room and collapsing early into bed. A good night's sleep would be just what he needed to make all of the badness of the day go by the wayside. And now, as his adrenalin rush diminished, his strength seemed to wane right along with it.

In the distance, he saw his car, the front door still standing open, and the interior light illuminated. The car couldn't have been more than thirty feet away, but the slow trudge back felt like Chad had been walking for miles in exhausted condition. The day's events had most definitely taken their toll, and Chad could feel himself mentally and physically crashing rapidly.

When he reached his car, he fell behind the steering wheel, and it took all of his strength to fasten his seatbelt and close the driver's door. Once inside the close confines of the car, Chad was immediately aware of just how rank he smelled. He started the engine and put down all of the windows. He felt as if he might begin to vomit all over again. Chad hoped that once he got moving and the wind started whipping through the windows, it might blow away the worst of the smell.

"Woo baby, I really stink!" Chad said aloud with an unexpected chuckle as the stress finally began to leave him, quickly and surprisingly replaced by an insane sense of glee. He was so relieved that he began to feel almost giddy. "I guess it's a good thing I'm not near Punxsutawney, or old Groundhog Phil might have seen his last shadow today." Then he began to laugh madly as tears of relief streamed down his filthy face. That was the exact moment when he felt the first lightning bolt of pain as a tiny pair of teeth sunk deeply into the back of his neck.

Chad tried to reach back and fight off whatever it was that was gnawing on his flesh but could not reach the thing. Then he heard a chorus of whistling, which sounded less like a warning cry and more like a war cry. He then felt dozens of other sets of tiny teeth chewing away at him in various places: his face, arms, legs, and throat. He screamed and thrashed about madly, trying desperately to free himself from the bonds of his safety belt while he could feel himself being eaten alive. Amid his wilt convulsions of agony, blood flew wildly, splattering the car's interior and windshield with gore.

The last thing Chad ever saw were two tiny, angry red eyes staring into his own eyes from the heavy, furry thing that had perched atop his head as it bent over, showing him its yellowed teeth, which popped one of his eyeballs like a grape. Groundhogs might traditionally be herbivores by nature, but these particular grundies had changed their ways to partake in a special feast of vengeance for at least this moment in time.

SCARY MONSTERS
(AND SUPER CREEPS)

Authors note: In late 2024, I was asked by Nocturnacorn Press to write a story referencing the David Bowie song "Scary Monsters (And Super Creeps)" for a charity anthology that was to be "A Literary Tribute to David Bowie," the proceeds of which were slated to go to a charity. I was unfamiliar with this particular Bowie tune, but with a little research and imagination, I wrote and presented this quirky and off-center story.

> *"Well, she could've been a killer if she didn't walk*
> *the way she do. And she do."*
> —DAVID BOWIE, "SCARY MONSTERS (AND SUPER CREEPS)"

> *"She asked for my love, and I gave her a dangerous mind."*
> —DAVID BOWIE, "SCARY MONSTERS (AND SUPER CREEPS)"

Steve Roscoe was an extremely intelligent young man with an IQ that bordered on genius, surpassed only by his didactic memory. He liked to think of himself as the ultimate David Bowie historian. Some might describe him as more of a rabid fan than a historian. However, those few who knew him best would likely say Steve was neither a historian nor a fan but a David Bowie obsessive to the point of being considered a maniac. He knew every song release date, sales statistics, every song David ever wrote, who he collaborated with on what songs, which studios where each song was recorded, the history behind every lyric, everything. There was no piece of David Bowie-related minutia too small to escape his capture and storage in that computer-like brain of his. Steve was also not shy about sharing all this information, ad nauseam, with anyone unfortunate enough to start a conversation with him.

As one might guess, with such a unique personality, Steve had few friends. In fact, he had only one. That was a young man Steve had known since childhood named George Caldwell. However, no one in town except for George's parents knew or called George by his first or last name. For everyone else, especially all available women in town (single, married, or otherwise), he was simply known as Boner, a nick-name which, as things turned out, was not wasted on him. Whereas the Good Lord had bestowed an incredible brain on Steven Roscoe, he had completely bypassed that gift with young George. However, as it is written, the Lord does work in mysterious ways, and in his infinite wisdom, he opted to give Boner other gifts that serve both him and his friend Steve quite well.

The two young men were sitting on recliners in Steve's basement apartment. Calling it Steve's "apartment" was somewhat generous as it was actually Steve's mother's basement. It appeared that employers didn't appreciate Steve or his condescending and belligerent personality any more than most people did.

Steve said, "I'm telling' you, Boner. If this woman existed, she'd be the wildest chick on the planet, and I'd have to find some way to meet her."

"Who are you talkin' about, Steve?" Boner asked.

"I'm talking about that crazy girl from what many people consider the ultimate David Bowie song," Steve explained.

Boner replied, "What Bowie song, Dude? Do you mean that chick from that Suffragette City song? You know, Wham bam, thank you, ma'am? That chick? Dude, I'd have to agree totally. She would be most righteous!"

"Seriously, Boner? Suffra-friggin-gette City? Listen to yourself. Is that the only David Bowie tune you know? That thing came out in 1972 and was originally meant to be the B side of the single, 'Starman.' It didn't appear on LP until 'The Rise and Fall of Ziggy Stardust and the Spiders from Mars' later in 1972. Then they re-released 'Suffragette City' again in the U.S. as a single in 1976, specifically for mouth-breathing, knuckle-draggers like you."

Boner said, "Yeah, Dude. That's right. 'Suffragette City.' Wham, bam, thank you ma'am. Yeah, is that the chick you mean?"

Steve was rapidly losing patience with his friend, Boner. This seemed to be happening more and more of late. Steve often wondered why he remained friends with Boner. At times like this, Steve some-times questioned what good it was for him to be a virtual walking, talking encyclopedia of all knowledge David Bowie related when his best friend on the planet was essentially a lumbering piece of barely human vegetation, whose entire knowledge of Bowie never got past the song, 'Suffragette City.'

To make matters worse, that limited knowledge consisted of Boner shouting "hey man" and "wham, bam, thank you ma'am" at hopefully the appropriate times when that ancient bit of recording history still came up decades later on the local fire company social hall jukebox. Steve considered that sort of deplorable ritual right up there with someone cueing up the 1963 Surfaries instrumental, "Wipeout," so the nastiest chicks in the bar could waddle out on the floor with their decades-out-of-date beehive hairdos, doughy flesh spilling from span-dex while shaking their former money-makers for all they're worth, which might be two bucks and a few food stamp coupons.

Maybe it was the fact that the same best friend happened to be an extremely handsome, albeit brainless hunk of masculinity with surfer boy, movie star good looks, who was also blessed to be hung like a donkey and who every woman in town knew. And despite his being dumber than a box of hair, the chicks Boner tossed aside were ten times hotter than any Steve could dream about scoring on his own, even if he were riding down the street in a stretch limo with hundred-dollar bills spilling from his pockets and buckets of cocaine sitting next to him.

Not opposed to being honest with himself, Steve was aware of his precarious place in the social and sexual pecking order. That being the case, Steve would always be standing by, at the ready, to shamelessly take advantage of Boner's trail of discarded gorgeous female breadcrumbs. Ok, so maybe Boner did have something to bring to the friendship table after all. Steve only wished sometimes that he might have some semblance of an intelligent conversation with Boner, preferably one centered around David Bowie trivia. That would be awesome.

Steve said, "No, Boner. I'm talking about the girl in Bowie's song 'Scary Monsters (And Super Creeps),' which was released on September 12th, 1980, and was the title track to Bowie's 14th studio LP of the same name. For that album, Bowie went above and beyond the call of duty to try to come up with a more commercially successful recording. He had a previously released trilogy that, although critically acclaimed, was not a commercial success."

Boner said, "Yup. Ya gotta make them record companies happy. Cash is king."

"Yes, that's a very astute observation, Boner," Steve said. He was a bit taken aback. Steve liked where this conversation was going. Perhaps he and Boner could actually have an intelligent discussion after all.

Then Boner grabbed his bulging crotch, snickered, and said, "Ya gotta keep the customer satisfied to keep 'em coming' back for more of your goods."

Steve's hopes were, once again, dashed. Although he had to admit that Boner had hit on an important principle of socio-economic theory, he had done so in a way that was 100%, Boner. Steve did a mental eye roll and said, "Anyway, the LP *Scary Monsters* was both a commercial and critical success, and many Bowie aficionados considered it Bowie's last great album. Several music scholars have gone so far as to consider it one of the greatest albums of all time. This was important because Bowie's final album, Blackstar, was released 36 years later on January 8th, 2016. The release coincided with his 69th birthday, and he passed away from liver cancer just ten days later. This high praise for Scary Monsters was also special since, according to Wikipedia, David Bowie recorded 26 studio albums, 9 live albums, 2 soundtrack albums, 26 compilation albums, 8 extended plays, 128 singles, and six box sets. And people were saying this album from 1980 might be his best record ever."

Boner stood silent for a moment. This often happened to him during a conversation that might require the young man to think excessively. It wasn't exactly like he suffered from narcolepsy or might be having a minor seizure. It was more like his brain was having trouble firing on all cylinders. Steve supposed it had something to do with humans having a limited blood supply and a single heart struggling to pump that blood throughout the body. In Boner's case, his heart was desperately trying to pump much-needed blood to all of his vital organs. Considering that one of those organs practically allowed his friend to run a three-legged race alone, Boner's heart might occasionally have to divert blood flow from his brain to other places, which might be the reason for the mental hesitation.

Steve often imagined two chipmunks working feverishly to get a hamster wheel to turn, but the darned thing refused to cooperate. Eventually, whatever obstacle had impeded the wheel's ability to spin would dislodge itself, Boner's brain would once again start to receive blood flow, and the conversation could recommence. As Steve looked on in morbid fascination, he could tell by the light slowly returning to his friend's vacant eyes that Boner was about to rejoin the land of the living.

Boner shook his head as if clearing out a few unwanted cobwebs, then asked, "So, you're sayin' this song, 'Scary Monsters,' is a pretty good tune, right?"

"Um, yeah, Boner. I suppose that's exactly what I'm saying."

Boner asked, "Can you play it for me?

"What?"

"The song, can you play it for me on your phone? I know you have to have it on there. If David Bowie farted during a recording session, you probably have a copy of that, so it only makes sense you'd have one of the greatest songs in the universe that Bowie ever recorded."

Genuinely impressed, Steve asked, "Boner? Do I detect a note of sarcasm in that statement?"

Boner chuckled, "From me? No way, Steve-o. We both know I ain't smart enough to come up with stuff like that, right?"

"Well, yes, I suppose," Steve said hesitantly.

"So, Dude. Play me the tune already."

Steve cued the song on his phone and played Scary Monsters. Boner listened intently, never letting his facial expressions give away his reactions. Simultaneously, Steve appeared raptured by the music and lyrics flowing from his phone like manna from Heaven. When the song finished, Steve released an almost ecstatic sigh and asked, "So, tell me, Boner. What did you think?"

Boner hesitated briefly, then took a deep breath and said, "I think it sucked!"

Steve was in shock, "Excuse me? Did you just say the song sucked?"

"Oh yeah. It sucked big time. I'm talkin' major inhalation. El sucka mundo, Dude."

"No way, Boner. This song is a classic and is considered one of Bowie's greatest."

Boner asked, "By who? Who said it was his greatest? It obviously wasn't any dude who liked to get down and funky with the babes. There ain't a chick in the world who could get into a tune like that. Hell, even a major player like me would end up going home empty-handed if I tried to turn a babe on with that sucky tune."

Steve explained, "But, Boner, it's a work of art, a creative masterpiece."

"Art, schmart, who cut a fart? That song is a joke. It would get laughed off of American Bandstand's Rape a Record."

Steve corrected, "First of all, Boner, the segment was called Rate a Record, not Rape a Record. And American Bandstand has been off the air for decades. What friggen' century do you even live in?"

Boner argued, "Alls I know is that tune doesn't have a great beat, and it ain't easy to dance to. Dick Clark would hate it too."

"Boner, Dick Clark died in 2012. That's over a decade ago."

Boner looked sad, "Oh man. Sorry to hear that. Everybody liked Dick Clark. He was like America's oldest teenager, Dude. You know what? Bowie should have sung Suffragette City on Bandstand; that would have been awesome. Wham, bam . . ."

"Just stop right there, Boner. Enough with 'Suffragette City' already. We're talking about Scary Monsters here."

"Oh, that thing. So, are you telling me that disaster is supposed to be some artsy-fartsy song about a chick?" Boner asked with a look of confusion still present on his face.

Steve said, "Yeah, some people say it's about this guy who has a painfully shy girlfriend, and he has conflicting feelings about her. He pushes her to have a normal relationship, but she becomes even more reclusive and eventually goes crazy. The Dude feels guilty because of his actions. He comes off as this bad guy, but he's not and has a guilty conscience about how he's treated her. He understands that he's responsible for pressuring the shy girlfriend, and his actions are essentially what turns her into a recluse and eventually drives her insane."

Boner said, "He sounds like a douchebag to me."

"It's more complicated than that, Boner."

"You got all that from that stupid song?" Boner asked.

Steve said, "Well, yeah, sort of. I mean, hundreds of music scholars discussed the song, instrumentation, vocals, and lyrics for countless hours to come up with a similar consensus. But yeah, that all came from that tune."

Boner was quiet for a few seconds again, then said, "Ok, so let me get this straight. The song's completely made up; it ain't about no real chick. But if it was about a real, shy, crazy babe, you'd want to meet her. Do I have that right?"

"Yeah, that's right," Steve said.

Boner added, "Look, Steve-o. You and I go way back. So, you know I ain't the sharpest bulb in the shed. But I gotta ask, why would you want to be involved with some borderline psycho chick like that?"

Now, it was Steve's turn to hesitate. Finally, after some thought, he said, "Even though the woman in this song never existed, she was as real in David Bowie's mind as if she had. I don't possess that sort of creativity or imagination, so the only way I can hope to experience such a chick is in real life. If I knew an actual woman like that and had to deal with her fragile emotional state, I might be able to understand more of what was going through Bowie's mind when he wrote the song."

"But you agreed that based on the song, she would be a major nutjob," Boner said.

"Yeah, I suppose she would be." Steve agreed.

Boner suggested, "And she might be dangerous, maybe even deadly, to be around. Do I have that right, too?"

"Yes, Boner. At some point, she might even try to kill herself or me."

Boner said, "Don't get me wrong, Dude. You know I love you . . . like a brother, not in any swapping bodily fluids way . . . but don't you think that kind of thing might be a little . . . um . . . obsessive."

Again, Steve was surprised, "You know, Boner. That was another very astute observation on your part. That's twice in the same day. I think that might be a new record for you."

"Why, thank you, kind sir. Coming from you, I'll consider that a compliment." Boner said, genuinely humbled.

Steve replied, "Take it as you will, my friend." He was happy to realize Boner was still Boner and had no idea when he was being insulted.

Then Boner surprised Steve by asking, "Suppose I knew a chick that fit the bill as being a really close match for that babe in that song. Would you seriously want to mess with some damaged chick like that? I mean, all things considered."

Steve was stunned, "Are you kidding, Boner? A woman like that is exactly what I would need to help me get inside Bowie's head and understand his thought process when he wrote that song. It would be practically like asking David Bowie himself. Do you know a girl like that, Boner? Do you think she's a Bowie fan?"

"I do know a chick like that, but I don't know her all that well. I don't know if she digs Bowie or not. From what I heard, she's kind of quiet. Her name is Cassandra. I know some of her friends."

Then Steve cautiously asked, "Boner . . . you didn't . . . um . . . you and her . . . you know?"

Boner looked momentarily confused, then said, "Me and Casandra? Bumpin' uglies? No, at least not that I can remember. She ain't exactly my type."

Steve said, "I'm going to assume that means she has a brain as well as a pulse. So, on a scale from 1-10, where would you say she falls looks-wise?"

Boner thought momentarily, then offered, "On a scale of what types of women I can get, she's about a five. But on a scale of what you can get, she'd be an eleven."

"Very funny, my friend."

"If only I was joking, Steve-o."

Then Boner suggested, "How's about I call her and have her meet you at Frank's bar in an hour or so? I'll set it up through one of her friends."

"Do you think she'll be available?" Steve asked.

Boner chuckled, "Um . . . Duh! She'll be every bit as available as you are, amigo."

"But if she's shy? Will she be willing to come out to a bar?"

"Sure. Not to worry, Bro. I'll lie and tell her you're shy, too. Maybe I'll even tell her you're fun to be around."

"Thanks, Boner."

Boner laughed, "Um . . . that was part of the lie too." Then Boner got up from his recliner, pointed upward toward the stairs, and said, "I'll be right back. I need to do this outside."

A few minutes later, Boner returned with a slightly distracted look on his face and said, "It's all set. You're good to go. Meet her at Frank's in an hour. I just sent you a picture of Cassandra that I just got from her friend, Megan. You remember Megan, right? She's the one who, by the way, I did. . . ."

"Too much information, Boner. I don't want to know."

Boner shrugged his shoulders and said, "Your loss, Bro. Anyway, Megan said Cassandra is coming off a bad situation with her former boyfriend and is a bit vulnerable. I assured her you were gentle and understanding. Translation: You should be guaranteed to be able to bang the doors off that thang!"

Steve said, "You're a prince among men, Boner."

"Whatever. Look, I gotta go, and you have a date to get ready for. I hope Cassandra meets your Bowie needs and other needs as well. Nudge, nudge, wink, wink. Try not to bore the poor girl to death."

As Boner left the house, heading for his own "apartment" in his mother's basement, he half-remembered something Megan had told him. What the Hell was it? He always got stuff mixed up, especially when talking to Megan. Was it something about Casandra and her fantasy football-obsessed ex-boyfriend? Did she say he ate, slept, and drank football statistics? Had she said the breakup had almost killed him, or had she said that Cassandra had killed him? That might be important to know. Boner thought the words chopping, knives, and pieces had been used somewhere in the conversation but wasn't exactly sure. Damn, something like that might be important too. Was there something about an upcoming trial and time spent in a mental institution? Boner couldn't remember. Then again, it hadn't been his fault. He had become distracted when Megan started talking dirty to him and reminding him about their last time together. He hated and loved when she did that. It was like the blood had left his brain for other places, and Boner had gotten confused. That often happened to him; he just didn't understand why.

Well, he hoped Steve didn't screw things up by spending the whole time talking about David Bowie. He could only hope that Steve didn't play that abysmal suckfest "Scary Monsters" for the poor girl. What Cassandra needed was a good old-fashioned dose of "Suffragette City."

Boner smiled as he bopped his head from side to side, walking along the street and singing, "Wham, bam, thank you, ma'am!"

CHRISTMAS STALKING

/ 1 /

The moon shone brightly across the snow-covered lawn as the snow fell that night, a week before Christmas. Several mighty pines, with their coating of white, glistened like a million diamonds in the moonlight. With the sidewalks unshoveled and the lawn covered with several inches of virgin snowfall, the scene presented a nearly perfect holiday image scarcely matched by even the most glorious Christmas card. It appeared perfect in every way. However, this night was anything but ideal.

Emma Wallington stood at the front window of her large brick colonial, mostly hidden by the thick velvet drapes, looking out into the winter wonderland. But she was not enjoying the picturesque holiday scene spread across the lawn. Although she may have wished to, such a desire would have to go unfulfilled. Emma had more important business to attend to. She was watching for him. These days, it seemed like she was always looking for him while simultaneously hoping he would not appear.

Although she had never seen him, even from a distance, Emma could feel him out there watching and waiting. She knew with certainty it was a man; she felt it with every sense she had. She didn't know his name or why he had chosen her, but she knew he most certainly wanted her. Emma couldn't understand why she had been singled out.

She lived alone, seldom dated, didn't use social media, and never spoke to strangers. Her day consisted of waking up, going to work, and then coming home to her cat, Ginger, who sat watching her mistress staring out the window.

For some unknown reason, this vile excuse for a human was out there stalking her. Emma knew she could never allow this maniac to get his filthy hands on her. She imagined all the tortures and degradations he would surely want to force upon her, all the sexual perversions this degenerate deviant would take great pleasure in putting her through. She had good reason for her imaginings.

Several months earlier, she had received a crudely written note that said, "I'm coming for you, Emma. You're mine, and no one can ever change that. If I can't have you, then no one will."

She had gone to the local police station to show the investigator the note, but when he examined it, the paper was blank. She couldn't explain what had happened; the message had been there earlier, plain as the nose on her face. Yet somehow, the message had vanished. Once that happened, the police wrote her off as some kind of crackpot. They paid no attention to her repeated pleas for help because she couldn't describe the man or offer any possible suspects for the police to investigate. Upon seeing her exhausted and agitated condition, one detective suggested as gently as possible that Emma might want to seek psychological counseling. That detective suggested that Emma had imagined her stalker, or worse, fabricating him to get attention. Furious, she stormed out of the police station because no matter what the police thought, she knew some maniac was out there, watching and waiting for the right opportunity to strike.

Emma Wallington was the twenty-three-year-old daughter of the late Frederick and Regina (Jacobson) Wallington. Her father and mother owned and operated a small grocery store in town, the income from which provided nicely for their family over the years. Sadly, Emma's parents were killed in a car accident when she was in her first year of college, and she had no choice but to leave school and take over the family business. Emma often wondered if their deaths might be more than an accident. Although she could think of no one who would want to harm her parents, in the back of her mind, Emma wondered, what if it hadn't been an accident? What if someone had killed them, knowing that it would force Emma home? What if it was the same person torturing her now?

As a child, Emma was a regular feature of the store and grew up with the store's employees. The townspeople had been accustomed to seeing the pretty little brunette helping her parents at the store, and everyone liked Emma. She continued working in the store in her spare time throughout junior high and high school. Her father often joked with customers that Emma knew more about running the store than he did.

Now, a young woman, Emma had survived her parents' tragic death, dropped out of college, and found her place in the store's operation. She was doing a fantastic job, and the business prospered under her management. Emma had kept all the employees on staff, including a young man named Jim Garland, despite her uncomfortable past with him.

Eventually, as the business began to run smoothly, Emma started delegating more day-to-day duties to her older employees, hoping she might find more time to have a personal life. She thought soon she might be able to start taking night classes at the local university. Things had progressed well in that direction until Emma received that awful threatening note. Now, she had essentially become a work/home recluse, leaving for the store early in the morning, returning home at night, and watching out for that horrible man to show himself eventually.

Not one to be forced into the victim role, Emma would do all she could to ensure she would be ready for him when that day came. She had found her father's 38 caliber revolver and a good supply of bullets in her parents' old dresser drawer. It had been years since her father had taken her into nearby woods and taught her how to load and shoot the pistol. As she recalled, the gun had quite a kick, but eventually, she learned to control it and became a proficient marksman. But now, if she found she had to use it in self-defense, Emma's target would be much larger and much closer. The day her mysterious stalker decided to make his move, she planned to be ready.

She still couldn't understand what had happened when the police had studied the note. How had the words vanished from the page as they had done? Emma knew they were there; she had seen them herself many times. Yet, when the police held the note, the words were gone. She had feared the dreaded text would return when she returned home and reexamined the note. Thankfully, it did not. Yet that did nothing to solve the mystery of how the writing had disappeared in the first place.

Sleeping fitfully most nights, as Emma tossed and turned, she wondered how long it had been since she had a full night's sleep. She couldn't recall. After a few more minutes of staring out the window at the falling snow, Emma decided to go to bed and try again to sleep. Since it was close to the magical season of Christmas, Emma hoped perhaps she might have a miracle and sleep through the whole night.

/ 2 /

James Garland was the youngest employee at Emma's store. He was only a few years older than Emma. Everyone called him Jimmy. He had started working at the store, stocking shelves part-time, when he was twelve, and Emma was eight. Over the years, they had become like brother and sister, having spent so much time together. Emma looked up to Jimmy, and he, in turn, watched out for Emma.

When they were younger, the two were inseparable and could talk to each other about anything. As Emma matured, Jimmy realized that his feelings towards her had grown from brotherly affection into true love. This troubled him terribly because he knew that if he proclaimed his feelings for Emma at the wrong time, their relationship could change negatively forever.

At the end of the summer of Emma's eighteenth year, she was preparing to go off to college. Her parents threw a going away party for her at the store. All the employees, including Jimmy, joined the celebration, although he was not in the mood for partying. Jimmy was heartbroken, knowing Emma would be going away to college without knowing how deeply he felt about her. She might meet a boy her age at college and fall in love, but then any hopes he had of them being together would be gone forever.

Toward the end of the evening, Jimmy walked outside alone with Emma and, with hesitation, said, "Emma, there's something I have to tell you, but I'm not sure how to go about it."

"Jimmy. We've been friends forever. You can tell me anything. I thought you knew that."

"I suppose I do. But this is something important that I really need to say, but I don't want to risk messing up our friendship."

"I think you know nothing can change that, Jimmy."

Jimmy took a deep breath and said, "Emma, I love you."

Emma smiled and said, "And I love you too, But you know that. I've told you before, you're like my own brother."

"That's not what I mean, Emma. I mean, I truly love you." Then Jimmy took Emma in his arms and kissed her passionately on the lips. Had this been a romantic movie, Emma would have given in to Jimmy's bold advance. But it was not, and Emma slapped Jimmy hard across the face. Then she stepped back and covered her mouth, wide-eyed in shock. Emma broke down in tears, turned, and hurried away. That was the last time Jimmy had seen Emma for over a year. He next saw her when she returned home for her parents' funeral and to take over the family store.

They had only briefly made eye contact at the funeral, but Emma and Jimmy never spoke. A week later, in her role as owner and manager of the store, Emma met with each employee individually to discuss the store's future and to assure them their jobs were safe. She also discussed the role each of them would play under her leadership. Emma deliberately delayed her meeting with Jimmy until the end.

As Jimmy entered her office and sat down, Emma said, "Hello, Jimmy."

He replied, "Hello, Emma . . . I mean . . . Miss Wallington . . . I mean . . . You are the boss now."

"Emma is fine, Jimmy." She said, her voice taking a serious tone.

Jimmy said, "I guess . . . I mean . . . Are you firing me?"

Emma hesitated momentarily, then said, "No, Jimmy, I won't fire you."

He asked, "But what about . . . You know . . . Before?"

"I'm willing to forget about that night, Jimmy, if you are."

He looked Emma in the eye and said, "I honestly don't know if I can, Emma. Everything I said to you that night is as true now as it was then. Maybe it would be better if I just quit, then leave town and find another job."

"I don't want you to leave, Jimmy. You are good at your job, and the customers really like having you in the store. I think you just need to give it time, and eventually, things will get back to normal, and we can be friends again."

Jimmy put his head down and said, "If that's what you want, Emma, then I'll try."

"I can't ask for more than that." She replied.

However, Jimmy knew he would never be able to go back to just being Emma's friend. He loved her too much. He didn't know how he would be able to work closely with her every day, knowing how much he wanted her. What if she found someone else? Would he be able to go on knowing that he had lost her to another? Jimmy felt that if he couldn't have Emma, then no one else should have the right to have her either.

/ 3 /

Emma tossed and turned all night long, her mind producing images of a shadowed, faceless man standing outside her home, looking in the window, watching her, and waiting for the opportunity to make her suffer. At first, she thought, what more could he do to her? Wasn't she already suffering enough? Then her nighttime imagination kicked in, and she once again envisioned all the sick and perverse things her stalker might do to her if given the chance.

Finally, she fell into a deep sleep. In her dream, she was at the celebration party her folks had thrown for her. It was a pleasant memory with her mother and father alive and well. One minute, she was cutting her cake and passing out slices to all the employees, and then she was outside facing Jimmy, who looked upset. His expression seemed to be in a constant state of change, moving from one emotion to another: happy, then sad, then angry, then confused.

In her dream, Emma asked, "What's wrong, Jimmy? You seem upset."

"I am upset, Emma, because of what I must do."

Emma was confused, "I don't understand, Jimmy. What is it you must do?"

Jimmy's face turned angry. Emma saw that he now held the knife she had used earlier to cut the cake. It had grown longer, wider, and sharper. How had he gotten that? Why did he have it?"

Frustrated, He shook his head and said, "I told you I loved you, Emma, but you refuse to accept my love. I can't bear the thought of seeing you with someone else."

"There is no one, Jimmy. You know I'm too busy running the store. I have no time for anyone else. I told you we can still be friends."

"I don't want to be your friend, Emma. I have plenty of friends. I want to be with you. I want you more than anything else in life, and if I can't have you, then no one can." Jimmy said as he raised the knife and thrust it at Emma.

Emma awoke, sitting straight up in bed. She was panting like a dog and was covered in a sheen of cold sweat. The early morning sun rose and shone through the crack in her closed bedroom drapes. She looked into the corner of the room and was certain she saw a dark shape lurking in the shadows. Emma reached over on her dresser and retrieved the revolver, pointing it directly at the figure. She shouted, "Come out of there, whoever you are. I have a gun, and I know how to use it."

There was no reply. Emma turned on the table light and realized what she thought was her stalker was nothing more than her coat tree with several items of her clothing hanging on it. She breathed a sigh of relief, turned, and set the revolver back on the nightstand.

She sat momentarily, getting her bearings, and the dream from the night before flooded back into her mind.

Sitting wide-eyed on the bed, she said to the empty room, "Oh my God, it's Jimmy. Jimmy is the stalker."

/ 4 /

The next day, Emma called Jimmy into her office to settle the matter once and for all. She hated dealing with it so close to Christmas but had no choice. Emma wasn't exactly sure how she would handle the situation or what she might say or do, but she knew she had to do something. If, after the meeting, she still believed Jimmy was the man who was stalking her, she would fire Jimmy and then go to the police and tell them her suspicions. Perhaps now that she had a face and a name to go with her concerns, the police would take her more seriously and start an investigation.

Jimmy came into Emma's office looking more than a bit concerned and sat in the visitor's chair across from Emma's desk. This put her in an assumed position of power, which was exactly what she wanted. Emma needed Jimmy to know who was in charge and who wouldn't sit back and be a victim. This would be challenging since she had scarcely slept well in weeks. The toll it took on her was as obvious as the dark circles under her eyes.

"I was told you wanted to see me," Jimmy said curiously.

Emma took a deep breath to calm herself, then said, "I'm having a problem, Jimmy, and I believe you are the reason."

"Me? Emma, I don't understand. I would never want to cause you any trouble. I love . . . well, you know."

"Yes, I most certainly do know, Jimmy, and that's part of the problem."

"How are my feelings a problem? It's not like I can control my emotions."

Emma decided to cut to the chase and ask him outright, "Jimmy, are you stalking me?"

"What?" Jimmy asked, appearing genuinely confused.

"I asked if you were stalking me."

Flustered, Jimmy said, "No, Emma. I could never do such a horrible thing to you. Why would you think something so terrible of me, knowing how I feel about you?"

Emma ignored his comment and pressed on, saying, "Did you send me a note, Jimmy?"

"A note? No, I never sent you a note. What kind of note?"

"A threatening note, Jimmy. And how did you make the message disappear?"

Jimmy had been concerned about Emma lately. She seemed to be exhausted as if she wasn't sleeping. Now, she was talking gibberish that made no sense. He said, "Look, Emma. I promise you, I have never sent you such a note, nor would I ever. I can't believe you would think I could do such a thing."

Emma was quiet. Now, it was her turn to be confused. Jimmy sounded legitimately unaware of what she was talking about. Maybe he wasn't the stalker, but then who was? No, she was certain it was Jimmy.

"Well, Jimmy, if you insist on saying it wasn't you, then I suppose I have no choice but to let you go."

"Let me go? You mean fire me?" Jimmy shouted, "How can you fire me? I'm one of your best workers!"

"I'm sorry, Jimmy, but I have no choice. You're fired. Now go empty your locker and leave."

"Fine, Emma. If that's what you want, I'm telling you you're wrong. I'm not that guy, and I hope you find the real stalker. When you do, you'll know I'm telling you the truth. Goodbye, Emma. Know that I still love you and always will."

Jimmy turned and left. At first, he was angry, not understanding how his beloved Emma could accuse him of such a thing. Then, as he got control of his emotions, he realized that Emma had a real problem. Jimmy knew he wasn't the one stalking Emma, so that meant someone else was. His heart sank at the thought of his Emma being stalked and in potential danger. Jimmy decided he would have to do what he had always done: watch Emma and protect her from her potential assailant.

/ 5 /

It was Christmas Eve, and Emma was once again standing by the front window watching, terrified that tonight might be the night her stalker would strike. She thought she saw some movement behind a tree toward the pavement but was unsure. Perhaps it was her imagination.

She started to doubt herself. What if the police detective was right? What if all of this was a product of her imagination? What if there was never any writing on the note? What if the stress of the death of her parents and taking over the store was more than she had realized? Could she really be imagining everything?

No, she was certain everything that had happened was real, and now she knew who her stalker was. It was Jimmy. His belief in his love for her and Emma's rejection of him must have driven Jimmy to do this. Now, Emma had to worry about what Jimmy would do next.

Outside, Jimmy ducked behind a pine tree. He could see Emma at her window. She had almost seen him. He wondered what she would have done if she had seen him. Would she have called the cops? If they found him lurking outside her house, they surely would believe he was her stalker. Now that he thought about it, his hiding in the bushes, watching her through the window, was a sort of stalking. But that was not why he stood out in the cold on Christmas Eve.

Jimmy was protecting Emma as he had always done. If that stalker came anywhere near Emma's house, Jimmy would be ready. He assumed the man might make his move tonight. There was something symbolic about attacking his victim on Christmas Eve. In his hand, Jimmy held a long butcher knife. If the stalker showed up, he would overpower him, keep him at bay with the knife, and call the police. Jimmy knew such a drastic move was dangerous, but he loved Emma and would not hesitate to risk his life for her.

In the living room, Emma backed away from the window. She decided she had seen nothing; it had all been her imagination. She went into the bedroom, put on her pajamas, and crawled into bed, pulling the covers up tight against her neck. She reached over and placed her hand on the revolver. If the stalker came, she would be ready. Emma was exhausted and cared more about getting some sleep tonight than worrying about her stalker.

When Emma was sound asleep, her orange cat, Ginger, jumped onto one of her end tables. Doing what cats do best, she knocked the light over and sent it crashing to the floor. The sound woke Emma, who, in her fright, screamed in the darkness of the bedroom.

Outside, a shivering Jimmy heard Emma's scream and knew the stalker must have made his move. Being one of Emma's father's most trusted employees, Jimmy knew where a key to the front door was hidden. He quickly ran to the front door, retrieved the key, and opened the door. Hoping to calm Emma and possibly scare away the intruder, Jimmy ran up the stairs, knife in hand, shouting, "Emma, it's me, Jimmy. I'm coming for you."

In the dark bedroom, Emma heard the front door open and someone running up her stairs shouting, "Emma, it's me, Jimmy. I'm coming for you." She realized she must have been right; Jimmy was her stalker, and now he was coming to get her. Emma reached over to her end table and grabbed her revolver. She decided to keep the bedroom in darkness, to make it harder for Jimmy to find her.

Jimmy raced down the hallway and threw Emma's bedroom door open. He stood, silhouetted in the hallway light, shouting, "I'm here, Emma. And now everything is going to be alright."

Emma saw the bedroom door fly open and the shadowed Jimmy standing there with a long knife in his right hand. It was just as it had been in her nightmare. Jimmy was her stalker, and he finally came for her. Emma raised her revolver and pulled the trigger. The blast was deafening in the small bedroom, but the gun had done its job well. The figure in the doorway flew back from the impact, hit the wall across the hall, and slumped to the floor.

Terrified, Emma ran out into the hall to Jimmy. The knife had fallen from his hand, and it was obvious he was dying as his lifeblood pumped from his body and puddled on the hall floorboards. Emma set down the revolver and put her hands on Jimmy's face, forcing him to look up at her.

Emma asked, "Why, Jimmy? Why did you do this?"

Barely able to get words out, Jimmy said, "I'm . . . not your . . . stalker . . . I was here . . . to protect you . . . I love you, Emma."

With that last declaration of love, Jimmy died. Suddenly, it all became clear to Emma. There was no stalker. There never had been. She really had imagined everything. The threatening note had been blank because there had never been any writing. She had imagined the whole thing. And now Jimmy, the only man who had ever loved her, was dead, and she had killed him.

"That boy was only trying to protect you from me, Emma." A voice she didn't recognize said from behind her, as a strong hand pulled back her hair and another covered her mouth with a wet cloth. She could smell a strange ether-like odor and could feel herself losing consciousness. The last thing she heard was a voice she didn't recognize saying, "I switched the note, Emma. You're mine now, and no one can ever change that. If I can't have you, then no one will."

THE PATH

"No one saves us but ourselves. No one can, and no one may.
We ourselves must walk the path."
—Buddha

The hot, stagnant space was encased in complete blackness as Winston slowly regained consciousness. The only available light came from a single candle burning at the far end of the blackened cavern. He instantly knew by the stinking hot and humid feel and the vile, recognizable stench that he was in a cave. Then again, each time Winston was forced to endure what he knew was coming, it was always in one cave or another. A familiar sulfurous, noxious reek permeated the air, along with the coppery scent he recognized all too well as the reek of coagulating blood.

As he gradually awoke, each nerve ending in his body began simultaneously sending rapid-fire messages to his sensory receptors, and he started to feel the pain rapidly increase from an unpleasant discomfort to overwhelming agony. When he finally regained awareness, Winston screamed with a painful howl as the tendrils of fiery Hell shot up and down his body like a relentless storm of white-hot electric anguish. It was always this way, again and again, time after time, seemingly without end. He had no idea for how long or how many times he had been forced to endure similar suffering; he had lost count a long, long time ago. Not that any measurement of time was relevant in this place.

Winston couldn't understand the physics behind how he was made to feel the horrible effects of the relentless torment, yet the pain was nevertheless always present and very real. He was aware that he was dead and had been for what seemed to him like an eternity. He understood he was now nothing more than a spirit, a tortured soul. He was no longer corporal and, as such—had no flesh, no bones, no brain, no physical apparatuses whatsoever—yet he was somehow forced to constantly endure the sensation of pain, which felt as agonizingly real to him as if he were still a living, breathing physical human being. Winston comprehended that he had been plunged into his own personal version of Hell for some unexplainable reason, which apparently was to be his fate for time without end. He couldn't imagine what he had ever done in his life to deserve such constant torment, but it must have been more severe than he realized. Why else would he have been forced to tolerate the existence of such never-ending suffering?

Tears flowed freely down his haggard face, and when he tried to move, he realized that, as was typical, he had been tightly secured and was incapable of any motion. Near the back of the coal-black cave, Winston saw another candle slowly come to life, followed by another and another. These unbearable sessions always progressed in the same manner. Winston would awaken to find himself in total darkness and suffering from intolerable misery. Then, slowly, the candles would light one by one until the room was awash with light. When all the candles were ablaze, Winston would once again see for himself what manner of torture had been put upon him as well as what type of heinous demon was assigned the responsibility of inflicting his pain.

Once that had been revealed, the fire in his nonexistent body would steadily grow to a level even more unbearable if such a thing were possible, spurred on by the addition of this visually terrifying aspect of his torture. Eventually, he would succumb to his pain and fall back into the blessed blackness. When his time in whatever particular room of torment was over, he would find himself outside the cave on what he thought of as the Path. Then, he would again be required to walk along the Path to the next available room, where, once inside, a new and even more horrifying form of torture awaited him. Oh yes, Winston had no doubt this was Hell.

As more of the candles sprang to life, the room became ablaze with their glow, and Winston could only see directly in front of him in his immobile state. Against the cave's far wall was a large area with an irregularly shaped reflective stone embedded inside. At first, Winston couldn't see well, but after a few moments of blinking away his blurring tears, he saw his reflection and then wished he hadn't.

Earlier, Winston had felt some pain in his forehead but had not known, nor could he imagine the cause, but now he suddenly understood the horrid truth. Winston could see some type of rusted barbed wire wrapped in a circle around his head in the reflective stone, and its sharp spines had dug deep furrows into the flesh. Dried blood tracks covered his face. He looked strangely like pictures he had seen of Christ with his crown of thorns. But there was no Jesus Christ in this unholy place. Then he noticed something previously inconceivable happening above the encircling barbed crown.

He had to strain to look more closely to ensure he was not imagining what he was seeing. He could not believe the sight before him. The entire top of his skull had been removed, and his brain sat completely exposed. As if that fact alone was not disturbing enough, he realized that dozens of thin, rusted metal pins or rods of some sort were scattered about and embedded deep into his unprotected brain. And although the horrifying sight repulsed him beyond his worst imaginings, strangely, he could not feel any pain in his skull other than the superficial pain he originally felt from the barbed wire. However, what he did feel was a fiery misery in his arms.

Winston followed his gaze in the reflective stone down along his body and saw he had been placed in a large wooden-framed chair, curiously resembling the electric chairs used in the early days of Earth's death penalty executions. The wood was thick, heavy, and deliberately uncomfortable. Winston could tell by the pain he was starting to feel in his buttocks that something had likely been placed on the seat to increase his level of discomfort; they always used something that felt like broken glass, metal shards, razor wire, or hot coals, but for some blessed reason he was not quite able to feel it as intently as he believed he should have. And that was fine with him because the pain he already felt in his arms was unbearable enough.

As he continued to determine the level of his unfortunate situation, Winston saw that he was naked, which was not a surprise, as he had been bare since arriving in this horrible place so long ago. In fact, it seemed like everyone in Hell was naked. But there was no sexual reason for the nudity. The obvious purpose of the exposure was to make access easier for the armies of pain-inflicting demons.

Then, in the foggy mirror-stone, Winston saw why his arms had been hurting him so badly. Oh my God, no! he thought as he bellowed out yet another blood-curdling scream. In a matter of a second, time seemed to stop as Winston took in the extent of what the vile demon of this particular torture chamber had done to him.

Both of his wrists were secured to the top of the heavy arms of the chair by two large, rusted spikes driven down through them, essentially crucifying him to the arms of the chair. He thought again about his wire crown, about Jesus Christ, and the blasphemy portrayed in Winston's own painful crucifixion. In the mirror, he could see that his fingers, which were curled around the front of the arms, had been relieved of all of their flesh and most of the musculature, leaving only skeletal remains, which he was strangely still able to move although doing so only caused him increased pain.

As if that was not bad enough, he could see that the area behind his wrists and up to the tops of his forearms had suffered the worst damage. Strips of bloody flesh, perhaps a half-inch wide, had been peeled back the length of his arms and curled up into rolls that were pierced and held together with long tarnished pins.

Each forearm had ten or more of these crimson coils of flayed flesh, and Winston could see his exposed red glistening muscles dripping with blood reflecting in the light. It didn't matter to Winston that what he saw wasn't physical because the agony he felt most certainly was.

He prayed for this particular session to soon be over long before the real pain began, yet he knew his prayers would go unanswered as they always did. Hell was no place for worship. Winston also understood once his time in this particular torture chamber was over, there would be another, even more painful period of pain waiting somewhere further up the Path.

"How you like me work? Good job, no?" Winston heard an ominous guttural voice, not possibly human in origin, say from behind him. Like most of the hideous beings responsible for inflicting pain, this one was no doubt another moronic monosyllabic beast whose sole purpose for existence was to exact untold levels of agony. Winston slowly pulled his eyes away from his throbbing arms and looked into the reflective stone to see an incredibly heinous-looking demon standing behind him. This abomination stood over seven feet tall and was rail-thin but sinewy with ropy muscles. Its fingers were long and bony and had great yellowed talons. Like the other creatures Winston had previously encountered, its face was pig-like in appearance with a pushed-up snout and a large, slobbery mouth from which long fangs jutted upward and downward. Its cat-shaped eyes bugged from the sunken sockets of its skull, and it had two long ram horns curling back from its forehead, continuing over top of a long mane of greasy black hair. It stank like a filthy barnyard animal, and its grayish flesh, sporadically adorned with long, rat-like hairs, glistened with sweat, adding to its already obnoxious stench.

The horrifying thing grinned sheepishly at Winston in the reflection and slowly lifted its clawed right hand upward toward the area atop Winston's head where his vulnerable brain had been stippled with so many pins.

"Humm." The horrid creature said, "It have too many pins. You don't feel 'nuff ouches." With that, the beast began to extract one pin after another from Winston's brain meticulously. With each pull of a pin, the pain level intensified until it reached its crescendo, and Winston once again found himself blessedly, albeit temporarily unconscious.

* * *

When he started to regain awareness again, Winston suddenly recalled the details of what he had just been through and reflexively grabbed for his head and arms, certain he would find them still ripped and exposed. But they were not. He was whole once again, still naked, outside of the room where he had just endured one of the worst sessions to date. He was also momentarily free of pain and knew he would have to enjoy whatever small amount of blessed relief he might have. It wouldn't last long, although it seemed time, at least as Winston understood time was meaningless in this place.

Long ago, a demon, in one of his many intervals of torment, mentioned to him that in Hell, a thousand years of pain could take place while only a few seconds passed in terms of Earth time. Likewise, a few moments in Hell might be a century on the other side. Although the creature was not intelligent enough to articulate what he wanted to explain, Winston could take the beast's grunts and half-sentences and turn them into what he thought might be a cohesive representation of the concept. He deduced that the relationship of time in Hell was not linear; neither did it always go forward. Sometimes, time stands still; sometimes, it moves backward depending on the particular need.

As Winston sat peacefully on the Path, he knew exactly what he had no choice but to do next; he knew the routine. He was never allowed to sit for very long. Eventually, he would have to get up and walk to whatever door he was supposed to find next. Failure to do so would mean more severe repercussions in the next room. He also knew he could not go backward and would not even consider doing so. He had made that mistake once shortly after his arrival and discovered he was forced to go through every single agonizing second of every torture he had previously encountered all over again from the beginning. That was only after five or six sessions. Now, with thousands of periods of suffering totaled, he didn't want to even look behind him, let alone try to go backward.

He stood up and looked out in the distance. Although he could only see about fifty or sixty feet ahead of him in the dimly lit cavern, he instinctively knew that the Path was endless. Spaced irregularly along both sides of the Path were doors made of large, heavy wooden planks bolted together with huge, rusted iron hinges. The doors had no windows and were mounted into the stone cavern walls providing the only access into or out of each chamber. Shortly after his arrival, Winston learned that the rules of Hell were simple: walk forward on the Path and look for the next open door.

As he slowly made his way along the Path, Winston heard the screaming of other unfortunate souls from behind the doors that were

closed. The large main cavern was ceaselessly resonant with the unending shrieks of the damned. But despite the screams of the multitudes,
Winston never met anyone else either in Hell or on the Path. That was
another apparent rule of Hell; he was always alone except for those
times of immeasurable suffering when he was in the capable hands of
a vile demon.

Next to each door hung a candelabrum formed from a real once-
living human hand, their withered gray fingers pointing upward as if
reaching to catch some unknown object falling from a nonexistent sky.
Melted fast to the cupped palm of each hand was a thick blood-red
candle; the hot wax dripping down forming puddles in the palm before
spilling over and sliding along its shriveled forearm. The candles never
seemed to burn down.

Not long after his arrival in Hell, Winston had been naturally curious and reached out to touch one of the hideous appendages, thinking them cast from stone because of their veined appearance, and was
frighteningly greeted with the icy chill of dead, rotting human flesh.
Then the hand had actually moved, ever so slightly, just enough to
send chills down Winston's spine and to teach him one of his first of
many lessons. It seemed to him that almost every minute in the horrible place, he was learning something new whether he wanted to or
not, and each new lesson was more horrifying than the last.

Winston kept the gruesome sconces in his peripheral vision as
he slowly walked along the Path, among the howls of the countless
damned, searching for the next open door, which he, unfortunately,
saw up ahead. He understood the opening was meant for him and
was his next destination. Dutifully but reluctantly, Winston stepped
through the doorway and was once again thrust into complete darkness to face whatever fate awaited him inside blindly. He heard the
thick wooden door slam shut behind him, as he had heard a thousand
times before. Then he stood in the blackness of the room, where he
awaited his next torture.

Suddenly, the room burst into light, and Winston had to shield
his eyes from the blinding brightness. After a few moments, when he
became accustomed to the light, he looked around and was shocked to
discover he was not in another stinking, fetid cave filled with devices of

inhuman anguish as he had anticipated but was in a room, a real room like he recalled from life.

He was standing in a brightly lit office, which was very similar to what he recalled his own office looking like back before he died. In fact, it was his office; he was certain of it. Winston was no longer naked but was dressed in a casual shirt, dress pants, and expensive shoes. The office was decorated exactly like his office had been, and it had the same large mahogany desk and a comfortable leather manager's chair positioned behind it. Winston turned to look at a certificate hanging on the wall. He was shocked to see it was his own college diploma.

"You are Mister Winston Peter James, is that correct?" a voice said from his left. He turned to face the desk again and saw that the chair was no longer empty but was now occupied by a peculiar-looking sort of man. The man was dressed in a business suit and sat up in a manner that appeared straight and proper, almost as if he were posturing and assuming what Winston supposed was the man's interpretation of how a businessperson should appear.

However, he was not doing a very good job of looking at the part he was trying to portray, as his suit didn't seem to fit him well, and he was somewhat rumpled and disheveled. He appeared to be about middle age, slightly built with a full head of thick brown hair, graying slightly at the temples, giving him a somewhat distinguished look despite the issues with his attire. He wore a pair of round wire-framed glasses, which sat askew upon a long, thin nose. He had a pencil-thin mustache and no other facial hair. His hands were folded and resting on the top of the desk, giving Winston the impression that the man was unsure what to do with them.

Besides the obvious incongruity of the office itself being recreated in its entirety in Hell and the presence of the odd-looking character behind the desk, Winston noticed there was also something else that was very wrong. It was the man's eyes. For starters, the skin around the eyes hung loosely and seemed to bag in places as if to suggest the flesh was not his own but was some sort of skin mask worn to cover whatever countenance lay beneath it. Likewise, the man's eyes were just as strange; they were not quite human but were more cat-like and seemed to stare out at Winston without blinking.

Winston suddenly feared he might now understand what was going on. He dreadfully suspected this might be yet another new form of torture, one that would start in a place familiar to him, such as his old office, and then quickly morph into another session of agony. Cowed by his time in the countless torture chambers, Winston found himself unable to lift his head to look further at the creature. The strange way that the creature's flesh appeared as rumpled and ill-fitting as his suit truly disturbed Winston, making him certain that the scene would change at any moment and he would once again find himself the victim of even more unimaginable tortures.

The weird man repeated his request, but this time with a bit more impatience in his voice. "I asked you a question, sir! Are you Mister Winston Peter James? Am I correct in making that assumption?" Winston could not bring himself to answer. He was not only terrified by the potential horror hiding deep inside this current scenario but had learned long ago not to engage these sick creatures in conversation willingly. He simply gave a cursory nod of acknowledgment.

"Well," the man said, "I suppose you are wondering what this is all about and why you are here with me, Winston. May I call you Winston?" Again, Winston gave a slight and suspicious nod. The strange creature continued, "By the way, Winston, it is perfectly all right for you to speak to me. After all you've been through while a guest here, I realize you might be a bit reluctant. But I assure you that no harm will come to you if you choose to reply. In fact . . . I insist that you speak and do so immediately." There was a look of cold, emotionless assertion in his cat-like eyes.

"All . . . all right," Winston said in a thin, raspy voice barely recognizable as the one he remembered. He had spent countless hours screaming in agony, and it had been what seemed like years since he had actually had an opportunity to speak to anyone in a normal conversational voice. "Wha—what . . . is this? Wh-why am I here?"

"Very good, Winston. Very good indeed," the being replied. Winston thought he saw the flesh mask on the creature's face slip ever so slightly. The man behind the desk said, "It's so good to have you actively participating in our conversation. It will make everything so much simpler. So please allow me to explain why I have arranged to meet with you here. Here is the situation in a nutshell, as they say."

"I suppose you've wondered since your arrival here in our fine little corner of Hell what it was you might have done during your lifetime to deserve such constant and relentless torture. You probably always assumed such punishment would be reserved for the lowest of the low; murderers, rapists, child molesters, and so on. Am I right?"

Winston kept his eyes averted and timidly said, "Y—y—yes . . . I wondered that many times . . . no . . . all . . . all the time."

"Yes, I'm sure you have," the strange man said and then released a loud guffaw of laughter, sending the most ungodly foul stench across the desk between them and directly into Winston's face. Winston felt his stomach turn over with revulsion at the smell of the vile stink. He noticed once again how the strange man's hands never left the top of the desk, making Winston wonder if those hands might be fused together into that pose to make whatever lurked inside that bizarre skin seem more human. Winston's eyes were focused on those hands, and he momentarily thought he saw maggots crawling between the intertwined fingers.

"NOW PAY ATTENTION, WINSTON!" the being shouted, momentarily losing his composure only to quickly regain it again and instantly return to his calm, business-like demeanor. "Let's cut to the chase, shall we?"

Winston nodded silently once again, then realizing he had not spoken as requested, he quickly said, "Y . . . yes. Please."

The man said, "All right then," and he explained. "Well, Winston, it appears there was a slight clerical error, which resulted in your coming here. You see, as it works out, you are actually not supposed to be here after all."

Winston felt his heart thudding in his chest. He thought to himself, How could that possibly be? Could I have really been made to suffer all this time over a simple clerical error?

"Cl—clerical . . . error?" Winston asked cautiously, not believing it was possible.

"Yes. I'm afraid so," the man replied nonchalantly."

"Wha—what do you mean?" he asked, confused.

"You see, every so often, the equivalent of one thousand or more earth years, we do an audit of our guests to make sure there have been no mistakes. And if we do discover mistakes, we do our best to try to make them right immediately."

Winston asked with a bit of uncertainty, "Mistakes?"

"Yes, mistakes," the being replied. "You see, here in Hell, we aren't perfect, nor are we expected to be. Those sort of high and mighty expectations are reserved for that other place." He cast his eyes upward. "Down here, we sometimes have the occasional unplanned faux pas, if you pardon my French. In other words, we have been known to make mistakes."

"Mistakes," Winston repeated now as a statement rather than a question. He had no idea where this bizarre conversation might be heading, but he felt very uncomfortable about it.

The creature behind the desk replied, "It appears you, Winston, have been the subject of our latest unfortunate situation. Winston expected the man to raise his hands and simulate air quotes when he said the word "situation," but he did not. He suspected the creature before him might not be able to move his hands at all. The longer Winston studied him, the more he realized the thing was not a man but perhaps a higher-level demon of greater intelligence than most he had encountered. He was wearing some sort of suit, apparently made of human flesh to make himself seem less offensive. Winston wondered why a place that had subjected him to countless bouts of humiliation and torture would even bother with such a ruse. It made no logical sense to him, but little had made sense in this place since his arrival.

The being said, "So, as I said, it appears you not only are not supposed to be here, but I am sorry to say you are not even supposed to be dead."

"W—what?" Winston managed to stammer. "N—not supposed to be dead?"

"Yes," the creature replied. "But that particular fact is somewhat irrelevant as you are now both dead and here as well. It appears what happened was that one of our minions was sent to retrieve the souls of the dead—I believe you call them Grim Reapers in your world—who mistakenly brought you to us instead of the human he was sent to retrieve. The error was only discovered a short while ago during a routine audit. You will be happy to know the minion who made that particular mistake is currently being punished for his failure, and I'm certain you can scarcely imagine what we are doing to him."

Before Winston could reply, not like he had any idea what to say anyway, the creature asked him, "Do you happen to recall exactly how you died?"

Winston most certainly did recall every detail of his death just as he remembered every single agonizing moment of every torture he had endured since his arrival in Hell.

"Shot." Winston replied, "I was shot during a mugging, a robbery."

"Yes, that is correct," the strange being said. "You were shot while being robbed by a very bad human named Wilson Johns, a man who you may recall was about your same age and physical build. You were supposed to overpower him, and he was supposed to end up dead, but our soul retriever incorrectly interfered, and the result was you are here, and he is not."

"But . . . but how?" Winston asked, "How could this have happened?"

The creature explained, "Actually, I see very clearly how something like this might have occurred. Think about it. Two men, physically similar; one Winston James and the other Wilson Johns, it makes perfect sense to me. Besides, after a few millennia, all humans start to look alike to us."

Winston could feel the anger and hatred build inside him. With more forcefulness than he would have believed possible, he asked, "You mean to tell me that worthless bastard has been alive, robbing, killing, raping, and whatever else he chooses to do while I've been suffering unimaginable tortures, which were really meant for him? Is that what you're saying?"

The creature looked directly at Winston with his strange, cat-like eyes and replied, "Yes. I'm sorry to say that is exactly what the situation is. So you can see why we are all somewhat embarrassed by this unfortunate oversight."

"Embarrassed? Oversight?" Winston said in a louder voice than he had used in a very, very long time. "This is not an oversight. That is . . . well . . . I don't know what the Hell to call it."

"Yes. You are most certainly correct and have a right to be upset." The being agreed, "And unfortunately, it's like trying to un-ring a bell. There is nothing we can do to restore you to life. You are dead and will remain so. However, there might be something we can do to help you get revenge against the man who was responsible for killing you in the first place."

Winston looked directly at the creature, suddenly interested. He was furious, and if he had an opportunity to right this injustice, he would jump at the chance to do so. Then perhaps the man who murdered him would be forced to spend eternity along the Path while Winston could move on to whatever place, presumably less painful than this, he was meant to be.

"How?" Winston asked eagerly. "How can I do this? What do I have to do?"

The creature gave Winston a sly look and said, "On Earth, it is currently October 31, Halloween night, the night of the dead. It is the one time during the year when we are permitted to allow certain souls to return to Earth to take care of unfinished business or do special tasks on Hell's behalf. We have arranged for you to return to Earth for one night to retrieve the soul of Wilson Johns and bring him back here to us.

Once this job is done, you will move on to another place, not heaven—you were never good enough for that, few are—but another level of Hell, much less unpleasant than this section is. All you have to do is return to the world of the living, confront Wilson Johns, take this special dagger, and plunge it into his heart." Suddenly, a long, sharp knife appeared in Winston's hand. "You do that, and we will do the rest."

"But . . . but, I can't do that . . . I'm not a killer. I've no idea how to do such a thing." Winston explained, his hand uncomfortably gripping the handle of the dagger.

Looking perturbed, the creature said, "Well, Winston. We are sending you back to get Wilson Johns. You will only have a few earth hours to do what must be done, and then you will be returned to us. If you come back empty-handed, you will return to where you left off on the Path and continue serving out a punishment rightfully meant for someone else. But, of course, the choice is entirely yours."

A moment later, Winston found himself standing in an alley in a city that looked familiar. He was wearing the same clothing he had been wearing the night he died. In fact, this alley was the very same alley he had tried to use as a shortcut when Wilson Johns had attacked, robbed, and murdered him.

In the distance, he saw someone entering the alley. As the stranger came briefly into the glow of a nearby streetlight, Winston was shocked to see it was no stranger but was him as he had looked the night he died. He then realized that the strange creature had returned him to Earth on the same night he had been murdered. Winston hadn't been murdered on Halloween night, but that didn't seem to matter in the strange juxtaposition of time that seemed to exist between the two worlds.

As the Winston of Earth approached the ethereal Winston, a man dressed in dark clothing suddenly sprang from the shadows. Winston realized it was all happening again, and this time, Winston was about to actually see himself being murdered. Reacting, not thinking, Winston forced his spiritual self into his earthly body just as Wilson Johns raised his gun and fired. Simultaneously, the spirit of Winston lifted his physical right hand and plunged the invisible dagger deep into the mugger's chest, piercing his heart.

Wilson Johns let out a howl and fell to the ground in a dead heap. Winston James floated out of his physical body and stood nearby. From the fallen form of Johns rose a stream of tiny red sparkling, glowing lights, which began to flow into the blade of the dagger, causing it to illuminate in a crimson glow. Winston knew this was what he had to take back to Hell with him to make things right. He looked down and saw his own dead earthly body lying on the ground. The creature had told Winston he could not undo what had been done but could only try to make things right.

Without warning, Winston started to slowly fade from the world of the living and, within a moment, found himself back in the room that looked like his old office, the dagger still held tightly in his hand.

The strange being was still seated behind the desk with its fleshy, gloved hands folded before him. "Very good work, Winston. I see you have returned the knife and acquired the soul we needed to right this injustice perpetrated on you." The knife disappeared from Winston's hand and then rematerialized on the top of the desk. The creature's hands did not move to pick it up.

"Yes . . . yes, I have," Winston said, still quite shaken from all that had happened. "I've done what you asked. Now, Johns can be punished as you require, and I can move on to wherever I have earned the right to move on to."

"Well," the creature said hesitantly, "about that. Well, there's a bit of a problem."

"What are you talking about?" Winston said, now with an air of defiance. "You said I didn't deserve to be here, that I was put here by mistake, and that I could move on to another place."

The creature wavered and then said, "Well, yes. But that was before you returned to your world and killed Wilson Johns. Now, my dear Winston James, you are officially a murderer."

"But I did that for you. I was carrying out your orders. I killed for you. If I didn't do what you said, I would have to continue down the Path," Winston said angrily.

"True, but the final decision to actually kill Johns was yours to make," the creature said. "And that made you a killer. You had your revenge, and you enjoyed it as well. The Path is exactly where murderers belong. It appears, my good Winston, as if you were damned if you did and damned if you didn't."

Then, before Winston had a chance to protest further, he found himself once again outside on the Path. He looked out at the endless road before him, hung his head in sorrow as he listened to the wailing of the tortured souls, and slowly began to trudge along the Path to his next stop.

THE SERVANT
(A NOVELLA)

"Service to others leads to greatness."
—JIM ROHN

"No time is better spent than in the service to others"
—BRYANT MCGILL

"The meaning of life lies in two major areas: your personal perfection and service to other people."
—LEO TOLSTOY

"There is no greater satisfaction for a just and well-meaning person than the knowledge that he has devoted his best energies to the service of a good cause."
—ALBERT EINSTEIN

"Wise people find purpose by serving others."
—MAXIME LAGACÉ

"The best way to find yourself is to lose yourself in the service of others."
—MAHATMA GANDHI

/ 1 /

The email read, "Dear Mister Gilbert, I must say that you are my favorite horror fiction author and have been for years. I've followed your work since the very first book I read and haven't missed a single one along the way. Your expertly crafted writing is both visceral and simultaneously thought-provoking. The images and feelings you create are so accurate and so vivid that they linger in my mind well beyond the final page. Sometimes, I wish the dark moods you create within your writing would stay with me forever."

Dan Gilbert read that paragraph again. It was part of another email his publisher had forwarded to him from someone with the email address "isurvu4evr@mymail.com." Typically, Dan enjoyed receiving emails from his few fans. He wasn't a world-famous author or household name by any stretch of the imagination. However, he had published more than two dozen books in the horror genre and had something of a small cult following. So Dan was happy to read whatever came his way.

This character, who called himself "The Servant," started sending emails via Dan's online portal a few months ago. Although both the email address and the pen name were suspicious-sounding, Dan chalked it up to being one of those weird internet privacy things, or it might be a bizarre horror fan thing. That might be more accurate. Chances were this guy was likely a loner, perhaps a young community college dropout living in his mother's basement. Dan was fine with that as long as the young man's critiques were positive. He hated the emails from failed, frustrated writers who thought they were simply misunderstood. Their reviews of Dan's books were scathing and often riddled with an equal part vile criticism and misspelled words.

The emails from "isurvu4evr@mymail.com" started out as typical fan letters, quite complementary, stating how much this person enjoyed his writing. Dan couldn't determine if the writer was male or female, but his gut told him it was a man and likely a young man. The timbre of the writing seemed like the young man might be trying too hard to appear older or perhaps more sophisticated than he actually was. Dan was in his early 60s and had been writing in one form or another most of his life. So, he felt he was adequately qualified to make such an assessment.

As each new email arrived, they began to take on stranger and stranger tones. It was nothing specific Dan had been able to nail down, but he felt something was definitely changing. That line in the first paragraph, "Sometimes I wish the dark moods you create within your writing would stay with me forever," took Dan aback. His "weird-o-meter" was beginning to inch into the red zone.

Dan was usually happy when his stories evoked some type of reaction from his readers. He didn't care what that emotion might be as long as he could press someone's buttons. Sometimes, people loved his stories; other times, they hated them. Their reactions didn't concern Dan as long as they reacted in some way. What Dan didn't want was for someone to consider his writing boring or mundane. He wrote to entertain his readers and stir their emotions. However, this particular fan, this "Servant," was something else entirely. This character was starting to sound downright creepy.

Against his better judgment, Dan decided to read more, taking time to consider any lines that might trigger the alarm bells in his gut. He read the next few sentences, "From the opening paragraphs of any of your stories, I, your most devoted reader, am instantly thrust into realms where the bizarre and the macabre reside side by side, in some sort of twisted, corrupted coexistence."

Dan thought, "Ok, that's not too bad. Sounds like the start of a positive review. It might be a bit overdone with words like "twisted, corrupted coexistence," but Dan could chalk that up to youthful over-exuberance if the writer was in fact, a young man. Or perhaps The Servant was simply trying to impress him.

The next line read, "You push the boundaries of modern horror, tapping into contemporary fears and anxieties with a skill seldom previously seen."

Dan felt comfortable again as these statements complemented his writing abilities. If Dan were asked to describe what he wanted to do as a writer, that line was exactly what he would like to say. Dan decided to commit those words to memory for future interviews. He imagined himself saying, "You see, I like to push the boundaries of modern horror, tapping into contemporary fears and anxieties."

Then the note began to drift into bizarro world again, "It's no wonder these dark and sinister thoughts linger so long and intently in my mind, refusing to fade. Only you have that power over me. You do more than influence and speak to me; you guide me. Perhaps more than that, you command me, and I, your humble servant, must obey. You are my messiah. I live to serve as you order me to do through your sacred, mystic commands." Now Dan found himself thrust again into the creepazoid zone. This guy was suddenly starting to sound like a full-blown wack-a-doodle.

Dan felt an icy chill slither down his spine. He decided he had better contact his publisher about this guy. Since all his fan emails were filtered through someone at their office, maybe his publisher could have them intercepted. All Dan knew was he didn't want to see any more wacko emails like this one. Dan might be a horror writer, but this guy seemed too authentically "out there" for him to deal with.

/ 2 /

"Honestly, Dan. Don't you think maybe you're exaggerating a bit? I know how you imaginative, creative types can be." Dan's publisher, Justin Thyme, suggested. Yes, that was the man's actual name. Apparently, his hippy parents changed their surname from Timmons to Thyme in the 1960s, probably during the height of Simon and Garfunkel's success with the song Scarborough Fair. The first name, Justin, was likely something they felt was a bit of cleverness they came up with during one of their drug-induced stupors.

Whatever the case, Justin never chose to change either of his names but to embrace them and use them to his advantage, which they did quite nicely. He used them to form and name his publishing company, Justin Thyme Publishing. The name worked on many levels, and Justin credited the company's catchy name for its rapid growth and financial success. He was sure that if his parents were still living, they would disapprove of his wealth as they had turned their backs on capitalism in favor of whatever weird Eastern philosophy they had been practicing on any particular week.

Justin was a young, relatively good-looking man with thick brown hair cut short and highlighted blond. He wore a long, full beard and mustache, rounding out his hipster look. Dan always found it funny how Justin was quick to criticize his late parents' hippy lifestyle, but years later, Justin dove headlong into an equally unusual life as a hipster.

Dan said, "No, Justin. I'm being serious here. Doesn't anyone read these emails before forwarding them on to me?"

"Of course not, Dan. You know my staff is busy with editing, manuscript formatting, cover design, and promotion. They don't have time to read every email sent to every author. The truth is, when we get an email through our online portal, the software is set up to automatically send it to the respective author."

"Well, Justin. This guy is starting to creep me out, big time." Dan said as he read several lines from the latest email.

Justin said, "Relax, Dan. I think we can use this. I especially like the references to how your writing 'lingers' with him. Imagine you . . . lingering in people's minds! Who knew? That gives me a great idea. Why don't you write a story about a writer who creeps people out? They can't forget his stories because they seem to unfold before them. Think about it. You can call him 'The Lingerer.' I like that name better than 'The Servant' anyway."

"Seriously, Justin? Do you think we should use this weirdo's creepy letter to inspire a story? I'm more concerned that he might be inspired to do bad things he reads in my stories. Don't you think maybe we should send it to the city police or FBI or some other alphabet agency?"

Justin said, "Why would you say that, Dan?"

"Think about it, Justin. Charlie Manson and his cult of murderers went on a killing spree because he thought the Beatles were telling him to start a race war through the lyrics of their song 'Helter Skelter.' You can't just ignore wackos like this, and we certainly shouldn't encourage them."

"If this guy did go out and kill a few people based on things he read in your stories, Dan, that might not be all bad."

Dan was stunned, "What are you talking about, Justin? That would be terrible."

"Maybe yes, maybe not so much."

"What are you saying, Justin?"

Justin replied, "Ok, maybe it would be bad, but remember, there's no such thing as bad publicity. If someone used your writing to go on a killing spree, it would make national news, maybe international. Your name and your books would become famous. Sales would go through the roof, and we might actually start making money off your writing."

"Well, while you're busy counting potential future dollars, can we do something about these emails in the meantime?"

"Ok, Dan. Here's what we're going to do. I'll get our computer geeks to fix it so all emails from this guy get rejected and sent back to him. What do you say?"

Dan thought, then said, "Maybe that's not the best idea."

"Why not?"

"Because all that might do, Justin, is piss the guy off. Maybe he'll just use a different email to sneak through. Or worse, if he really is a wack job, maybe he'll find some way to track me down. No, here's a better idea. Have your geeks forward those emails to a special location to store them. That way, this weirdo won't know they aren't being read."

Justin asked, "Why, Dan? Are you thinking you might want to read them someday after all?"

Dan said, "No, nothing like that, thank you very much. I think if this nutcase ever does go postal, it would be good to be able to go back, read them, and see if he continued to escalate. That might come in handy with the cops, should the need arise."

"Ok. I think that might be doable. I'll see what our tech boys can come up with."

"Thanks, Justin," Dan said, relieved.

/ 3 /

A week or so later, Dan awoke early in the morning when his doorbell rang. This was followed by persistent knocking on his front door. Dan trudged down the stairs, determined to give whoever had disturbed him a piece of his mind. He angrily opened the door and was stunned to find two large square-jawed men in cheap suits glaring at him, looking serious. One was white with short, dark hair, was clean-shaven, and sported aviator sunglasses. The other was a large black man with a shaved head, a neatly trimmed, close-cropped beard, and a mustache.

He wore no sunglasses, so Dan had a good look at the man's piercing dark eyes; cop eyes.

Dan immediately identified them as two plainclothes police detectives. He had watched enough cop shows to know the stereotype. Dan had often said that sometimes things were stereotypical for good reasons. As such, he decided to think of them as Salt and Pepper, which, although a bit bigoted on his part, he nonetheless found the idea humorous. Dan must have picked it up from one of those police cop shows as well. He noticed that Pepper held a transparent plastic bag with a copy of a novel Dan had written called "*It Came from Hell* " in his hands. The bag was sealed with red and black tape that read "EVIDENCE." The book appeared well-worn, with rippled pages, bent corners, and what looked like a few makeshift book markers inserted periodically. Ominous-looking dark stains were visible on the cover.

Salt was the first to speak. "Excuse me, Sir, are you Daniel John Gilbert?" Dan was certain the pair knew exactly who he was, not because of his limited fame but because, in his experience, cops rarely asked questions they didn't already know the answer to. However, the way the detective said his name caught Dan off guard. Usually, when cops apprehended serial killers or active shooters and addressed the press, they always used their full names, for example, John Wayne Gacy. Now, an assumed police detective was standing on his front porch, using his full name, Daniel John Gilbert, as if he were some sort of criminal.

All Dan could come up with was, "Excuse me?"

Salt repeated, "Daniel Gilbert, the horror author. Is that you, Sir?"

Dan regained his composure and said, "Yes. Yes, that's me. And who may I ask, are you two gentlemen?"

Salt said, "I'm Police Detective Sam Wheatly, and this is Detective Darnell Johnson." He nodded his head at Pepper. Detective Johnson nodded, never taking his piercing cop eyes off Dan. Dan suspected Wheatly was also giving him the death stare, but he couldn't see the detective's eyes through the cop's blackened shades. Although Dan wore an athletic tee shirt and long pajama bottoms, he suddenly felt naked under those scrutinizing eyes. A cool breeze blew a few fallen leaves across his front lawn, signaling the oncoming end of summer and sending a chill across Dan's surprisingly sweaty skin.

Wheatly asked, "Are you alright, Mister Gilbert?"

"Um . . . Yes, I'm fine. May I see some form of identification, officers?" Dan asked.

"It's detectives, not officers," Detective Johnson corrected. The two produced leather fold-out wallets and displayed their detective shields.

Dan explained, "Thank you, officers, I mean detectives. Sorry for insisting, but as you know, there are a lot of not-so-nice people walking around these days."

Johnson held up Dan's book and said with a less-than-friendly tone, "Yeah. We know that very well, better than most. That's what we're here to talk to you about. Did you write this book, Mister Gilbert?"

Dan looked at the plastic evidence bag as if double-checking the book he already knew was his and paying closer attention to the dark splotches on the cover. Again, he understood that this was one of those questions the detective knew the answer to. Then again, his name was prominently displayed on the cover. Dan stared at the dark patches. The book looked like someone had gripped it with dark paint-covered fingers, or perhaps bloody fingers would be a more accurate description. Dan silently chastised himself for letting his writer's imagination get the better of him. Then again, two police detectives had his book in an evidence bag, so maybe the idea of bloody fingerprints was not all that much of an imagined assumption.

Dan replied calmly as he could manage, "Yes, that is one of mine. I believe that might have been my third or fourth published novel. It's hard to recall exactly."

Detective Wheatly asked, "So, you've written several books, Mister Gilbert?" Dan wondered if these ridiculous questions would ever end. He was sure these two cops knew exactly how many books he had written. They likely had a complete list of all his works. For the first time, Dan began to think perhaps he should call a lawyer. Then again, he didn't know any lawyers. Maybe his publisher, Justin, might have someone on retainer.

Dan decided to let things play out for a bit and said, "I've written several dozen books, actually. Some are novels, and others are short story collections. I tend to lose track of how many. Periodically, I go back and check, but it's been some time since I've counted."

Detective Wheatly smiled and said, "We'd like to come in and talk to you for a bit, Mister Gilbert, if possible."

"Certainly. Please come in and sit down. You'll have to forgive my unkempt appearance; you literally woke me from a sound sleep." Dan said, feigning confusion. The last thing he wanted to do was have a "little talk" with these two, but he decided it might be better if he tried to go along to get along. Dan stood aside as the two large men walked by. He caught the faint scent of cologne under the more noticeable smell of coffee, cigarettes, and sweat. These two had obviously been working most of the night.

Wheatly replied, "Yes, Mister Gilbert. I should apologize for waking you. It's just that because of the nature of this case, time is critical."

Detective Johnson remained silent as he walked past Dan, studying the living room as if it were a crime scene. Dan realized he had been right. The detectives had been working on some important case all night long. Detective Wheatly removed his sunglasses and tucked them into his sports coat's inner pocket. As he did, Dan saw the butt of the detective's service revolver in its holster inside the coat. Dan wasn't fooled by Wheatly's insincere apology. The two detectives had deliberately arrived at his home at this early hour to catch him at his weakest and most vulnerable time. But why?

"What case?" Dan questioned, watching both detectives for reactions that did not come. Their stone, expressionless faces spoke volumes about their level of experience.

Then Detective Johnson spoke. "We'll get to that shortly, Sir. For now, we need to be the ones asking the questions." His voice was a deep baritone, and his delivery was flat and direct. It reminded Dan of Joe Friday on the reruns he had seen of the old TV show Dragnet. Only this detective's voice was much deeper and richer. That observation only served to make Dan more apprehensive of the detective. Dan assumed that if they were going to pull the "good cop/bad cop" routine on him, Johnson would be playing the role of the bad cop. Perhaps the game was already in play.

Then Dan mentally chastised himself again for feeling so paranoid, despite the feeling he might have good reason to feel somewhat unsure of this situation. After all, he had never been approached by two police detectives before, and these two were doing nothing to make him feel comfortable. In fact, they were making him feel like he might be guilty of something, although he knew he was not. He recalled an expression he had once heard, "You're not paranoid if everyone really is out to get you."

Then Wheatly spoke in his fabricated compassionate voice, "You see, Mister Gilbert, we're investigating a murder, a most horrendous murder. We thought perhaps you might be able to assist us." Dan decided he had been right yet again. Wheatly would play the good cop, likely because he was white and might be perceived as less threatening.

Dan asked, "A murder? Me? How could I ever be able to help you?"

Johnson held up the evidence bag and, in a menacing tone, said, "Can you tell me, Mister Gilbert, why this blood-soaked book, with your name on the cover, was left at the scene of one of the most gruesome murders in this city's history, and why the site was staged to look exactly like a murder in this book?"

/ 4 /

Dan was shocked to silence for two very good reasons. First, he didn't write murder-type books where one human being kills another. He always felt plenty of other writers were doing the slasher and splatterpunk thing. He wrote horror fiction, and his brand of horror primarily featured monsters and demons. Granted, many of the scenes were violent and gory, but not the sort of thing one human could perpetrate on another, not acts someone would construe as murder. Secondly, because he remembered all the bloody death scenes from his books and couldn't imagine any human capable of the strength required to recreate one of those horrid scenes in real life.

When he felt he could speak, Dan said, "I don't understand. I write monster stories and horror fiction. I don't do murder scenes. I'm not sure what you're talking about."

Detective Wheatly took out a notebook, pointed to the book in the evidence bag, and asked, "Mister Gilbert? Do you have a copy of that book in your house?"

Dan said, "Um . . . Yes. I have copies of all my books."

Wheatly continued, "Sir, would you be kind enough to go get your copy of the book?"

"Ok. It's right over there in the next room, on the bookshelf in my office." Dan stood, walked into his office, over to a wall of shelves covered in books, withdrew a copy of "*It Came from Hell*," and brought it to where the police detectives sat waiting.

Dan said, "Here it is."

Wheatly asked, "Mister Gilbert, would you be so kind as to turn to page 234 and, starting with the third paragraph, read the scene you described?"

Dan said, "I suppose I could, but I don't understand . . ."

"Just read the damned passage!" Johnson insisted, looking both angry and disgusted simultaneously.

Dan said, "Fine, fine. Very well, if you insist."

Johnson said firmly, "Oh, I most definitely insist."

Dan turned to the page as directed and started reading, "The scene looked like a charnel house. Body parts were strewn across the blood-soaked floor, so many that it was almost impossible to determine which limb went with which dismembered body. The stench of blood, urine, and released bowels permeated the air, which was already thick with evening moisture. It was obvious by the strips of sinewy bloody muscle and tattered ligaments dangling from the ragged ends of the arms and legs that the limbs had been torn from their sockets, likely while the victims were still alive and screaming in agony.

"Around the room, several severed heads were displayed on wooden poles as if bearing witness to the carnage that had taken place. Then again, since all the eyes had been plucked from their sockets and shoved into their mouths, these heads wouldn't be witnessing anything. George had no idea what sort of monster could have caused such a horror, but he knew no human could have possibly been responsible. This was the work of a real demon, summoned for this vile purpose."

Dan looked at both detectives in confusion, then said, "Ok. I read it. Now what?"

Wheatly asked, "In your book, who was responsible for what happened in that scene?"

Dan said, "It wasn't a 'who' but a 'what.' It was a demon sent from Hell to wreak havoc on the people in that room who were self-proclaimed demon hunters. Unfortunately, they weren't very good at what they professed to be. As I've read to you, the result was not pretty."

"If you thought it horrendous in your book, you should see it in reality," Johnson said angrily, as he held his electronic tablet out for Dan to see a full-color crime scene photo of a tableau depicting in real life what he had read seconds ago.

Dan's eyes bulged with shock and horror. He got up from his chair, covered his mouth with his hand, then turned and raced to the nearby powder room. The detectives could hear retching sounds as Dan involuntarily freed space for a breakfast he would have no desire to eat. A few minutes later, the toilet flushed, and the sink water ran. Dan stood momentarily in the powder room doorway, holding the door jams for much-needed support. A sheen of cold sweat covered his pallid face.

Dan stumbled over to his chair and fell into it with a plop, looking like something the dog had dragged in, eaten, and then thrown back up. He sighed and managed to ask, "Was that really necessary, detectives?"

Johnson smirked and said, "I guess I just assumed that anyone capable of coming up with a scene like that out of his imagination wouldn't have had any trouble with it. However, I could tell you didn't find it very pleasant by your reaction."

Dan said angrily, "What I do is fiction, gentlemen! Complete and total fiction. You said it yourself, Detective Johnson. It's all made up from my imagination. No one real is involved! No one actually gets hurt. It's all pretend."

Tapping his tablet, Johnson said, "Well, this certainly wasn't pretend. Somebody went to a lot of trouble to recreate this scene from your book."

Dan stammered, "But . . . But that's not even possible! No human could ever have the strength it would take to do something like that!"

Wheatly said, "Unfortunately, someone found some way to do it, and it looks like we're going to need your help to catch this guy."

Dan said, "Of course, I'll help in any way possible. I have no idea what I can do for you, but I'll try. Just let me know what I need to do."

In his typical surly tone, Johnson said, "Look, Dan. We assume the type of writing you do tends to attract a certain less than desirable segment of society." Dan noticed how Johnson had stopped calling him Mister Gilbert in favor of the less formal and deliberately less polite "Dan." Dan wasn't sure what, if any, inference he should take from this change in the detective's attitude. Maybe it meant nothing. However, it could just as easily be a bit of passive/aggressive disrespect.

Wheatly saw Dan's reaction to Johnson's comment and decided it was time for the good cop to take charge again, "What Detective Johnson means to ask is, might it be possible that a fan of your writing could be someone who would take your writing and interpret it in a way you never wanted it to be?"

Dan said, "I'm not sure I follow you, detective."

"I assume, as a writer, you get fan mail from people who are your regular readers. Is that correct?" Wheatly asked.

"Yes, I do occasionally. I'm not that famous as to get it regularly. It comes to me through the company online portal." Dan said as he suddenly remembered the strange emails from "isurvu4evr@mymail. com."

Wheatly asked, "Is everything ok, Mister Gilbert?"

Dan said, "Yes, sorry. I was just thinking. There was someone, a guy, who wrote weird emails to me. He called himself 'The Servant' and wrote all sorts of creepy stuff. He said my writing lingered in his thoughts, and I was commanding him through my writing. It was really wacky stuff. I had my publisher redirect his emails to a junk folder so I wouldn't have to see them anymore."

Johnson said, "We need to see those emails ASAP!"

/ 5 /

"Justin, thank you for taking my call," Dan said.

Justin insisted, "You do realize how early it is, Dan. If this was anyone but you, we wouldn't be talking. I most certainly hope this call is as important as you seem to think it is."

"Believe me, Justin, it is."

"Well then, Dan. Let's get on with it. What's so important that you had to rouse me from a sound sleep?"

"Justin, so you know, I have you on speaker. I'm here at my house with two police detectives who woke me about a half hour ago."

Justin said, "Police detectives? What the Hell happened, Dan? Do you need a lawyer? Don't say another word until I get Harry Jacobson over there. He'll take good care of you."

Wheatly interrupted, "Excuse me, Justin. I'm Police Detective Sam Wheatly, and next to me is my partner, Detective Darnell Johnson. Neither you nor Mister Gilbert is in any trouble at this time. As is your right, you may request your attorney to be present for these informal discussions, but at this point, I don't feel one is necessary. And time is extremely critical to our investigation."

Justin said, "Yeah? Well, that's what you cops always say, then the next thing you know, we find ourselves up to our eyeballs in legal trouble."

Johnson asked, "Are you speaking from experience?"

"No, not at all. I just know how things work in this world."

Dan said, "Listen to what the detectives have to say, Justin. We don't have to answer any questions, but you need to hear them out. There have been some murders, and the Police are asking for our help finding the guy responsible."

Justin shouted, "Murders? Our help? How the Hell are we going to help them, Dan?"

"I think I might have an idea who's responsible, Justin."

"You do? How could you possibly know any . . . any murderer?"

"Maybe I don't. I'm spitballing here. I'm just trying to help is all. Do you remember that wacky guy who was writing all those crazy emails a few weeks ago? He called himself 'The Servant.'"

Justin said, "Yeah. I remember him. He was a real nutter, that one. He was the guy who said he lived to serve your every command. What makes you think it was him?"

"I'm not sure what to think, Justin, but if it will help stop a killer, then I have no choice but to do whatever I can." Then Dan said, "Do you recall me asking you to forward all his emails to some directory where we could get to them if needed? I think it would help the detectives if they could read his emails. They might be able to use them to catch the guy."

"I remember you asking me to send the emails to a special directory, and although I did ask my techies to make it happen, they couldn't make it work for whatever reason. The best they could do was reject his emails so we wouldn't get them anymore."

Dan shouted, "No, Justin. I specifically told you we didn't want you to do that. I said that would be the absolute worst thing to do. Remember how I said that might only piss him off and get him to do something really bad. Remember? I can't believe you let the techies get away with that! I hope you realize that single act of stupidity might have been enough to push this loony over the edge."

Justin said, "Me? No way, Jose! I didn't push anyone. Look, Dan, if this guy is crazy, then he was crazy long before either you or I entered the picture. You know what? I think this situation is getting way out of hand, Danny Boy. I'm sorry, but I gotta call Harry Jacobson in on this. You probably already said more than you should have. I'm warning you, Dan, don't say another word to those cops. There are so many ways this disaster can come back to bite us square in the balls. If you value your relationship with this company, you would be wise to put a cork in it and not say another word until Harry gets there."

Detective Johnson spoke up angrily, "Look, man. I don't know who you think you are, but we're already neck-deep in one of the most horrendous murders this city has ever seen, and I have no reason to think we've seen the end of it. This guy, this so-called "Servant," is on some kind of homicidal rampage, duplicating scenes of carnage right out of Dan's books, books that your company published. And this guy apparently has some kind of weirdo boner for your author. It's obvious the guy is a real wack-job for sure and very possibly our killer. What's worse is he seems to think Dan is commanding him to do these things. Like it or not, that puts you both in the middle of this mess."

Wheatly added more calmly, "Look, Justin and Dan, it's true we need your help, but if what you've told us so far is accurate, then you may need our help as well."

Justin asked, "I'm not sure I know what you mean. What are you saying, detective?"

"I'm suggesting that if this 'Servant' character is the one who committed these murders, then he is plenty angry. If so, he's probably angry with your company, Justin, for rejecting his emails. He's also probably angry that his emails didn't get through to his favorite author, Dan. I don't think he would do anything to hurt Dan as he needs him for his writing, but he might come looking for you, Justin."

Justin said, "Wonderful! Just friggin' wonderful. Ok, detectives, the ball's in your court. What do I need to do not to end up as the star of one of Dan's bloody death scenes?"

Johnson said, "The first thing you need to do is take the block off the crazy guy's emails. We need to see them flowing again. That will tell us many things, and if we're lucky, the guy might even brag about what he has done and confess."

Dan said, "But something still doesn't make sense to me."

Johnson added, "Welcome to the club, brother; none of this makes sense to me."

"Maybe so, detective. But what still doesn't add up for me is, even if this guy turns out to be the killer, where did he get the strength to rip someone's arms and legs right out of the sockets?"

Wheatly said, "I don't know, Dan. Maybe when we catch the guy, we will get the answers you want. For now, I just want to stop him."

/ 6 /

It didn't take long for "The Servant" to renew his email writing campaign, as he began just a few days later. The first email arrived at 10:17 A.M. A group consisting of Dan, Justin, Harry Jacobson, the lawyer, Detectives Wheatly, and Johnson sat in the walnut-paneled conference room at the offices of Justin Thyme Publishing. Harry Jacobson was an older middle-aged man with an off-the-rack blue suit and a substantial middle supported inadequately by red suspenders that matched his clip-on bow tie. He was bald with a somewhat unruly fringe of white hair connecting his elephantine ears, which sprouted their own crop of white whisps. Harry was clean-shaven with a chin so weak that it was hard to tell where his pudgy face ended and his neck began. Combined with large, droopy-lidded eyes, this feature gave the lawyer a turtle-like appearance. Attorney Jacobson took a deep breath and then read the contents of the email for the gathering.

"My most dear Mister Gilbert. I'm so glad to see that whatever glitch had befallen your publishing company's computer system has been rectified, and you are, once again, I assume, receiving my emails. Needless to say, when I started seeing rejection notices for emails I sent, I became quite upset. It wasn't so much that I was concerned you might not be able to send me my orders, as those always come through your published books. However, it bothered me that you might be unable to read and enjoy my letters. I feel it's crucial that you know how much your writing and more importantly, your ideas are to me. As I'm sure you have learned by now, I decided that your publishing company's disrespect towards me could not go unpunished. I had been planning for some time to begin turning your amazing descriptive commands into physical works of art, but I was missing one crucial element: rage. Your publisher's actions, whether intentional or accidental, provided me with that rage I so desperately needed.

"That being said, I decided to pick one of my favorite scenes from one of your earlier works and duplicate it to the best of my ability. I was quite nervous about this first attempt, as it was, as they say, my maiden voyage. I've always been particularly fond of that book, "*It Came from Hell*," for a variety of reasons which I won't get into now. Although it wasn't your first book, it was the first of your books that I had ever read. As such, it holds a place near and dear to my heart. And that particular scene, where the demon arises from the bowels of Hell to rip those pretenders to pieces, is perfectly descriptive. Those are the types of thoughts that linger most for me. Those are the images you paint for me with words in such incredible detail that it makes it so much easier for me to create my own art. If I may be bold enough to suggest this, I suppose that makes us a creative partnership.

"I'm sure, being the great creator and the originator of these visceral images, you are wondering how I managed to duplicate your grizzly horror in such accurate detail. The strength required to rip human beings to pieces is extraordinary, if not superhuman. Unfortunately, that must remain my secret for now as well, but I'll be happy to share it with you sometime soon. I have no idea who those poor souls featured in my work of art were, as they lived to serve a greater purpose. They lived to serve me as I live to serve you, now and always. Perhaps our new friends, Detectives Wheatly and Johnson will be able to identify them if they haven't already. Although those people were strangers to me, simply flesh figurines for my art, they resembled the would-be demon hunters you described in your book, so that was good enough for me.

"Are you surprised I know about Wheatly and Johnson, Mister Gilbert? You shouldn't be. After all, it was I who left the copy of your book at the scene, knowing they would make a beeline straight to you. I'm sorry I had to involve you, but it was necessary. It's all part of my game. I think this is all so much fun, don't you agree? I was curious if they did the good cop/bad cop thing I always see on TV cop shows, not that I have much time for television. My guess is that Wheatly played the good cop and Johnson the bad. I'll also guess that you, Mister Gilbert, predicted the same results I did. See, great minds do think alike.

"By the way, I must apologize for the sad condition of the book. It's one I picked up specifically for this project. Don't worry, my spirit guide. I still have my original autographed copy of your book on my bookshelf at home. That's right, Mister Gilbert. You probably don't remember, but you signed my copy at a book event over a decade ago. Perhaps that's a clue for our detectives to pursue, maybe not. Ten years is a long time, and I'm sure you've signed many books since then.

"Anyway, thank you, as always, for your descriptions and for those incredible thoughts that linger. Here's a gift from me. It's something our two Sherlock Holmes wannabes don't know about yet. I just completed my second work last night. It's based on a particularly graphic scene from your short story, "*Hell Hath No Fury*." Best of luck finding the location of my latest creation, detectives. I hope you find it soon before things get too decayed. Corpses in that condition tend to rot quickly and can really add a nasty stink to a place. I encourage Mister Gilbert to help you in any way possible. It makes the game so much more fun and, dare I say, exciting! In case you're wondering, I am well aware that I won't be able to continue creating my art for very long. You know how society is with its rules and morals. No matter how inept, sooner or later, the powers that be will find me, capture me, and likely kill me. I'm ok with that. Sacrificing myself in the service of Mister Gilbert's inspiration is all I could ever ask for. Then again, I do have another reason not to fear death. I believe I have seen where I will go after I die and know I will have a place of honor there.

"By the way, I'll give you two detectives until tomorrow morning to find my latest flesh sculpture. If you haven't found it by then, I'll send an anonymous tip to our local TV station, and they'll get to see my masterpiece first. I'm certain that would prove to be a real kick in the balls for the police department."

"As always, yours truly,

The Servant"

/ 7 /

Johnson said, "Oh boy, this guy's crazy train just went off the rails in one big hurry."

Dan and Justin stood silently as Harry held the printed email in trembling hands.

Doing his best to keep the investigation on a logical course, Wheatly said, "Ok. So, what do we know here? We know this Servant character is our guy. He not only admitted it, but new details nobody else knew."

Dan asked, "What kinds of things do you mean?"

Wheatly replied, "He knew Johnson and I were on the case, and he knew we would identify the victims based on fingerprints and dental records. Five people were killed. Three were homeless vagrants that no one would miss, and two others were not. He also knew exactly what we would find and why he specifically chose his victims. The three homeless male victims were the toughest to identify. The final two victims were a male and female passing through the area, we assume on vacation. Their names were Sid and Grace Halbert from Ashville, North Carolina. The couple physically matched the couple in Dan's book. If I'm correct, they were called Bob and Sharon Andrews in the book.

Dan said, "That's right. But in my book, they were the leaders of the group of demon hunters."

"The other three males were not given the extensive detailed descriptions as the Andrews were in your book, so our killer had some latitude when selecting them." Wheatly said.

Justin added, "The killer also chose a location similar to the one in Dan's book if I recall correctly."

"Yes. In the book the demons met and attacked the hunters in an abandoned warehouse, down by the waterfront. But in the real-world scene, the warehouse wasn't abandoned." Wheatly pointed out.

Dan said, "That was probably deliberate since the Servant wanted to ensure that his "art" would be found quickly."

Justin asked, "Why do you think that should matter?"

"Think about what his email just said. I suspect he wants his creation to be found as quickly as possible because of degradation from rot and decay. He wants his sculpture to look as much like a scene from my book as possible, and the more it decomposes, the less it resembles my description." Dan said.

Johnson added, "That makes sense to me, assuming any of this makes any kind of twisted sense. That also reminds me of a question I had for Dan."

"What question is that?" Dan asked.

Johnson asked, "Why in the Hell did your story have the five victim's heads mounted on wooden poles, then have their eyes plucked out of their sockets and shoved into their mouths? That's pretty weird stuff. It's also illogical."

"How so, Detective Johnson"

"Well, Dan, I may not be a high-falootin' big-time horror writer like you, but logically speaking, I'm fairly sure once a head is removed from a body, the eyes ain't seeing nothin' anymore. So, popping their eyeballs out is kind of redundant. Then, shoving the peepers inside the victim's mouth is unnecessary and overkill. I guess I don't get whatever artsy-fartsy point you were trying to make."

Dan stood silent momentarily, uncertain how to answer the detective's question. He wasn't trying to make any point whatsoever in that extra bit of gore. He was just writing horror, the only way he knew to write it. That was the unique thing about horror fiction; the reader either accepts it at face value or does not. Dan often used the analogy of telling a joke that requires you to accept the premise in order for you to enjoy the punchline.

Dan asked, "Detective Wheatly. If I were to tell you a joke that started like this, 'A Rabbi, a Nun, and an armadillo walk into a bar,' what would your reaction be?"

Wheatly responded, "I'd want to hear where this joke was going. You know. I'd want to know what happened inside at the bar."

Then Dan asked, "And you, Detective Johnson, what would your response be?"

Johnson said, "I'd want you to explain what a Rabbi, a Nun, and an armadillo were doing walking around together, let alone walking into a bar together."

Dan smiled and said, "Exactly! There is the difference. Detective Wheatly instantly accepted the premise of the joke without question and, as such, was ready to receive the punchline. Detective Johnson, on the other hand, was so busy questioning the premise that he had no interest in learning the punchline."

Johnson said, "Ok, Dan. I get that, but what does that have to do with severed heads and mouths full of eyeballs?"

"Everything." Dan insisted, "You see, detective, we horror writers expect much from our readers. We want them to accept the impossible at face value without question. You're right that there was no logical need for the overkill in my story, but that's where the creative license comes into play. Horror fans constantly want and expect you to go over the top, especially regarding graphic scenes. When I write and feel like I might have gone too far, I say, 'Now it's time to go further.' The readers appreciate that. It's what I think of as the 'Ugh! Factor.' It's when the reader knows you've gone too far, and their only reaction is to do a mental 'Ugh!'"

Johnson said, "Until their reaction is to think you are their messiah and that you are commanding them to carry out your orders in the flesh."

Dan hesitated, then agreed, "Yeah. There is that."

Wheatly said, "We have several priorities here; each one is equally important. We have to try to figure out who this lunatic is and attach a name and face to him. We also only have a day to find and secure his latest kill site. If we don't, then the press will be notified, this will be broadcast everywhere, and we could have a citywide panic on our hands."

Dan asked, "What can we do to help?"

"Dan, I'm going to need a copy of that short story The Servant mentioned."

"Sure thing, Detective Johnson. The story was called "*Hell Hath no Fury.*" It's part of a short story collection we published called "*Tales from the Bowels of Hell, Volume 5.*"

Johnson asked, "Volume 5? How many damn volumes have you published?"

Justin said, "I believe we are up to volume 12. In addition to his many novels, Dan has written more than 260 short stories. He's our most prolific author."

Johnson shook his head and said, "How did we get so friggin' lucky?"

"Dan, can you get Johnson a copy of that short story and see if you can figure out what scene this wacko might have used and where we might look?" Wheatly said.

Dan agreed, "I'll go to my place and get it now. My house is only about fifteen minutes away. But before I do, I've been thinking about that book signing the Servant mentioned. Ten years ago, my book signings attracted very few people. Most of the time, I was part of a multi-author event with writers from all different genres. Usually, if someone ever bothered to stop by, it would be a real horror enthusiast. This one character had large, strange eyes, thick glasses, and a disturbing smile. Justin, do you remember the show we did at that Convention Center near Philadelphia? It was a horror convention, and you had brought a box of my books for me to sign and give away for free?"

Justin said, "Yeah, I remember that one. You, Cathy Jones, and Bill Barrow all shared a table. What I remember most about that day was how hard it was to give away free, signed horror books. Nobody wanted any. People actually had no problem shamelessly saying they didn't read; they watched movies instead."

"If I remember correctly, Justin, you took a bunch of promo pictures at that event. Some were with me, posing with people who got books. Maybe you inadvertently got a picture of this Servant guy. Do you still have those pictures?" Dan asked.

"I might have them somewhere in the digital archives on the company server. I'm a digital packrat and never throw anything away." Justin admitted.

Wheatly said, "That would be awesome, Justin. Why don't you and I get on your computer now and see if we can find those pictures."

Dan added, "As I recall, it was in late September or early October of that year, in time to take advantage of the Halloween season."

Justin said, "We can go track those down immediately."

Johnson added, "I'll go with Edgar Allen Poe boy, here and see what we can dig up with his short story."

"Harry, if you want to call it a day, that's fine with me. You can go back to your office and do whatever lawyer stuff you normally do. I think cooperating with these detectives is the right thing for us to do. Don't you agree?" Justin said to his lawyer.

Harry reluctantly agreed, "Well, ok if you say so, Justin. However, after reading that email and seeing the crime scene pictures, I may find it hard to return to my normal, boring everyday 'lawyer stuff.' But I'll give it a shot. I'll tell you what. I'll continue to monitor the email account to see if the Servant sends anything more.

"That's fantastic. Thanks, Harry." Justin said.

/ 8 /

"Here's the collection I was telling you about, Detective. Now give me a moment to find the short story." Dan said.

Johnson was staring wide-eyed with his mouth open at Dan's home office's rows and columns of shelves filled with books. "That's a lot of books, Dan. Did you write them all?"

Dan flushed with pride and a bit of embarrassment. "No, I only wrote the books on the first three shelves in this middle cabinet. All the rest of the shelves in this cabinet are filled with anthologies from other publishers that have featured one of my stories along with other authors. There are also a bunch of magazines that featured my stories."

"Wow!" That was all Johnson said. Unless Dan was mistaken, there seemed to be a tone of genuine respect in the detective's brief but honest reply.

Dan said, "Yeah. I don't make much money from those anthologies, but it's a good way to get my name out there and for people to start recognizing it. The other cabinets hold my personal collection of signed books from other authors."

Shedding most of his bad cop persona, Johnson asked, "You really are a busy boy. So tell me a bit about that story, '*Hell Hath No Fury.*'"

"No problem. It's a story based on the expression, 'Hell hath no fury like a woman scorned.' It's a typical love triangle theme with a twist. The woman in the story, Jill, is in love with and is faithful to her husband, Lance. The same can't be said of Lance, who takes his name far too seriously, as he feels the need to impale virtually every woman he meets. Jill is somehow unaware of Lance's extramarital sexual jousting. The couple has been unsuccessful in trying to have a baby for several years. One day, Jill learns that her best friend since childhood, Sandra, who was also Jill's maid of honor, is pregnant as the result of an affair she had with I-can't-keep-it-in-my-pants, Lance."

"Rutt row." Johnson offered.

Dan continued, "Rutt Row is right. So, our girl, Jill, has just been scorned big-time by her husband and bestie. What neither fornicator knows is that Jill has a secret of her own. She has been studying the occult and has become a full-blown, closet Satan worshipper. She has also developed some occult powers. Jill lures the couple to a remote location in a nearby forest. In the story, I call it Woodland Forest. She sedates them, and when they awaken, the cheating couple find themselves tied to trees, unable to move but perfectly capable of screaming in a place no one will hear them."

Johnson said, "Why do I have a feeling this is where we will find the scene in the story we are looking for?"

"Because it is. Listen to this." Dan replied.

Then Dan began to read a passage from the book, "An icy chill crept down Lance's spine as he slowly opened his eyes, examining the dark forest around him. He could tell by the cold he felt on his skin and the rough feeling of tree bark against his back that he had been tied, naked, spread-eagle between three trees. A rope around his neck held him to the center tree, and four other ropes bound each of his hands and feet to two adjacent trees. Lance heard a moan, and as a sliver of moonlight shone between an opening in the canopy of tree branches above him, Lance looked across the small clearing to see Sandra secured in the same way. Her formerly flat stomach was just starting to show signs of the baby growing inside her, his baby. Lance tried to call out to her but could not seem to form the words.

Jill said, "Don't waste your time trying to speak, dear husband. The drug I gave you will prevent you and your baby mama from boring me with your pitiful explanations or pleas for mercy. It will not, however, prevent you from screaming, a sound I can't wait to hear."

"Then, Jill began uttering some strange-sounding incantations in a language Lance had never heard before, and things started to happen. A crack appeared on the forest floor, spreading between the two lovers. As the crack widened, a foul stench of sulfur, rotting meat, and decomposing flesh permeated the air. Flames shot upward from the gash in the forest bed as dozens of serpentine, snake-like creatures crept from the opening. These hideous monstrosities were greenish-brown in appearance, covered in a flaming slimy ooze, about two inches thick, tapering almost to a point at their tips. At the smallest end of the taper, a nearly imperceptible flaming red tongue flitted in and out of the orifice.

"Jill uttered a few more guttural chants, and the creatures slithered from the fiery crevice in both directions and began systematically flaying the flesh from the bodies of the couple as they screamed in agony. Within minutes, all screaming ceased, and all flesh had been rendered, leaving bloody skeletons covered in patches of crimson musculature. The faces of both victims were hideous ruby skulls dripping with blood and fragments of remaining flesh. The lovers' eyes bugged from bloody sockets, and their grins were captured in a hideous rictus of death."

Dan said, "That scene is what we have to assume we will find."

Johnson stared at Dan with disbelief and finally said, "Jesus, Mary, and Joe Christ the carpenter, man! Where in the unholy hammers of Hell do you come up with this horrible crap? That just ain't . . . it just ain't normal."

"Well, I suppose you're right about that, Detective. If it were normal, I would never have been able to get a reaction like I just got from you. See, that's the whole point of writing horror, to shock, sicken, and entertain simultaneously; to generate some kind of reaction."

"If that was supposed to make me feel all warm and fuzzy around you, Dan, it failed miserably," Johnson confessed. "That is some really twisted stuff."

Dan shrugged his shoulders and said, "It's just what I do."

Johnson shook himself back into focus and said, "So this park or forest you're talking about, this Woodland Forest. Would that be, by any chance, a reference to Woodward Park, or is it referencing Woodly Forest?"

Dan said, "When I wrote the story, it was only a few days after I visited Woodly Forest, so that was what I had in mind."

"But what about this Servant character? Do you think he'll understand which one you meant? We don't have the time or manpower to search both sites. We'll be lucky if we find any location before he releases the information to the press."

Dan thought for a moment, then said, "Yeah. I'm pretty sure he would have chosen Woodly. Woodward Park is a much more urban and busier area with very few secluded places. Woodly, however, is a forest that has several places that could match what I wrote. I can take you to the area of the forest I visited before writing the story. I'd say that would be the best place to start since I described it in detail in the story."

Johnson said, "Sounds like a plan; let's head back to the office and tell Wheatly. We can see how he and Justin made out locating a picture of this scumbag."

/ 9 /

"I'll bet money that's the guy, Detective Wheatly!" Justin said excitedly. "Thanks to these pictures, I'm starting to recall more stuff about that event." Justin was looking at three pictures he had printed from the file of pictures he had taken at the show. Two of the photographs were of Dan with young women, and the third was with Dan and an odd-looking young man.

As he stared at the strange man in the photo, Wheatly said, "I have to agree with you on this one, Justin. That character does look really strange."

The picture showed a smiling Dan standing beside a bespecled young man in his late teens or early twenties. It was hard to determine his age as the man was clean-shaven and had thin, longish blond hair that was clearly receding, even at his young age. Wheatly suspected that the man might have lost most of his hair a decade later and opted for the shaved-head look. His glasses were as thick as the bottom of soda bottles and magnified the young man's eyes to the point of looking particularly strange. The character seemed especially disturbing when you combined the googly eyes and his wide jack-o-lantern grin.

Wheatly said, "What about the women? We haven't ruled out the possibility that our suspect might be female, although my gut tells me we're looking for a male. Not just because of the physical strength it would take to accomplish what he did, but women are seldom serial killers."

Justin asked, "If you look at that guy's build in the picture, you'll notice he's pretty frail looking. He would have had to spend the past decade pumping iron and gulping steroids to become strong enough to rip a person's arm off."

Wheatly agreed, "Yeah. I noticed that, too. In fact, the burly girlie in that second picture looks like she could break that skinny guy in half."

"So, maybe we need to keep our options open regarding gender, Detective Wheatly."

"I always try to keep an open mind, Justin. The key to being a successful detective is to go where the evidence takes us. I think these pictures will help stimulate Dan's memory and get us pointed in the right direction."

The office door opened, and Dan and Johnson walked in, looking confident. Dan said, "We believe we know the location of the second killings."

Justin said, "And we believe we may have found a picture of The Servant."

Johnson said, "Excellent work. Why don't we do this? The four of us will head to the location, which we believe to be Woodly Forest. On the way, Justin can review the pictures you found with Dan, and maybe we'll find a way to catch this lunatic before he can kill again."

On the way to Woodly Forest, Dan looked over the printout of the pictures and said, "Yes, that's the strange character I was thinking about. Now, if I could only remember his name."

Wheatly said from the shotgun seat, "Check out the other two pictures as well, Dan. Just to make sure."

Dan said, "But they're women. You don't really think a woman would be capable of something like this, do you?"

Johnson added, "Remember what happened in your story, 'Hell Hath No Fury,' Dan. We're on our way to find this psycho's recreation of what happened in that story. And the killer in that story was a woman."

Dan said, "But in the story, she could conjure demons from Hell to do her bidding. The demons had the strength and did the actual killing. That's all fiction, stuff I made up."

Justin said, "Detectives. When Dan and I started working together a long time ago, I asked him if he believed in such things as the occult, demons, ghosts, and monsters. I also asked if he thought they might exist in the real world. Dan, tell them what your answer was."

"My answer then was the same as it is now . . . absolutely not. There is no way I could write the kinds of stuff I write unless I was completely sure it was 100% fiction. That would freak me out way too much."

The car pulled into a parking place near a sign reading "Woodly Forest. Open Dawn to Dusk Daily." Wheatly said, "Here we are, gentlemen, Woodly Forest."

As the four passengers left the automobile, Johnson said, "Let Dan take the lead since he can take us to the exact location he visited right before he wrote the story. That will be the most likely location for this crime scene. We'll be right behind him. I should warn you, Wheatly and Justin, if we find this scene, and it accurately depicts what Dan wrote in his story, it's gonna be bad, real bad."

Wheatly said, "It will probably be dark under the trees, and the sun will set in a few hours. We'd better get in there, or we'll be doing this by moonlight and flashlights."

The four entered the forest, with Dan taking the lead, followed by Johnson, Wheatly, and finally, Justin, who was starting to question his sanity for going along with this project. But what else could he do? He felt as responsible as Dan did. It was true that Dan wrote these stories, but Justin published them. He also had to admit he was curious; who wouldn't be? But he wasn't a cop or even a writer. Justin was a businessman and a book publisher. He nearly tossed his cookies, seeing pictures of the previous crime scene. What would he do with the real thing? Justin always read all of his authors' works before publishing, and as such, he started to recall the details of Dan's short story. He prayed he might be remembering the details incorrectly. If Dan actually led them to the latest recreation, and it was a depiction of what he recalled, Justin was sure he might puke, pass out and crap himself simultaneously. Before Justin could think of a way out of his dilemma, he heard Dan call out.

"Oh dear Lord in Heaven, it's here. He did it again." Then, they heard the sounds of Dan vomiting behind a tree.

Johnson looked on in disbelief. The horrible tableau presented in the forest was illuminated by several battery-powered lights. The

Servant had strategically placed the lights, giving the team a stomach-churning view of the incredible horror. As in the story, two naked bodies, one male and one female, were tied to trees spread eagle in an "x" pattern. All the flesh had been rendered from their bodies, and the stench surrounding the flayed corpses was revolting beyond description. Insects had already begun landing on the bloody remains and laying their eggs.

"Oh, sweet mother of God!" Was all Justin could eke out before collapsing to his knees and joining Dan in a barf-a-thon.

Then Johnson noticed something and called, "Dan, quit your pukin' and get over here. There's something you have to see."

Dan rose shakily to his feet, pale and weak-looking as he croaked, "What? What is it, Johnson? What do you want me to see?"

Johnson was pointing to a huge crack in the forest floor stretching from the male corpse to the female. It was over ten feet long and about two feet across at its center, tapering to nothing at the ends. The crack still had burning embers all along its edges, and smoke was still billowing from inside. A vile stench of sulfur and rotting flesh also rose from the crack.

Johnson asked, "Tell me, Dan, If you thought ripping arms out of their socket was impossible, then how the Hell did our guy manage to pull this trick off? How could he open a fiery crack in the forest floor? It is exactly as you described it in your short story."

Dan staggered over to the edge of the split in the earth and looked into the opening. It was like staring into the center of an active volcano. It was so deep that Dan couldn't see the bottom, but as far as he could see were walls of flaming, molten rock. Dan felt as though he was looking into Hell itself. That was when his mind became full of what sounded to Dan like the screams and anguished cries of millions of damned souls.

An image appeared suddenly in Dan's mind. It was a giant wall of undulating flesh over a thousand feet high and countless miles long. The surface of that wall was in constant motion as millions upon millions of bodies slid over, under, around, and through each other in a tortured ballet of the damned. Every creature on the wall was naked and bald and of indeterminate sexual origin. They were covered in a flaming, napalm-like gelatinous substance. The name "Wall of Lost Souls" suddenly appeared in Dan's mind.

Dan was about to tip over and fall forward into the gash when Johnson grabbed him and pulled Dan to safety. Sitting on the ground several feet from the crack, Dan looked around at his sickened comrades and said, "Gentlemen, it appears our problem just got one thousand times worse."

/ 10 /

"You can't be serious, Dan," Justin said, not believing what his normally rational author and friend had just explained to the group.

Dan sighed and said, "I've never been more serious about anything in my life."

Wheatly added, "But we just had this conversation a few minutes ago, Dan. You made it clear that you didn't believe in ghosts, demons, or all that mumbo jumbo. Now, you're telling us you do? I don't get it."

Dan said, "I'm not necessarily saying I do. To be honest, I'm not sure what I believe anymore. But if you could have heard what I heard and saw what I saw in my mind, you would be questioning your entire belief system as well."

Johnson jumped into the discussion, "Yeah, yeah. You said you thought you heard the sounds of millions of tortured souls screaming in torment from the bowels of Hell."

"I did hear that, Detective Johnson."

"So you say. Look, I heard you and I got what you said. But think about it logically for a minute. Although I agree something caused that crack to open and catch fire, that doesn't mean this is some kind of portal to Hell. Maybe it is nothing more than the result of an explosion set by that lunatic, Servant. Then you went over and got much too close to check it out; maybe you were overcome by, I don't know, maybe natural gas or sulfur. This made you hallucinate. If I hadn't pulled you back, you might have done a header right into that flaming slit."

Dan asked, "But what about that wall of tortured souls I saw in my mind? How do you explain that?"

"It's all part of the same hallucination, Dan," Johnson said. "Anything else simply doesn't make logical sense."

Dan said, "Fine, so let's look at this logically. Since we've got questions about both of these murder scenes and our list of suspects consists of two women and a frail, scrawny man, where did the superhuman strength come from? I'm telling you all, whoever this killer is, he is getting help from somewhere. And since both crimes were based on my stories that involved summoning demons from Hell, isn't it logical to assume whoever is doing this must have found a way to actually summon creatures to do their bidding?"

Johnson shook his head in frustration and said, "So let me get this straight. You're saying for the first murders, this Servant called a huge, monstrous demon to come up from Hell to dismember the five victims?"

"That's what happened in my book. In fact, I even gave a detailed description of the monsters' appearance, gargantuan size, and strength. I'm saying that the demons I described in my book could have easily created the horror of that first crime." Dan said.

"And this one, Dan? What about this one?" Johnson asked.

Dan said, "I read the passage to you, detective. You know what kinds of demons I described. The horror you see hanging from those trees could result from such monsters."

Wheatly said calmly, "Look, we're all a bit emotional here. Things might seem to make sense that really have no business in our criminal investigation. Let's think about this for a few minutes. I'm going to call for a Crime Scene Investigative team to come out and do their thing, just like we did with the last scene. We'll put our emotions aside and let the facts and evidence lead us wherever it does."

As the group listened to Wheatly's call for rationality, the ground began to tremble. The flaming crack in the forest floor began to close itself until, after a few seconds, nothing remained but a thin line of smoldering pine needles leading from one corpse to the other.

Dan shouted, "Ok, people. Will someone please explain to me what just happened out here?"

Before anyone could offer an opinion, Justin's cell phone rang. He looked at the caller ID and said, "It's Harry. There's been another email."

Justin told the lawyer, "Harry, I'm going to put you on speaker so you can read the letter to everyone." He pressed the speaker button and said, "Go ahead, Harry."

Harry cleared his throat as if preparing to give a summation in open court and began, "Good evening, Justin, Detective Wheatly, Detective Johnson, and, of course, Mister Gilbert. Allow me to congratulate you all on your excellent accomplishments. I see you've successfully found the second tribute to my inspiration, the wonderful Mister Gilbert. If I may be so bold as to toot my own proverbial horn, I must acknowledge that this might be my finest work so far. Then again, I have only completed two of these die-a-ramas so far, so I have little to compare it with. But I can assure you that will change soon. However, before I expound any further, I feel I must apologize to Mister Gilbert for making him ill. His reaction caught me by surprise. I assumed anyone capable of creating such incredible images of agonizing death and mayhem would not be affected in such a negative way. Again, my apologies, Mister Gilbert, and to you as well, Mister Justin Thyme. I would recommend that when I create my next masterpiece, both of you do not attend the live presentation in person. If this one bothered you, I have no idea what your reaction to the next one will be.

"Speaking of which, I have decided that my next work will be based on a scene from Mister Gilbert's short story, '*Theater of Terror.*' I apologize for not having finished reading the story, but once I got to the kill scene, I figured the rest of the story could wait until I had more time. I think that one will be quite a challenge for me, but I believe I have the power to make it a reality. How many innocents were slaughtered in that story, Mister Gilbert? Dozens? Several hundred? Please be so kind as to bring the two Keystone Cops, Wheatly and Johnson, up to speed regarding that story. They'll need all the help they can get if they intend to try and stop me. Unfortunately, there is nothing they can do. My power and my abilities have grown far too strong to be thwarted by mere humans.

"I have learned so much since I first met Mister Gilbert all those years ago. I also discovered an interesting tidbit about my favorite author through reading blogs and online interviews. I found that even though Mister Gilbert does an incredible job describing both the powers and horrors of Hell, he is not a believer. This information does not make me think any less of the source of my ideas and the reason I live and breathe. On the contrary, it inspires me to take my work to the next level and, in doing so, convince my influencer, Mister Gilbert, that what he thinks is fantasy is actually my reality. I hope this latest demonstration has helped him believe and appreciate just how accurately his stories depict what the powers of Hell can do. That is why Mister Gilbert is so amazing; he is my messiah, and I am his humble servant. He has motivated me to learn how to make his nightmares real, even without being a believer himself.

"My parting gift, a clue if you will, to our less than exemplary police department is this. You can stop considering females as you conduct your futile attempt to identify me. I am a man. When I met and had my book signed by my mentor, Mister Gilbert, I was but a teenager. Somewhere, there is a photo of me standing next to my hero. I haven't seen it, but I suspect I looked starstruck, as any young man might be, upon meeting someone who would become his god. The years have passed, and for the record, I no longer look the same as that boy in the picture. It's amazing what adding a little muscle, a shaved head, some contact lenses, and a nice demonic-looking beard and mustache can do to change one's appearance. So, there you have it, gentleman. It is a fairly good description of my appearance, but it will not help delay the inevitable.

"Well, I suppose that's all for now. Special thanks to my messiah, Mister Gilbert. This next slaughter will be a crowning achievement for me and for the powers Hell has bestowed upon me. As always, I am but a humble servant of Satan, using the genius of Mister Gilbert to bring evil into a much deserving world."

Very truly yours,

The Servant"

/ 12 /

Johnson said, "Shissh! Don't say another word until we put some space between this mess and us." He signaled everyone to follow him away from the forest bloodbath.

When the group was an acceptable distance away, Wheatly asked, "He was watching us, wasn't he?"

Johnson replied, "Yes, and listening too." I'm unsure where he hid the cameras and mics, but I'll have the forensic team look for them."

Dan asked, "What if there were no cameras or listening equipment?"

"What are you talking about, Dan?" Johnson said, "He has to have planted something out there. He saw your reaction to his display. He knows you're starting to believe his hocus-pocus balonie. That's why he is claiming to be in league with some demonic forces. He's trying to pull us into his psychopathic fantasy. He believes he can call up the powers from Hell, and he wants us to buy into it as well."

Justin asked, "But why, Johnson? Why does he want us to believe?"

Wheatly added, "I think I get what you're suggesting, Johnson. You're saying this wacko wants to convince us that he can somehow call demons to duplicate the killings in Dan's stories."

Dan repeated, "I have to ask again, what if forensics doesn't find any equipment?"

"What are you suggesting, Dan?" Johnson asked, not wanting to hear his answer.

"I'm offering the following scenario. Please humor me here, as it will likely sound crazy. Suppose, just suppose, The Servant has actually found some way to call demons from Hell to do his bidding. If we are willing to accept that premise, then we can better know what to expect."

Johnson interrupted, "Sorry, Dan, you lost me."

Dan continued, "First, for the sake of argument, let's assume we believe it is actually possible for a human of a certain ilk to call creatures from Hell. No one knows what these demons would look like or what powers they might have. Now assume that since these monsters consist of the damned souls of former living humans and, as such, would be noncorporeal or without any physical shape or form. Enter the Servant. Somehow, he learns how to summon these beings. In order to use them to kill, these creatures need to have some physical structure. What form these damned souls take will be determined by whoever summons them. In my writings, I use my imagination to describe what I think these demons should look like based on the scene I create. The Servant studies my writings closer than most people would do. It's logical, then, that he would use my descriptions to give substance to his summoned demons."

Johnson said, "Now wait a minute . . ."

Wheatly interrupted, "Let him finish, Johnson. I want to hear the rest."

Dan said, "Thanks, Detective Wheatly. For his first scene, The Servant probably took my descriptions of the demons right from my book. I had described them as gigantic, muscle-bound hideous creatures with snot-dripping pig-like snouts, large mouths full of fangs, rams horns, and long, greasy hair. These creatures could rip arms and legs from their sockets with ease. And for this latest scene, he used my description of snake-like tentacles with flaming tongues to create creatures to flay the flesh from those two bodies back there."

Johnson said, "Fine. You've had your say. But it's not the 1600s, Dan. Nobody believes in summoning demons from the great beyond. Maybe he's an amateur illusionist. Those guys can make people think they can make the Statue of Liberty disappear. Maybe he uses tricks like that. One thing I do believe in is psychopathic murderers. And that's exactly what we are dealing with here. You heard what he said in his email: he had put on some muscle in the past decade since you saw him. Here's what I think. I believe this wacko has spent the last ten years pumping iron, probably excessively, since these wackos always want to do things to excess. He's also likely been taking anabolic steroids to increase his strength and build muscle faster. My theory is this guy honestly believes he can summon demons, but in reality, he is the only monster, him and roid rage. Yep, he's probably so messed up on steroids, and God only knows what other drugs, that he has convinced himself he can call demons from Hell."

Wheatly said, "I have to agree with Johnson, Dan. What he is suggesting is a more logical and most likely scenario. This Servant has carried out these murders alone, with no help from demons, unless you count the ones in his insane mind."

Dan said, "If that's the case, he'll never be able to create his next work. He said it would be based on my story, 'Theater of Terror.' There's no way he could possibly pull that off alone, roid rage or not."

Johnson said, "Tell us about this story; at least give us an overview of the scene he will be trying to recreate."

Dan agreed, "Since I don't have that book with me, I'll give you the five-minute summary. The crucial scene in the book takes place at a local theater called The Magnificent Theater. It happens during a sold-out live stage presentation of a play. The name of the fictional play is 'The Struggle,' although in our situation, whatever is playing is irrelevant. What does matter to us is the name of the theater. I referenced our Majestic Theater here in the city and used it for my description. That means we can assume The Servant will use that theater for his next attack.

"The antagonist in my story is a frustrated actor who jumps onto the stage in the middle of the play and begins summoning demons to attack everyone in the theater. A giant swirling portal opens like a whirlpool suspended in the air. As the play comes to a halt and everyone stares up at the swirling mass above them in terror, winged demons begin dropping from the portal and attacking everyone in the theater. I go into great and brutal detail about the slaughter, including limbs ripped off, eyes gouged out of their sockets, flesh flayed from bone, all happening as our antagonist laughs and watches through wild, mad eyes."

Johnson said, "Man-o-man, Dan! You just keep the horror coming. I'm glad you're not more popular. I can just imagine a hundred loonies like this one in cities around the country, slaughtering people to duplicate your gory scenes."

Justin said, "I don't think you'd have to worry about that even if Dan were the most famous horror writer in the world. This 'Servant' character is a freak, an anomaly, a twisted excuse for a human being. If Dan had never written a word, I'm certain this mutant would have found some other author to glom onto."

"But either fortunately or unfortunately for us, he chose Dan." Wheatly said. Then he turned to Dan and said, "How do you think he's going to pull this one off, Dan."

Dan thought for a moment, then said, "He can't. No one can. To duplicate that scene, someone would genuinely have to be able to open a giant portal to Hell and call the same demons as in my story."

Johnson said, "Unless he used illusion to create the whirlpool effect in the ceiling, released hundreds of bats or birds in the theater, then set off explosive charges to blow the audience to pieces. The carnage following something like that would probably look very much like the aftermath of the attack in your book, Dan."

"When is the next big event at the Majestic? Does anyone know?" Wheatly asked.

Justin was already scrolling through his cellphone feed and said, "Holy crap! It looks like they have a special showing of the play, 'Godspell,' Two weeks from now on Saturday night. It's a charity event to raise money to fight childhood cancers. It looks like every big wig in the county will be there, including a special visit by the Governor."

"He'd have to be insane to try something at an event like that. There will be security up the ying-yang." Johnson said.

Wheatly added, "But he is insane, and what's worse, if he truly believes he has the powers of Hell on his side and is being commanded by his messiah, Dan, he won't hesitate to take out as many people as possible, even at the risk of dying. Remember, he said he realized his days are numbered. Although it is also possible he may believe he has reached some level of immortality. These psycho types often do."

Dan said, "I think he will be there for that event, and it may be your only chance to get him. I want to be there when you do."

"I don't know, Dan. If this guy is using explosives, he could very likely be on a suicide mission. It won't be safe." Wheatly suggested.

"I agree, Dan. You and I should both stay away." Justin added, sounding less concerned about saving Dan's skin than his own.

Dan said, "Detective Wheatly is right about one thing. This will be The Servant's last event if he follows my book through to the end."

"What do you mean, Dan?" Johnson asked.

"In my story, after the demons slaughter everyone in the theater, they turn on the one who called them, and they rip him to pieces."

Johnson said, "But if he didn't read the story to the end, and he has no idea that's what supposed to happen, then in his version of the story, it won't happen."

Dan agreed, "Unfortunately, you are probably correct."

Wheatly said, "However, he does plan on this being his last and greatest accomplishment."

"I plan on taking his sorry butt out for good before he gets to harm a single hair on anyone's head," Johnson said.

"I can only pray you do, Detective Johnson. Or several hundred innocent people are going to die at that show."

/ 13 /

The night of the performance at the Majestic Theater, security, as predicted, was extremely tight, with metal detectors at the entrance and a major show of uniformed police officers as well as big, muscular men in tee shirts with SECURITY stenciled on them covered at every exit. In addition, plainclothes detectives were scattered throughout the audience. All the security personnel were given an artist's composite sketch of what "The Servant" might look like. It was based on taking the original photo from a decade earlier and the description from the killer's email.

Detectives Wheatly and Johnson were stationed on both sides of the stage, watching for suspicious activity. They had read the short story "*Theater of Terror*" and knew that The Servant would have to appear on stage at some point. Dan Gilbert was seated in the center section, five rows from the front of the stage. He asked Justin to come along with him, but Justin refused. The publisher had been traumatized by the two previous scenes of butchery and had no intention of being anywhere near this one.

The show was about to start. The audience was seated, and the theater was dark. The curtain was open on an empty stage. An organ in the orchestra pit played a deep introductory chord, which it held and allowed to resonate throughout the theater. Suddenly, a spotlight showed on one of the back entrances as a long-haired, bearded young man dressed in bright multicolored clothing stepped forward and, using a thin, head-mounted microphone, slowly sang with an incredibly melodic tenor voice, "Prepare, ye the way of the Lord."

Soon, he was joined by other similarly dressed young men and women who sang with him. Then the drums crashed, the tempo picked up, and within seconds, all the colorfully dressed performers danced in the isles, making their way toward the stage, singing that opening tune. Before long, audience members standing in their seats sang and clapped along to the song. After all the actors had made their way to the stage, they stood in front, singing along with the crowd, until they sang the song's final refrain, and the audience gave a cheering standing ovation.

When the clapping subsided, and one of the actors was about to say his first line, the stage began to rumble and shake. The actors wobbled, and some fell to the surface of the stage, many crying out in pain from injured arms and legs. One or two actors fell from the stage, crashing into the orchestra pit and injuring themselves and the musicians.

Over his communication device, small, almost invisible earbuds, Johnson shouted, "It's happening. Wheatly, do you see anything?"

"Negative, Johnson. Something's wrong with the stage. Several actors and musicians have been injured. Do you see what's causing this?"

"Sorry, Wheatly, I got nothin'. I see no sign of The Servant, but I'm sure he's behind this and is here somewhere."

Dan watched the stage tremble as actors, struggling to remain upright, tripped and fell. Female actors screamed, and the males moaned as they struggled helplessly with their injuries. People in the audience were shouting and beginning to panic. As the house lights came back on, a voice came over the sound system saying, "Please be calm, ladies and gentlemen. There's no need for panic. It appears we may have experienced a very minor earthquake. Security will be opening the exit doors shortly, and we ask that you proceed to your nearest exit in an orderly fashion. Please do so cautiously, and everyone will be evacuated without harm."

Before even one of the exit doors could be open, something ominous happened. At the high ceiling of the theater, a reddish-gray mist seemed to form from thin air and swirled around and around, creating a whirlpool of spinning fog. Dan looked up, knowing what was coming next. At the front of the theater, the center of the stage pushed upward, then split open as the actors stumbled for cover. Smoke billowed from the opening as a figure emerged, seeming to float upward. Despite the great changes to the man's appearance, Dan recognized The Servant immediately. The two made eye contact, and The Servant smiled with an evil, knowing grin.

The Servant was no longer a weak, sickly boy, but he was now a large, muscular man more than six feet tall, with a shaved head, a mustache, and a goatee. The man no longer wore the thick glasses he had worn a decade earlier, but somehow, seeing his eyes was even more disturbing. If eyes truly are windows to one's soul, The Servant's eyes revealed a person with no soul to view. As he stood on stage, the man was shirtless, his body covered in strange symbols and pictures of people being ripped apart by monsters. A golden amulet hung from his neck on a thick gold chain.

Dan couldn't determine the inscription on the medallion, but he was certain he knew what it said. Just as he knew what even the smallest symbol on the tattooed landscape of the psycho's over-muscular body said. Dan should know since all those symbols, including the medallion, were products of his imagination. He had described them all in great detail in his stories. The Servant simply stole them and made them his own.

"That's him!" Johnson shouted as he climbed the stairs to the stage, pulled his service pistol, pointed at the man in the smoke and shouted, "Freeze, scumbag! You are under arrest."

Likewise, Wheatly took the stairs at the opposite side of the stage, gun drawn, shouting, "Police. Hold it right there, punk!"

The Servant ignored the two detectives. He raised his arms high in the air, not in a gesture of surrender but one of confidence. He was grinning like a madman as the air around him suddenly filled with glowing red and white sparkles. They rose around him, encasing The Servant in a giant sphere of sparkling particles.

Dan looked on in stunned silence, knowing that his worst and most impossible fear was coming true right before his eyes. Somehow, this lunatic was causing the stage to shake, the actors to fall, and the smoke to rise from the stage. Dan wanted to believe it was a trick, some type of illusion. No matter what he saw, Dan's mind wouldn't allow him to think it was happening until The Servant commanded the sphere of sparkling particles to form around him. Dan saw the two detectives storm the quaking stage with their guns drawn, shouting to The Servant to surrender.

However, he did not obey their commands. In fact, he acted as if the two detectives pointing loaded guns at him were as insignificant as annoying gnats. A second later, flames shot upward from the opening on both sides of the stage, creating a wall of scorching heat, forcing the detectives backward. Johnson was able to get off a shot that struck the outside of the sparkling sphere but never reached The Servant. The bullet was stopped in mid-flight, dissolved, and was absorbed into the protective shield.

The Servant shouted in a voice that was so loud it overcame the roar of the screaming crowd, which was stampeding toward the exits. He yelled, "Everyone stop and be silent and return to your seats. I have things to say, and you must hear them."

Incredibly, the audience did as The Servant commanded, turned, and slowly and quietly sat back down in their seats, waiting for whatever was to come next. Sadly, a few dozen patrons had been crushed to death under the trampling feet of the panicked crowd. Their bloody remains lay near the still-closed exit doors. Dan watched the people returning to their seats, resembling mindless zombies, as if they had no will of their own. He knew they were now under the control of The Servant.

The stage had stopped shaking, but the fiery gash in the center of the stage continued to spew smoke and flames. The Servant stood tall in his sparkling protective particle sphere, unharmed by the fire and untouchable by the Police. He looked like an ancient statue as he prepared to address the crowd.

The Servant said, "You have all been gathered here for a very important reason. You have been awarded the greatest of all honors. You have been chosen to be part of my flesh sculpture, which I will call 'Theater of Terror,' a tribute to my messiah."

Dan was amazed by how everyone in the theater, including the security staff, seemed to be staring at The Servant in awe, in what appeared to be a surreal, hypnotic reverence. It was as if they had forgotten how, moments earlier, they had tried to storm the exits to escape. They seemed to not notice the bloodied, crushed, and trampled bodies of the people killed under their rampaging feet. Dan could see Detectives Wheatly and Johnson standing at each side of the stage, slack-jawed, staring in wonder at the sparkling sphere and the person inside. They appeared to be equally hypnotized.

The Servant announced to his raptured audience, "You may wonder where I got my inspiration for this magnificent work of art I'm about to create. I am honored to have the famed horror writer and my inspiration in the audience tonight, Mister Daniel Gilbert. Please stand, Mister Gilbert, and please, folks, give him a round of applause."

Like programmed automatons, the entire auditorium erupted with several hundred hands clapping. Dan reluctantly stood up, not certain what would happen next. Then, a name suddenly appeared in his mind, Garth Copely. Had The Servant put that name in his mind, or did Dan suddenly recall it from briefly meeting the man a decade earlier? Dan realized it was neither. The reason he thought the name was because some kind of mental connection had formed between himself and The Servant, which told Dan the man's real name was Garth Copely. Dan wondered, if there really was a connection between them, could he use it to stop The Servant?

/ 14 /

Giving up any rational or prejudicial concepts he may have previously held, Dan decided to go with his writer's imagination and accept the premise of what was happening. The Servant, Garth Copely, had found some way to make Dan's stories a reality. Somehow, Copely had also found a way to call demons from Hell to do his bidding. No! That wasn't correct. Dan suddenly realized the flaw in his thought process. Although Copely had developed some sort of mystical power, it wasn't the power to summon Hell's minions. It was more complicated than that, which is why Dan had missed it. Perhaps being just a few feet from whatever source of power Copely had acquired had given Dan the ability to perceive the truth.

He realized the Servant had found some way to take Dan's words and manifest living, breathing versions of those ideas in real life. For his first kills, Copely had somehow created monsters from Dan's book's descriptions and used them to rip his victims to pieces. Then for his second kill scene, Copely caused a fiery slit to open in the earth and snake-like creatures to emerge from it to flay the flesh from his next victims. Now, he was mysteriously duplicating yet another horrid scene. Dan looked up at the ceiling, which was now a swirling, chaotic mass of crimson mist, from which Dan knew horrors too terrible to imagine would soon sweep downward to kill everyone in the theater. Dan had to do something.

Dan shouted at the stage, "Garth Copely, hear me. That's right, I know your true name. I am your master, and you must follow my commands. Is that not so?"

"As it is written, so shall it become real. I receive your commands through your writing, and as such, I, your humble servant, must obey." Copely said.

"Then, Garth Copely, I command you to stop what you are doing, remove that sphere surrounding you, and turn yourself into the police," Dan ordered.

As Garth looked at Dan, several expressions passed over his face in a matter of seconds: confusion, realization, anger, and a look of pure, insane rage. The Servant shouted, "How dare you try to order me, Dan Gilbert! I don't obey the worthless spoken words that flow like sewage from Dan Gilbert's mouth! I only accept commands from the great Mister Gilbert's incredible and immortal prose. Apparently, that is something the 'Dan side' of Mister Gilbert does not understand. Isn't that right . . . Dan?"

Dan sensed he was in big trouble. Until now, The Servant had never referred to him by his first name nor disrespected him. Now, however, something had drastically changed. Just as Garth Copely and The Servant were apparently two parts of the same being, The Servant considered Dan as two separate beings in one. There was Mister Gilbert, who wrote the stories that inspired and motivated The Servant by speaking to him through written words, and there was Dan Gilbert, whose verbal commands were disrespected and useless in the eyes of The Servant.

Then Dan came to another important realization. Everything that made The Servant who he was had come directly from Dan. The man's physical appearance, power, and the ideas for the atrocities the man had committed came from Dan's creative mind. Dan recalled one of the earliest stories where he had described a villain physically identical to the man standing on stage. If The Servant had never discovered Dan's writing, he would probably still be the frail, bespeckled character Dan had briefly met that day at the book signing. Although Dan had no idea how the man had developed the strange powers he now had and assumed he probably never would, he knew Garth Copely was using some unknown but awesome powers. Still, the man would be nothing without Dan's creativity.

Dan looked up at the swirling mass on the ceiling and knew the first of dozens of horrific winged demons would soon be exiting the cloud, just as they had done in his story. He knew what would happen next because he had created the scene. These demons would continue to come out by the dozens, flying down from on high and tearing the audience members to pieces. The Servant remained on stage, arms upward, protected by his flames and sphere of particles.

Then Dan knew what he had to do. He was the one with the imagination. It didn't matter how The Servant had gotten his powers. Dan still remained the source of the ideas. He was the creator. Now, he was somehow mentally connected to the maniac on stage. Dan began to focus all his thoughts and energy on strengthening the link between himself and The Servant. Then Dan concentrated on the final scene from the story, his story, his creation. It was the part of the story The Servant never read and knew nothing about.

From the center of the swirling crimson cloud above, hideous leathery winged demons began to emerge. They were terrible-looking creatures with thin but muscular arms and legs bearing tallon-like claws. Their faces resembled bats with pig noses, bulging eyes, and large mouths full of long fangs meant for ripping flesh.

From the stage, The Servant commanded, "Come down, my children. Come by the dozens and feast."

Dan stood focusing, his face a sheen of sweat. He kept replaying the same scene from his story over and over again. Several dozen of the winged monstrosities flew downward toward their waiting prey in the audience. But something happened as they got close. It was as if an invisible force high above the crowd prevented them from reaching their intended victims. They flew in circles above the audience for a few seconds, unable to penetrate the protective barrier.

"Kill them, you fools, I command you!" The Servant shouted from the stage. "Rip them to pieces!"

All the flying creatures suddenly turned as one, their bloody red eyes now focused on the stage. Concentrating harder than he ever would have believed possible, Dan replayed the story's ending again and again. He looked directly into the eyes of The Servant as the evil man stood defiantly on stage, and for the first time, Dan thought he saw fear in those eyes.

Then, the flying demons plunged toward the stage, attacking the sparkling sphere surrounding the madman. The first dozen or so slammed into the sphere and were instantly vaporized. But as each subsequent demon hit the object, it began to weaken. It flickered as it grew weaker, and holes started to open on its sparkling surface. Finally, the holes grew wider, and the sphere was no more.

The first flying demon to break through the protective ball dug its clawed hands into The Servant's raised right arm and bit his fingers off instantly. Another tore his tattooed chest open while biting into his nose and tearing it from his face. Others attacked his remaining arm and legs, ripping through his pants to get to the tasty flesh below. Soon, the screams of agony from The Servant ceased as what remained of his tattered body collapsed in a heap on the floor.

Dan heard a commotion behind him and realized the audience had awoken somewhat and were once again stampeding toward the now-open exits. The remaining flying monsters helped themselves to generous portions of the dead Servant's body, grabbing flesh and bones and then returning upward to reenter the spinning bloody vortex. As the last creature entered the swirling mass, the opening closed, and the crimson cloud was suddenly gone. On stage, most of The Servant's body had been destroyed, save for a few recognizable fragments like a hand, part of a leg, and a fleshless skull, with the left eye dangling from a hollow socket. A puddle of blood pooled on the stage floor. The flames had gone out, and the smoke had dissipated. The audience had cleared out, leaving Dan standing in his fifth-row seat. He saw the detectives shake their heads as if awakening from a dream.

/ 15 /

Detectives Wheatly and Johnson walked from their respective sides to the center of the stage, looking down at the carnage that had once been The Servant. They looked into the now-empty theater and saw several dozen bloody bodies near the exits. Then they saw Dan Gilbert walking uneasily down the aisle toward them. He appeared shocked and confused.

Johnson was the first to speak, " What the Hell happened, Dan? Where's The Servant?"

"He's gone, Detective Johnson. Whatever you see there on stage is all that remains of him."

Wheatly asked, "What happened, Dan?"

"What do you remember, Detective Wheatly?" Dan inquired.

Wheatly hesitated, then said, "I remember calling to him to surrender, and I recall Johnson taking a shot but nothing else."

"Yeah. Me too." Johnson said, looking at the gun he still held in his hand. "I got nothing' else."

Dan asked, "What do you remember about The Servant? Anything?"

"I vaguely remember a muscle-bound bald guy with a beard, no shirt, and lots of tats," Johnson said.

Wheatly added, "I remember a bright red light . . . but nothing after that. Did you see what happened, Dan?

Dan found himself at an important junction regarding what direction he should take the conversation. He believed he had several options and had to choose the one he felt would lead to the best result. He could join the detectives and say he couldn't remember anything.

Dan was certain the audience would remember nothing either as they, too were hypnotized, so this might be a possible logical road to consider. However, doing so would result in no answers for the police investigation. They would never know The Servant's real name and might never be able to close the first two cases. Perhaps they could get DNA from what little remained of the man, but if he were not in the 'system,' they would never identify him.

He could tell them the truth but knew the detectives would never believe him. Dan could scarcely believe it himself. Dan had no idea how Garth Copely had acquired the mysterious power to become The Servant. To make matters worse, Dan had even less understanding of why he had been able to stop The Servant by willing the flying demons to destroy the killer. He decided he couldn't tell them the complete truth for the same reason as his first idea. None of those unexplainable events could appear in a police report, meaning the cases would never be closed.

Dan suddenly came up with a story that he believed would work. It wasn't exactly the truth, but it was the only likely scenario that any sane person would be expected to accept.

He took a deep breath and said, "I saw some of what happened. When The Servant blew up part of the stage with explosives of some type, everybody panicked. Unfortunately, when they did and ran for the exits, more than a dozen poor folks were trampled underfoot, crushed, and killed. The rest of the audience escaped. I think The Servant would have tried to use more explosives to kill them, but then he saw me sitting in the audience, and I managed to distract him long enough for everyone to escape. I was able to speak with him briefly and did my best to pretend to understand him so that I could get on his good side. It apparently worked. He even told me his real name was Garth Copely. Then, either accidentally or as a final suicidal act, the floor beneath him exploded, essentially vaporizing him. I suppose what you see up there is all that remains of Garth Copely, The Servant."

Detective Johnson looked again at the remains and said, "Ok, Dan. That's what we'll run with. I'll call a forensic team down here to analyze the scene, and then we can wrap this up. We should be able to verify this Garth Copely's identity and hopefully clear the other two cases as well."

Wheatly looked suspiciously at Dan and asked, "Is there anything else you want to add to your account, Dan?"

"No, Detective Wheatly, I think that summarizes what little I can recall, and hopefully, that will help you close these investigations."

"In that case, Dan. I think you can leave for now. Johnson and I will take care of this with the investigative team, and if I need to ask you anything else, we'll get in touch."

Dan said, "Thanks, Detective Wheatly. Please let me know what you learn about this Garth Copely. I'd love to know what made him tick."

Johnson added, "We'll probably find out he was a nutball on the verge of a major meltdown for years. But whatever we learn, we'll let you know."

/ 16 /

Several days passed, and Dan's front doorbell rang early one evening. When he opened the door, he saw Detective Wheatly standing and waiting to talk to him.

"Detective Wheatly, please come in," Dan said, wondering where Detective Johnson was since the pair seemed to be joined at the hip.

Wheatly entered and went right to a chair in the living room and sat down. He watched Dan close the door, then Wheatly walked over and sat in a nearby chair. Dan sensed something was off with the detective. He wasn't wearing his trademark sunglasses, and Dan could feel his cop eyes watching him closely. The detective pulled a notebook from his breast pocket and opened it.

Dan asked, "So Detective Wheatly. Have you discovered anything new about Garth Copely? That is, anything you can share."

Wheatly hesitated, then said cautiously, "Well, Dan. It's not so much about what we discovered as what we didn't discover."

"I'm not sure I follow you, Detective Wheatly."

"That night at the theater, you said you believed Copely was vaporized by an explosion. Is that correct?"

Dan realized he would have to tread carefully and possibly back-peddle his way out of this inquiry. He said, "Yeah. That's what it seemed like to me."

Wheatly continued to bore holes in Dan with his eyes and said, "Well, here's the thing, Dan. Our forensic team went over the crime scene and what little remained of Copely, and the funny thing is, they didn't find a single trace of any explosive media whatsoever."

"Explosive media?" Dan asked.

"You know, things like gunpowder or any incendiary liquids or even signs of burning on the remains. We found nothing, Dan."

Dan said, "Ok. What does that mean?"

Wheatly explained, "The lack of explosive residue, combined with some other things we found, tell a different story."

"Other things?"

"Yes, we found a few strange things. For example, we found a broken claw sunk into the skull that appeared to come from a large hawk or other bird of prey. Also, there was an unknown substance that, when analyzed, was determined to possibly be a type of bat guano. But not any type they could find in any database."

Dan asked, "Bat poop? That makes no sense, does it?"

Wheatly replied, "No, it doesn't. Unless one was to read your story to the end, which Johnson and I did. You talk about flying creatures with bat-like faces."

Dan asked, "Surely, Detective, you're not suggesting that The Servant was able to manifest winged demons from thin air, and they turned on him, ripped him to pieces, then disappeared? I thought we had this discussion earlier and decided such a thing was impossible. Besides, how would something like that look in your police report?"

"Trust me, Dan. That will never find its way into any report I ever write. I like my job and future pension too much to risk such a thing. Still, it makes me wonder."

Dan looked the detective in the eye and said, "Look, Detective Wheatly. That night was extremely chaotic, and it's quite possible I may have confused some of the facts. I may not know exactly what happened, but I can assure you nothing supernatural, ghostly, or demonic occurred. I may have been temporarily spooked out in Woodly Forest when we found those bodies. But that was a one-time thing. As I always say, I couldn't write the scary stuff I write if I believed any of that mumbo jumbo."

Wheatly gave a slight, knowing smile, then said, "Well, Dan. I just wanted to give you an update on the situation. We were able to close all three cases and name Garth Copely, AKA The Servant, as the perp. The exact nature of how he died remains unexplained for now, but to be honest, no one is really too concerned about what happened to him. Let's say we're glad he's gone, never to return. He was guilty, and now he's dead. End of story."

Wheatly closed his notebook, stood, and headed for the front door. Dan opened the door, and the detective turned and said, "Do me a favor, Dan. If you receive any weird letters from your fans, call me right away. I don't really think anything like this will happen again, but as they say, 'one never knows, do one?'"

Dan said, "No problem, Detective. You'll be the first one I call."

As Wheatly walked out on the porch, he turned and said, "Maybe you might want to consider changing your genre to . . . I don't know, maybe nonfiction or historical books?"

Dan smiled and said, "Thanks for the suggestion, Detective, but in the immortal words of Popeye the Sailor, 'I yam what I yam, and that's all that I yam.' Horror is my thing."

The detective walked to the street, got into his car, looked back at Dan, nodded, then drove away.